THE SUBURBAN SAGA

BOOK SIX

THE SUBURBAN JUDGMENT (PART I – DISCLOSURE)

BY

MARION KILLE

"Your secret is your prisoner; once you reveal it, you become its slave."

Solomon Ibn Gabirol

AUTHOR'S NOTE

Thank you for buying this book. Because of the complexity of bringing a satisfactory conclusion to the multiple storylines, The Suburban Judgment is without a doubt, a massive undertaking. I had a choice – release it as one monster novel, which would easily span seven hundred plus pages and as a result, be expensive to buy, or to divide the book into manageable chunks. That being the case I decided, through Facebook, to seek advice from my readers, asking what they would prefer. The unanimous opinion was to publish the final Suburban instalment in four sections.

So, I have great pleasure in presenting Part One (Disclosure) – well over 80,000 words and therefore, a novel in its own right.

I hope you enjoy. If you do, I'd be grateful if you could take the time to post a review on Amazon and Goodreads. Thank you.

Please keep in touch and follow any updates on:

www.marionkille.wix.com/author

www.facebook.com/TheSuburbanSaga

To Muriel
Love Marion xxx

ACKNOWLEDGEMENTS

Many thanks to my proofreaders who between them, have hopefully managed to spot all those deliberate little errors that I put in purely for entertainment purposes just to keep them on their toes – Andy Kille, Kevin Etheridge, Michael Buchan, Beryl Buchan and Mandy Harley-English.

Thank you to Zak Woodman for the front cover.

Many thanks to Inspector Ian Ashmore for the in-depth tour of Chichester Custody Suite and to Ben Pranczke for his advice on the Prison Service. And finally, special thanks to my Editor, Albion Winslow Land.

And of course to my readers. I really hope you enjoy the story.

This book is dedicated to my family, friends and colleagues who are always there to offer support and encouragement.

OTHER BOOKS BY MARION KILLE

The Suburban Saga in Book Order:–

The Suburban Cage

The Suburban Coven

The Suburban Vendetta

The Suburban Sinner

The Suburban Shadows

The Suburban Judgment (Part I – Disclosure)

The Suburban Judgment (Part II – Perception)

The Suburban Judgment (Part III – Truth)

The Suburban Judgment (Part IV – Justice)

CHAPTER ONE

"I'm sorry you died," was all he could think of to say to her. Four short words, expressed so bluntly, were hardly adequate to describe the lifetime of misery and regret that engendered them.

The woman watched him curiously from the mirror, her lips twitching in a faint smile. He could not believe she was actually here, that he could see her. Was it a dream? Please don't let it be a dream. His throat tightened, making it difficult to speak. He swallowed hard.

"I'm sorry I killed you," he managed to rasp as tears rolled unbidden down his cheeks. He was so relieved to have finally told her. The only thing he needed now was absolution.

She cocked her head slightly to one side, her eyes constantly surveying his face.

He searched for signs of resentment or anger in her gaze – any hint that she blamed him for cutting short her life – but he found no trace of either. Instead, she sat before him cast in a serene golden glow, and all he could read in her cornflower blue eyes was compassion and love. There was so much he needed to say since that fateful day, and he feared that this special fleeting moment would be over before he had the chance. He had to make her understand – to tell her of his pain, the burden of which he'd dragged around like a dead weight from the very instant she left him. He needed to explain how guilt had infected his heart and poisoned his soul and that his only desire was to be with her.

Sniffing loudly, he cautiously reached out to touch her, surprised to discover how small and childlike his hand had become. This aberration was the least of his concerns, and he chose not to question it. He simply revelled in the fact that he could feel the silkiness of her hair. Pale blond fronds caught the light as they glided effortlessly through his fingers. Ah yes! He remembered her hair, how he used to stand for hours on tiptoe and brush it. If he was able to touch her then it couldn't be a dream, could it?

Her reflection continued to study him. His eyes never strayed from her face. He feared that if he broke eye contact for even a second she'd be lost to him forever. He inched closer to the mirror so that his reflection came into focus and he gasped in surprise when the image of a child stared back at him. Being a little boy again made him feel secure.

"Stay with me," he whispered, a crippling yearning pressing on his heart. As she opened her mouth to speak, he sensed they were no longer alone. A shape emerged from the corner of the room. Tall and foreboding, it floated forward. The boy tried to ignore it.

The woman beamed a beautiful smile in greeting, momentarily dazzling him.

"You know I can't," she replied.

Her voice was sharp inside his head. It was clear and tinkling, like cut crystal. Memories flooded his brain.

"Then let me come with you," he begged.

"Let him come," spoke the voice of his father.

Craig blinked and turned his head. The shape metamorphosed into the image of his dad. In his arms, he carried a baby. Craig realised with a jolt that it was his brother, Alex. Time had stood still for his family. They all looked exactly as he remembered. They would never grow old. He turned back to the mirror. The little boy had vanished, and he was a man again.

"No," his mother's tone was forceful.

"Please," Craig whimpered. "I want to be with you; I've always wanted to be with you. Don't leave me alone again. I can't stand it."

"Let him come with us," his father implored.

His mother shook her head with sadness.

"It's not his time," she said adamantly.

"I can't live without you. Can you not see that? Take me with you," he sobbed.

Her pity was almost palpable, but she remained resolute.

"Come with us," the voice in the corner beckoned. It didn't sound so strong anymore. He shifted his gaze and watched in despair as a beam of white light streamed down from above, turning his father and brother into shapeless entities. They were disappearing. Craig's eyes darted frantically back to the mirror – his mother was fading too.

"Please, no. Let me come with you," he screamed.

She didn't answer but locked him in her gaze. He held on, staring into her eyes for as long as he could – committing her beautiful face to memory. Then he blinked and all that remained was his own reflection, now horribly disfigured.

* * *

St Richards Hospital, Chichester

Nurse Beverly Hutchins couldn't believe what she was seeing. All her professionalism seemed to fly out of the window as she watched the crash team encircle the patient's bed. Having watched his heartbeat on the monitor, she had seen the regular rhythm suddenly stutter out of control. She took a step back, feeling useless, trying not to get in anyone's way whilst her colleagues endeavoured to save him.

Could this really be Dr Craig Donohue? she asked herself – the same man she had admired from afar and secretly fantasised about. Now he was barely recognisable. His handsome features had been melted by fire into the parody of a hideous Halloween mask. Such a crying shame. She felt bereft even though she was painfully aware she'd never have stood a chance with him, what with her mousy frizzy hair and ample figure. He was always out of her league.

She heard the noise of the defibrillator charging and watched as one of the team applied the pads to the patient's chest.

"Stand clear," shouted a commanding voice. Through the throng of bodies, Beverly saw Donohue's motionless form suddenly wracked by a violent spasm and almost levitate from the bed. The team paused for a second to assess his heart rate. Beverly craned her neck, but her view of the screen was obstructed.

"Again," shouted the voice.

The process was repeated. Beverly held her breath. Out of the corner of her eye, she saw them approaching – waiting like a cluster of vultures for an update on the patient. For some reason, Craig Donohue had captured the interest of the police. She spied their anxious faces pressed up against the glass panel as they awaited news of his condition. She had no idea if he was being regarded as a criminal or a victim, but they hadn't strayed from the premises since he'd been admitted earlier in the day.

"Stand clear!" One final attempt to tame his volatile pulse rate. She wondered what sort of battle was raging inside him. A bolt of electricity shot straight to his heart. They waited – all eyes focused on the screen. Once again, the team looked pensive, fearing that he might flat-line at any moment.

Beverly watched their shoulders sag in unison and released a regretful sigh. Such a waste. Such a shame. Then suddenly a steady bleep. They all stared unblinking at the monitor. Nobody moved – too afraid to speak lest they tempt fate. But the signs were encouraging. He appeared to have settled down again – the gentle regular rhythm of his heartbeat restored.

The crash team began to murmur amongst themselves. Beverly gauged their reaction. She heard one of them say, "It's okay. He had us going there for a while, but he's stable now."

She sensed their relief and turned eagerly towards the officers peering into the room. She nodded affirmatively in their direction and witnessed the ghost of a smile in reply.

CHAPTER TWO

It seemed as if Rosemary Kent had lost the ability to speak. Sat huddled in the front of the police car, she was engulfed in a shroud of numbness that deadened her mind and staved off the pain in her tattered heart. She was being taken home by a kindly faced female officer who would occasionally cast a concerned glance in her direction on the ten-mile drive.

PC Susan Llewellyn was grateful for the lack of conversation. She was trying to come to terms with the heated half-whispered rumours doing the rounds at Chichester police station. She didn't want to believe them but, judging by the state of the crumpled female sitting beside her, they would appear to be true.

She had met Detective Sergeant Adam Kent's wife at a couple of barbecues at their house – a pretty woman, petite of stature with large brown eyes and enviable long blond hair. She was the perfect match for Sue's fanciable colleague, but not today. Rosemary looked as if she'd aged a decade – her skin red raw from grief and her luscious locks reduced to matted coils, which hung like limp dreadlocks around her narrow shoulders. Sue shook her head, trying to dislodge an assortment of controversial questions from her brain as the police radio crackled softly in the background.

In her world, Adam Kent was a rising star – a competent and well-thought of member of the team, with a host of successful arrests under his belt and in line for The Queen's Gallantry Medal for bravery. So what had gone wrong? Right now he was sitting in a police cell after being arrested for murder. How could his shining future be so monumentally snatched away? Sue shivered. It was every policeman's worst nightmare being banged up. But the one question burning on everyone's lips was – had he done it?

Her instructions were to drive Mrs Kent home and to stay with her until she settled down – whenever that might be. But appearances were deceptive, and Sue suspected this might well be the calm before the storm. At the moment, the woman was anaesthetised by shock but what state would she be in when that wore off? Sue had already seen Rosemary become hysterical – it had been a major ordeal getting her out of the police station, so desperate was she to stay close to Adam. It wasn't until Detective Inspector Nick Marshall bluntly told her that she would do her husband no favours by neglecting the rest of her family. He'd swiftly followed with the promise to be in touch the moment he had some news.

Nick's straight talking must have penetrated her brain, because Rosemary reluctantly obliged. She walked like a zombie towards the awaiting police car and climbed in. She hadn't even acknowledged Sue, who had been grateful for that small mercy. When they did eventually reach their destination, she would need to get Adam's wife safely indoors without any hysterics. For now, she had to concentrate on driving.

The sky darkened and the first plops of rain hit the windscreen. Sue noticed hordes of children, dressed in a variety of different school uniforms, hurrying home before the weather got any worse. Rosemary saw nothing. The journey melted away, and the speed camera that signified they were getting close came into view. Sue applied the brake, keeping just below the 30 mph restriction. She wanted to ask how Rosemary was doing, but feared that might sound lame and, worse still, she didn't want to set her off. Best to get her inside as quickly as possible, she thought.

"My car," Rosemary suddenly spoke out in a monotone voice as if she had just remembered abandoning her Volkswagen Beetle haphazardly in the front car park of the station.

Sue steered the police vehicle left into Orchard Road.

"It's okay," she reassured her. "Someone is driving it back."

Rosemary said no more, just watched blankly as they weaved their way past a host of obstructions before arriving at the house. Then she shivered and crunched over, clutching at her stomach, trying to catch her breath.

"What's wrong," Sue asked. Stupid question really but it was an automatic response. Is she in pain? Does she need a doctor? Adam's wife seemed to be in severe discomfort with her swollen eyes scrunched tightly shut and her lips suddenly devoid of blood.

"Oh God," Rosemary gasped as she raised her head and stared nervously towards the well-tended frontage of her home. "What am I going to tell the children? What am I going to tell Sophie?"

CHAPTER THREE

Today was the worst day of DS George Robin's career. No, rewind that – the worst day of his life! He stared miserably out the window of the incident room, situated on the upper floor of Chichester police station, watching the storm clouds rolling in. They gathered pace and converged above the building in a coordinated attack. The weather had been beautiful that morning, with a totally unblemished sky, but the atmosphere was now oppressive and sticky. Thunder bugs appeared from nowhere, crawling all over him and making his bald head itch.

George sniffed. His eyes were sore. It had been years since he'd cried, but he didn't care what anyone thought. To see the big man reduced to tears must have been a sight to behold. George's last memory of being so upset was when he was just a kid. He was only eleven-years-old, and his dog had been put to sleep. A couple of decades later, despite the horrors and heart-rending scenes he had witnessed as a police officer, nothing could compare to the misery he was enduring today. Even now, he was unable to get his head around what his best friend, Adam Kent, had pressured him into doing. Adam had literally forced George to arrest him for the murder of a man named Jason Sadler. He was furious with Adam, not only for committing such a heinous crime but also for having put him in this impossible position.

In the background a phone rang. George didn't even turn. Detective Inspectors Brian Proctor and Nick Marshall were also present in the room, discussing the disastrous situation in low voices. Nick answered the call. His tone was abrupt, bordering on rude. The first blobs of rain began to fall, smacking against the pane. George blinked. He heard a distant rumble of thunder and noticed a flash of lightning zigzag across the blackened sky. How apt, he thought, even the weather is in tune with my mood.

His colleagues moved quietly around the room behind him. Brian had only just returned from the unpleasant task of booking Adam into a cell. George was outraged that they were treating him like this. There was no better officer than Adam. In the eyes of his colleagues and the public, he was a hero. It was that fucker Guy Kane's fault. Their colleague hated Adam, whom he had been secretly investigating for the murder, and he had pressed the bosses to follow procedures and not award him any special treatment.

"Are you okay?" Brian asked, cutting through George's gloomy thoughts.

"I've been better," he mumbled dejectedly.

He felt the weight of their stare but couldn't bring himself to face them. Since Nick had returned from informing Rosemary Kent about what had transpired, George had turned his back on his superiors and on the room displaying evidence of Adam's crime. Even though he chose to ignore the grisly photos, he couldn't block out the misery in Nick's voice when he relayed what had been said.

"It was awful," Nick had muttered, after Brian prompted him. "Fucking awful. She's a mess."

Brian closed his eyes and pinched the soft skin at the top of his nose, as if nursing a headache.

"She'll need our support. They both will," he said.

Nick nodded in agreement and turned his attention to George.

"Just to warn you, mate, Guy Kane is on the warpath. He's threatening to make a complaint against you."

"Because I almost punched his teeth down his throat?" George replied tartly, addressing the window pane.

Nick nodded, saddened to see this officer acting so aggressive. This wasn't the gentle George Robins they all knew. Being forced to arrest his best friend was a big deal and had affected him deeply – affected them all.

15

"Anyhow, I thought I should warn you, just in case. Hopefully he'll calm down," Nick sighed.

"Guy Kane can go fuck himself," George spat, turning away from the window to stare at his superiors through wild tormented eyes. He returned his attention to the world of grey beyond the glass.

The two Inspectors resumed talking quietly. George couldn't make out their conversation, but occasionally picked up a stray word – 'brief'; 'interview'; 'guilty'. He swallowed with difficulty, trying to stem another surge of emotion. Adam Kent was his best mate; they had been together through thick and thin. God! George had been his best man – at both of his weddings!

A vision of Adam uttering those devastating words returned to the forefront of his mind.

"It was me. I killed Jason Sadler."

George would never forget his reaction. Naturally, it was disbelief at first. But Adam had appeared far too unhappy to be playing some kind of sick joke. Ever since that moment, George had engaged in the futile exercise of wishing he could erase time. How far back would he have to go? Certainly long before Adam had got that crazy idea into his head and pulled the trigger. Why hadn't he confided in him, told him what he was planning to do? George could have hopefully talked some sense into him and avoided this catastrophe. It wouldn't be the first time a police officer wanted to avenge a wrongdoing, but you just don't go around taking the law into your own hands.

For six months, George and his team had struggled to unravel the mystery surrounding Jason Sadler's murder. That had led to their investigating his wealthy estranged family, the Sinclairs, and the clients of Jason's lurid child sex business. But the police had never known that Sadler, who was married to Adam's ex-wife, Jessica, had raped Adam's twelve-year-old daughter and killed Jessica. Until today, Adam had kept that to

16

himself.   Premeditated? Christ, mate, I hope not, George thought.

As a single tear rolled down his cheek, he promised himself that he would back Adam one hundred percent no matter what he had done. He would defend his friend's character to the ends of the earth. And anyone who questioned it had better watch out.

A Nokia ringtone interrupted his thoughts. He heard Nick answer.

"Yes, thank you," he said before ending the call and addressing Brian. "His brief's here."

Brian Proctor then coughed in such a way as to seize George's attention. Both he and Nick were now hovering by the door.

"Go home, George," Brian said pointedly. "It's been a long day. We'll take it from here."

"What about Adam?" George gasped, thrown into a whirlwind of panic. He didn't want to leave him here, alone. His best friend would need him.

Brian smiled kindly. George noticed a flash of pity in Nick's eyes.

"We're going to see him soon and try to make some sense out of this disaster."

George opened his mouth to speak but then thought better of it. It would be no good requesting if he could sit in on this interview, purely as moral support. He knew exactly what they'd say.

"Don't worry, George," Brian said, sensing his distress. "We'll be gentle with him. I promise."

17

CHAPTER FOUR

Adam knew the routine, not that he'd ever been a custody sergeant or, before today, a prisoner. He just knew the routine.

He hadn't moved from where he sat on the holding cell's bench-like bed for what felt like an eternity, not trusting his legs to support him. A tray of what looked like chicken and rice lay cooling beside him untouched, its basil and tomato sauce congealing by the second. The meal had been delivered by the custody assistant – a civilian and the only human contact Adam had had since the door had been locked behind him. There was no way he could eat the stuff.

Instead, Adam just focused on breathing, keeping his eyes tightly closed and trying to block out the sounds around him. Aggression and indignation seemed to permeate these smooth magnolia-coloured walls, along with protestations of innocence. Breathe in, breathe out, breathe in, breathe out. Adam's stomach see-sawed several times. Occasionally, he would open his eyes and stare warily at the smooth moulded toilet bowl that hundreds of prisoners before had used to relieve themselves. No, he didn't want to use that either! For one thing, there was no privacy and, even though it looked to be relatively clean, Adam could see brown stains around the water line. There was a sink of sorts, really more of a hole in the wall.

Past experience had played a major role in the design of these cells. There were no sharp corners anywhere – nothing that could cause injury. No bars on the windows, just toughened, thick glass squares set into smooth concrete. A convex mirror was positioned high above in one corner and a CCTV camera angled downwards from another. Everything was in place to protect those in police custody. An intercom system had also been fitted to each cell so that prisoners could contact the staff in emergencies, but this luxury was often abused and could be switched off via the central Bridge.

The high-tech structure of the Bridge was the first thing people arrested would encounter when they entered the Custody Suite. At any one time, four or five people worked from behind it, operating various computer systems. Its sophisticated design wouldn't look out of place on a spaceship – the green, marble-effect construction rising up before prisoners as they were guided to stand on foot-shaped marks painted on the floor. It wasn't meant to be intimidating, but detainees were forced to crane their necks and look up at the person booking them in. Looming above, like giant hawks, the officers could be confident that this fortress protected them from any sudden outbursts of violence. Custody had come a long way since Adam had joined the police, and now he'd had the misfortune of experiencing this new phase of technology from the wrong side.

His memory of being booked in was already hazy. He had tried to keep his feet squarely on the marks whilst DI Brian Proctor outlined to the astonished Custody Sergeant what had occurred. It was all a bit of a blur now. Adam remembered swaying unsteadily from side to side – irrationally scared that he would stagger from his spot and be punished. He guessed he was in some form of shock, the numbness of which was slowly wearing off and gradually being replaced by unpleasant pinpricks of anxiety. It wouldn't be long now, he was sure. He knew what they were doing, what procedures were being put in place. Adam could see them in his mind's eye, imagine them discussing how they were going to play this.

"Have you no fucking idea who I am?" an indignant upper-class voice suddenly shouted. "Have you nothing better to do? Go and arrest some real criminals for fuck's sake! Don't forget my taxes pay your salary!"

Adam didn't hear the officer's reply but knew what he would have said. He opened his eyes again and stared down at his hands, feeling a wave of crippling sadness when he noticed the absence of his wedding ring. He'd had to hand it over to the custody sergeant, along with a number of other possessions, including his warrant card. It had become part of him, as precious as any limb, and it's loss was crushingly painful.

The white band of naked flesh on his finger now dominated his line of sight and reminded him of the devastating sequence of events that had led to this very moment. He was sure he would never be able to rid his mind of the horror he had encountered at his home earlier that day – when he caught fellow detective Guy Kane in his bedroom, having just engaged in an illicit tryst with Adam's beautiful wife. From thereon, everything that followed seemed totally surreal.

"Look, can we talk about this?" The well-spoken man had suddenly calmed down, although Adam could still sense his unease. He sounded closer, having inevitably arrived in the grim reality of a police cell. "Please, can you get Superintendent Tarring. I-I play golf with him – quite regularly. There's been a mistake."

The man continued to cry out, switching effortlessly from over-the-top politeness to full-blown 'Hooray Henry' tantrum. Adam had no idea how much longer he would have to endure the man's self-pitying protestations.

Get over yourself, he thought, as niggles of temper broke through his depression, miraculously making him feel marginally stronger and more like the policeman he was. Be man enough to acknowledge the blame and accept your punishment.

However, this surge of emotional strength evaporated the moment he heard the viewing window to his own door being slid open and the slightly embarrassed face of the custody assistant peering through.

"Um," he hesitated, obviously unsure of how to address Adam. Christian name? Surname? Skip? The young man decided to skirt around the issue. "Your brief is here," he muttered quickly before unlocking the door to Adam's cell.

CHAPTER FIVE

The moment Sophie Kent let herself into the house, she knew something wasn't quite right. It was too quiet, eerily so. She checked her watch, to make sure she wasn't early, and realised that her stepmother and half-siblings should already be home by now.

Sophie dropped her school bag at the base of the stairs and wandered into the lounge, feeling almost as if she was in the wrong house. Her eyes swept the room as she strained her ears, trying to pick up on any reason for this unexplained absence. The steady ticking of the clock on the wall was the only sound she heard.

She cut across to the answering machine to see if anyone had left a message. The red light was flashing, indicating that there was one pending. That might explain things. Her heartbeat quickened and she crossed her fingers, praying that nothing bad had happened to Luke or Paige. As she pressed PLAY, she glanced out of the lounge window and noticed that the driveway was empty. Her dad's voice suddenly filled the room. It was a message for Rosemary.

"Baby, I'm just checking on you. I guess you must be asleep or in the shower. I'll be with you shortly. Something's happened at work and I need to come home and change. I hope you're feeling better. See you soon. Love you."

The message ended.

Of course, Rosemary was ill – Sophie remembered. Her father had dropped her off at school that morning. She'd had such a shit day. What with worrying about her best friend Ruby, who was in hospital after being raped and left for dead, and her boyfriend Dale giving her the cold shoulder, she'd totally forgotten about her stepmother being sick. But Rosemary's car was absent, so what was going on? Adam's voice sounded strained, but that was nothing unusual lately. There was always

21

some horrible murder to solve, and Sophie's dad worked long hours. Had he already come home and gone back out again?

Sophie decided to change out of her uniform. She was a little unnerved by the emptiness of the house, remembering how Ruby had been alone the night she was attacked. This fear dominated her mind as she crept slowly up the stairs, listening out for intruders. Every time she heard an odd noise or one of the floorboards creak, her heart almost stopped beating. By the time she reached the landing, she was panting with trepidation.

She stared wide-eyed at all the partially closed doors, wondering if somebody was lurking behind one of them. Her imagination was running on overdrive. It was typical that the day she'd heard the horrific news about Ruby was the one time nobody was home. Okay, it was still daylight, but the circumstances leading up to Ruby's attack were similar. A large part of Sophie wanted to turn tail and run from the house and wait outside on the drive until her father or stepmother showed up.

She pulled her mobile phone from her pocket. She could call her dad, or Rosemary, but decided not to. Instead she felt the best thing to do was to enter 999 on the keypad just to be on the safe side. Then, if someone were to jump out and attack her, it would only take a nanosecond to press the green button. With her arm extended, Sophie bravely nudged open the door to her bedroom.

After looking behind the door, in the wardrobe and under the bed, she concluded that the room was exactly as she had left it. Even her trainers were in the same position – with the left one lying on its side. A bit less frightened, she moved on and repeated her actions in Luke's room, followed by Paige's and then the bathroom. Feeling a little more confident after no one had leapt from the shadows to pounce on her, Sophie finally entered her dad's and Rosemary's domain.

There was an odd smell clinging to the air – like rubber. Sophie wrinkled her nose in distaste. Everything was in disarray – bedclothes strewn everywhere, as if there'd been a pillow fight or something. Her stepmother's white, satin robe lay crumpled on the floor. Sophie stepped further in, uncomfortable because she didn't make a habit of intruding. She was surprised that Rosemary had left the room in such a mess. Maybe, even though she was ill, she'd been forced to pick up the children, but then Adam had said he was coming home. Was Rosemary in hospital or something? Why hadn't anyone left her a message?

Finally convinced that there was no stranger waiting to kill her, Sophie made a move to leave the room when she noticed something strange on the bedside unit. Little foil packets – open ones She peered closer, recognising them straight away to be condom wrappers. Please, she thought, totally disgusted. Have some class! She didn't need evidence of her dad's surprising trip home staring her in the face. Sophie knew that they did *it*, but it was very unlike them to leave the revolting debris lying around. She hurried towards the door, her eyes suddenly snagging a used pink rubber, knotted at one end, protruding from the hem of the valance sheet. She pressed her hand to her mouth, feeling sick. For God's sake, control yourselves.

Totally pissed off, Sophie left in a huff and stormed into her own room, slamming the door behind her. She tore off her uniform and changed into a pair of jeans and a sweatshirt. No kid liked to think of their parents having sex, and it wasn't normal for her dad and step-mum to be so indiscreet. They obviously couldn't contain themselves. Grimacing at the thought, she dragged the scrunchy from her hair, allowing the golden curls to hang loose before stomping downstairs. Hopefully, very soon, someone would enlighten her as to what the hell was going on.

Sophie didn't have to wait long. As she entered the lounge, she saw through the window a marked police car slowly drawing up outside the house.

CHAPTER SIX

Detective Constable Guy Kane was furious that he hadn't been the one to arrest Adam Kent for murder. And he was even more incensed that, after all his weeks of meticulous planning and some very risky groundwork, that twerp George Robins had got there first and stolen his thunder. It was obvious Adam had contrived his arrest by George as a final "fuck you" to Guy. But an hour or so down the line, he was feeling marginally better. Keeping busy was the key to all this, and he revelled in the knowledge that it would be he who would have the final word.

He glanced down at his list. One more to go. One more chance to twist the knife. Guy dialled the number, drumming his fingers on the desk whilst listening to the ring tone. He warily eyed the closed door to the office in which he had ensconced himself, crossing his fingers that nobody would stumble upon the intrusion. The room was used by the Criminal Justice Support Inspector, whom Guy had seen leave for the day, and Guy prayed that he would be left undisturbed. Occasionally, he heard footsteps passing on the landing just beyond the threshold, but nobody entered the office and asked him what he was doing there.

After working his way through a number of automated options, he was finally rewarded with an upbeat live voice at the other end of the line.

"News of the World," a woman said. Guy could almost imagine her cheesy smile.

Guy asked to be put through to the editor-in-chief, stating that he had valuable information which he was sure would be of interest to them. When he finally got through, he made his sensational announcement.

"A serving police officer in Chichester has just been arrested for the murder of Jason Sadler."

And just as with the telephone calls that had preceded this one, Guy rang off before the man had an opportunity to ask him to elaborate. He also refrained from giving his name.

Guy replaced the handset, rested back in his seat and smiled. That would surely knock Adam Kent off his pedestal in the eyes of the public, not to mention the top brass. He scooped up his notes and pen, returning them to the safety of his jacket, and exited the room. He glanced left and right. The corridor was empty.

He had debated whether to make a complaint against George Robins for attacking him but decided against it. Guy's unsubtle enthusiasm over Adam's arrest clearly hadn't helped matters and, while his neck was very tender from the assault, he didn't think going down the grievance route would do him any favours. Better to take the moral high ground and let everyone think for a change that he was a thoroughly decent chap for not taking things further. It didn't mean he wouldn't let George sweat a bit though. He was justifiably upset to learn that his best friend was about to spend a substantial amount of time behind bars. And bad things always seem to happen to coppers in prison, Guy thought maliciously.

CHAPTER SEVEN

Twelve years of marriage down the drain. Tracy Peterson did expect to be more upset but instead, she was angry. Angry at her own pathetic display of emotion when confronted by her husband's mistress, Jenny who had delighted in telling her that the affair had never ended. Angry, because her husband Gavin had managed to fool her these past few months. It had been wonderful to believe he had learned from his mistake – that he was truly sorry for ever running off with that woman and how Tracy was the only one for him. How stupid was she? The tears burning in her eyes had nothing to do with self-pity. She wanted to lash out – to be honest, she actually felt quite violent. Instead, she was forced to curb her temper and was sat curled up on her bunk, sipping a cup of hot, sweet tea whilst her cellmate, Charlotte eyed her quietly from across the room.

Arrested and sent down for five years on a manslaughter charge had been a bitter pill to swallow. Tracy had never set out to kill anyone but her initial reaction to her husband's cruel abandonment had led her to make some very reckless choices. She was desperately sorry for the death of Kevin Evans. During her crusade against all men hellbent on cheating on their wives, she had only ever intended to drug him, before leaving him in a humiliating position. How was she to know that he would suffer a fatal, allergic reaction to the medication she had slipped into his drink? The other men she had entrapped were fine – whether their marriages had survived remained to be seen but at least their spouses could make an informed decision on their future happiness.

"Peterson, are you okay?"

An imposing figure blocked the doorway to the cell. Both women looked up to see the uniform clad body of Mark Bowson. Over six feet tall and muscle bound, sporting a fair, military haircut and warm, green eyes, he had witnessed the angry display between Tracy and her husband the moment she asked for a divorce. Mark had watched the fireworks from afar, which had culminated in Tracy stomping away from the visitor's room. Within five strides he was beside Gavin, using firm but gentle resistance to prevent the man from pursuing his wife into the restricted zone of the prison.

Mark was new to Granville. Until now, he had only worked in men's prisons, and some people had told him that female prisoners were worse. That was open to debate, but Tracy Peterson having been brutally raped by three fellow inmates with a metal bar and nearly bleeding to death certainly gave credence to those claims. Every prison has its bullies, Mark thought soberly. It's a dark unforgiving place where reason and compassion are in short supply. Granville was no different.

He watched her now – shoulder length copper-coloured hair pulled loosely into a ponytail, exposing the delicate bone structure of her face. Like his, her eyes were green – a little darker perhaps. With no makeup on her pale, almost translucent skin, Tracy's freckles stood out prominently. She had killed a man, Mark knew this from the gossip in the staff room, and was doing five years for the privilege. But the long slim fingers that encircled the precious mug of tea were caring hands, those of the nurse that she had been – not those of a killer.

Tracy attempted a smile to show that she was fine, but the corners of her full lips barely twitched. Mark flicked his gaze to Charlotte, who gave him a small resigned shrug.

"Well, I'm around and about if you need anything," he muttered before turning on his heel and heading off in the opposite direction.

Because of his good looks, Mark attracted much female attention, especially from the bunch of sex starved inmates banged up in here. As usual, he tried to block out the constant kissing sounds and suggestive winks from the clusters of women he passed. Most of his colleagues also took the piss out of him, which didn't help matters. It had been a choice between coming here and Marden – the notorious men's prison but Marden, with its horrible reputation, was probably the most

27

violent of them all. By taking what Mark considered the softer option, being subjected to a continuous stream of sexual attention was something he was going to have to put up with. Though what was concerning him more than anything was his undeniable attraction for Tracy Peterson. It wasn't healthy and he was determined to rise above it and maintain a high level of professionalism. After all, Prisoners and Prison Officers were certainly not a match made in heaven.

CHAPTER EIGHT

When Gavin Peterson stepped off the train onto the crowded platform at Chichester Station, his ears were still ringing from Tracy's unexpected and vitriolic attack. After she had virtually thrown him out, he would be getting home much earlier than planned. He still couldn't quite come to terms with how sour the whole day had turned.

Gavin pushed past hordes of travellers and fought his way out of the railway complex. He was exhausted, mentally and physically. It wasn't as if the journey was particularly easy, navigating his way across London to visit his wife in Granville Prison. And now that he was on half pay at work, the hefty rail and taxi fares hadn't made the excursion cheap. He didn't begrudge the money – far from it – but it would have been nice if Tracy could have just stayed there for the time they had been allotted and given him a chance to explain instead of her storming off in a huff. Surely, twelve years of marriage had to account for something?

A divorce? That's what she said she wanted. A divorce! He couldn't quite bring himself to say the word out loud. It was a curse, even though he had demanded the same of Tracy last year after he left her for Jenny. But that was when he'd lost his way. He'd been confused, his mind all over the place. Tracy seemed pretty level headed today.

As Gavin left the station behind, he could hear the bells and chimes of the level crossing gates closing again, signalling the arrival of another train. He trudged forward, focusing solely on what had transpired. God, he could kill Jenny for what she'd done. His ex-lover was certainly losing the plot with her bunny boiling antics but to confront his wife with her lies – well, that was unforgivable. When he had called Jenny to give her a piece of his mind, it was clear she had lost her grip on reality and continued to live in a make-believe world. Did she truly think that he would still want to marry her after all she had done?

Not that he ever had – well, not seriously. She was a raving loon, and he wished he had never set eyes on her.

As he walked to the house, he wondered if their marriage really was doomed? Judging by the disdainful expression on Tracy's face, he didn't hold out much hope for a reconciliation. She looked as if she hated him. What would the boys say about all this? It was bad enough that their mum was in prison. It would surely destroy them completely to learn that their parents were going to split up as well. Adrian and William had struggled to come to terms with the temporary loss of their mother, though they had adapted. But Gavin feared there was no way they'd be able to shoulder another major setback.

He crossed the road to his house, his mind feverish, constantly churning as he tried to come up with a solution. He clung to the hope that maybe, after she'd calmed down a bit, Tracy would have a re-think. He would give her a bit of space. With luck, his wife would consider the welfare of their children before her own. She wasn't a selfish woman, and Gavin hoped that this tiny smidgen of possibility might make the difference.

CHAPTER NINE

If nothing else, Adam Kent was grateful to be in the new custody facility. Gone were the tired interview rooms with their insipid green walls permeated by years of tobacco smoke, the stench of which no amount of redecoration could disguise. Now the environment was civilised and brightly furnished in clean lines. It was considerably more pleasurable to work in as a policeman and, in his current situation, made him feel less like a prisoner when he wasn't confined to his cell. Since Jason Sadler's body had been unearthed, this room had featured many times in his nightmares – nightmares that had now turned to reality.

For the past half hour, Adam had been speaking to Terry Brown, a solicitor he had a lot of time for. Now he was depending on Terry. But for what? To keep him out of prison? That wasn't going to happen. Terry was good, but he was no fairy godmother. Another wave of panic crashed through Adam when the door opened and Detective Inspectors Nick Marshall and Brian Proctor came in. Christ! This was for real.

"Hello Adam," Brian said gently as the two entered cautiously, unsure how he was going to react. "How you doing?"

Adam shrugged and shook his head.

"To be honest, I'm not really sure," he mumbled. He glanced across at Nick. His boss appeared to have aged considerably since he'd last seen him. Only hours earlier, he had been at his side, united in saving a witness from a house fire. Nick couldn't meet his eyes. He said nothing.

All four men settled down. Adam knew the procedure. Several times he had to pinch the skin on his arm to remind himself that, this time, he wouldn't suddenly wake from a terrible dream. His brain was having difficulty dealing with this surreal situation, perhaps as a coping mechanism. He had to keep the words spinning around in his head before he totally lost his grip on reality. Yes, he had discovered that his beautiful wife, Rosemary and his colleague, Guy Kane, were sleeping together. And yes, her deception had been the catalyst to make him confess his crime to George Robins. If Adam hadn't felt so betrayed, would he be sitting here under these circumstances? Probably not – at least, not yet. He tried to quash the bitterness swelling inside and concentrate on what Brian was saying. He was informed that the interview would be tape recorded. Either Nick or Brian, he couldn't remember which, asked him if he would like a glass of water or a coffee. He politely declined the coffee but said yes to water.

* * *

Half an hour earlier, he'd been escorted from his cell to consult with Terry. Prior to that, whilst still in a daze, Adam had been fingerprinted and photographed, the details of which would be forever held on the National Database. When he finally entered the interview room, he noticed the shock and sorrow portrayed on Terry's face.

"Please tell me this is some kind of joke," Terry had said when presented with the staggering truth. DS Adam Kent was one of his favourites. He was professional, courteous and good at his job. Now he needed his help. Murder? Hell – it didn't get much worse than that!

As Adam had given him the rundown on what had occurred, Terry could read the despondency in his eyes. His voice had been depressingly monotone – masking any fear or panic he was undoubtedly feeling. Terry prayed that he had come across supportive and positive, although he honestly didn't hold out much hope. As Adam relayed the circumstances surrounding his crime, all Terry could think of was how to build a defence that would limit his suffering. The fact he was a police officer made it very likely they would throw the book at him. In his opinion, there was little he could do to keep Adam out of prison, but he withheld this shattering information. Best to keep optimistic for now. However, he thought the easiest thing to do on this occasion was for Adam to go 'no comment'. Terry needed the time to make sense of a few things. He had to get Adam out on bail and talk further when they weren't under such a stringent time constraint. Unfortunately, they fell at the first hurdle. Adam didn't want to go no comment.

"There's no point," he had said, rejecting Terry's advice. "It only infuriates everyone. I've been on the receiving end of such interviews and, don't forget, I've confessed."

Adam appeared to be in self-destruct mode, and Terry could only hope that his client's candidness would be looked upon favourably by the criminal justice system.

* * *

Throughout the entire interview, the air was heavy with awkwardness, but somehow, Brian managed to steer them through it in a calm proficient manner. Much like Terry, Nick Marshall sat quietly observing Adam through haunted eyes. It was difficult to set personal feelings aside and remain professional. The fact that Brian didn't know Adam quite as well as Nick at least kept procedures tightly in place.

After the usual introductions and caution, Brian launched into the meat of the interview.

"Adam, can you tell us the circumstances leading up to the death of Jason Sadler?" he asked. Brian's voice was gentle, almost seductive. Adam shot a look at Terry who signalled with a small shake of his head to say nothing. He licked his lips and swallowed.

"Jason Sadler raped my daughter." Adam didn't recognise his own voice. He sounded gravelly. He cleared his throat and continued. "When my wife informed me of this, I saw red. I went looking for him and eventually tracked him down at the Scarlet Hotel."

The ramshackle hotel, north of Chichester, had been the focus last autumn of Operation Gargoyle. Jason Sadler was involved with a man named Jeremy Salander in human trafficking and forced prostitution, and the premises was being used as a cover for that. A number of innocent people, as well as some very guilty ones, lost their lives during those dark days.

"What happened when you caught up with him?" Brian probed. "Was he alone?"

Adam nodded and placed his hands on top of the table, threading his fingers as if in prayer.

"Yes, to begin with. I was insane with fury. I went for him and got him by the throat, up against the wall."

"Did you want to kill him?"

Adam pressed his lips shut and glanced at Terry. Once again, Terry shook his head.

"You don't have to answer the question," he reminded him.

Adam turned back to Brian.

"Yes. I did want to kill him, but I didn't really know what I was going to do. Hit him? Yes. Put him in hospital? Most likely."

"Did you hit him?"

"A couple of times – in the gut."

"And then what happened?"

"We were interrupted. Jeremy Salander appeared."

Brian frowned and looked across at Nick, waiting for his colleague to jump in. Operation Gargoyle was a little before his time at Chichester. Nick opened his mouth to speak. He remembered the events as if they had happened only yesterday, although what Adam was telling them now was all new to him.

Adam had been held prisoner in the basement of the hotel before being rescued. But back then, he'd managed to glaze over the finer details of how he'd ended up there alone, without backup. His official statement was full of holes but because Jeremy was killed in a plane crash and Jason had disappeared, everything had been put on the back burner. Nick didn't recall Adam's account being quite so comprehensive.

"Jeremy Salander. Anyone else?" Nick asked, finally finding his voice, all the while observing the man he thought he knew so well. He could still see a little soot on Adam's face – a physical reminder that they had jointly saved a murder suspect from that fire. God! That now seemed like years ago. Nick made a mental note to allow Adam to take a shower before he went back to his cell. It was the least he could do.

Despite the severity of his situation, Adam attempted a weak smile. Soon they would all know everything and the reason why.

"His daughter, Miranda, was also present, along with one of their henchmen. They had a gun trained on me, so I was forced to let Sadler go. Then the other bodyguard arrived. I was beaten and thrown into a cell in that bunker. I could see the relief on Jason's face. He suspected that I would never live long enough to see the light of day – that Jeremy Salander intended to kill me."

Adam face crumpled in disgust as bitter memories pervaded his mind. He reached for the cup of water and took a sip before continuing. He was still suffering from smoke inhalation, and his throat burned, the cool liquid only offering temporary relief.

"Jason actually gloated about what he'd done to Sophie before adding that he'd also killed her mother, my ex-wife Jessica," he spat. "And then Reg McGee turned up. I thought he would help me but, as it transpired, he was in Jeremy Salander's pocket."

Brian frowned and consulted his notes. The room fell silent.

"Remind me again, who this Reg McGee is?" he asked. "I've heard the name before."

Never taking his eyes off Adam, Nick cleared his throat and explained that McGee was a fellow detective who had committed suicide shortly after Adam had been taken hostage. Often off sick and the bane of Nick's life, Reg had left a parting note, apologising to Adam's family. Reg had been present when Adam was captured and he had failed to help him.

Adam, lost in those memories, focused his attention on the table in front. He curled and uncurled his fingers, reminding himself of why he was here. He remembered the smug expression on Jason Sadler's face after admitting to raping his daughter, the hurtful things he had said and the way he had gloated. Adam knew without a doubt that, if he had his time over, nothing would change. He would happily kill him again.

"So, tell us exactly what happened in that bunker, Adam. We know some of it, but I'm guessing a lot more went on than you previously divulged," said Nick.

Adam closed his eyes for a second or two before addressing his boss. It all came flooding back – the terror, the pain. He'd forgotten how afraid he had been. He was going to die, and nobody but McGee even knew where he was. He would never see his children or his wife again. The taunts of Salander's bodyguards haunted him. "The drain in this cell is for your blood. When Jeremy has finished with you, we will wash you down the plug hole!"

"Jeremy Salander believed I had killed his son, Tony, which you know I did not do. In fact, as you will recall, it was his sister Miranda who ended his life. But Jeremy didn't know this, and had the two thugs beat me again. I was shackled to the wall and couldn't even defend myself, much less fight back. Then, for some reason, one of the thugs released my left arm. I think they wanted me to retaliate, to make it more sporting, but by then, I was in no fit state. It was during this time, I became aware of the others – of the half a dozen Romanians that Jeremy had trafficked over.

"What made them stop, Adam? Why didn't they kill you?"

"They were never going to kill me," Adam replied quickly, locking eyes with Nick. "Jeremy wanted that pleasure for himself. It was Miranda who eventually stopped the beating. The thugs left us alone, and we had a brief conversation in which she acknowledged that it was she who was to blame for her brother's death. Obviously she was afraid of her father and so was happy for me to take the fall. However, unbeknownst to her, Jeremy had been hiding in the shadows and heard everything she said. That's why he shot her."

"Just like that? His own flesh and blood?" Brian blinked and turned to Nick, who nodded in affirmation.

"Jeremy Salander was a little extreme," Nick interjected.

"You don't say," muttered Brian, raising his eyebrows before addressing Adam again. "Please continue."

Adam exhaled and bit down on his lip until it hurt. He didn't like returning to that day. Until now, he had managed to suppress the fear, but these intrusive questions were forcing him back. Suddenly, all the crippling terror began to take hold. He could almost smell the dampness of the bunker and feel the chill in the air that had seeped into his skin. His hands began to tremble. He had nearly died that day.

"He turned the gun on me and pulled the trigger," he said quietly.

For several seconds, nobody spoke. Nick swallowed hard as he stared at his friend. He'd had no idea – no idea that any of this had occurred. Adam should have been counselled after his ordeal, but how were his colleagues supposed to know what he'd been through if he hadn't told them?

"So, he pulled the trigger …" Brian coaxed.

"It jammed," Adam said bluntly, locking eyes with him. "As he was trying to figure out what went wrong the police had just entered the grounds and he was forced to abandon his plan to kill me and flee. In a rage, he threw the gun on the floor. "

Ah, that makes sense now, Brian thought.

"So you were able to take possession of the weapon?"

Adam nodded.

"Yes. I managed to secrete it just before my colleagues arrived and rescued me."

"And when you took the gun, did you know what you wanted to do?"

"You don't have to answer the question," advised Terry, his voice laced with caution. This was where his defence could crumble beneath their feet. Everything hung in the balance, and his biggest fear was that Adam was about to throw everything away in one fell swoop. A premeditated crime was considered a damn sight more serious than a crime of passion.

Adam contemplated his answer very carefully. He knew what his solicitor would want him to say. But while he was now deemed a criminal, he would always think of himself as a police officer. Integrity and honour ran through his veins. If he didn't have that, what did he have?

He fixed his eyes on the officers across the table – his friend and boss, Nick Marshall – a man who had, on many occasions, stood by his side. And Brian Proctor, not so well known to Adam but someone he had a great deal of respect for. They were watching him closely. One more glance at Terry's wide eyes confirmed the tension in his solicitor's face. Adam answered the question.

"Yes. I believe I knew exactly what I wanted to do," he confessed.

CHAPTER TEN

DS Amanda Black watched in horror as the dishevelled man dropped to the floor at her feet. She'd had the misfortune of babysitting the hapless Vince Taylor and learned that he wasn't afraid to display his emotions. Melodramatic was the best way to describe him. It could have so easily gone the other way, Amanda mused, as he curled himself up in a ball and buried his head in the crook of his arms – Vince was prone to lash out violently too. He began to sob loudly.

"Mr Taylor, please, as yet, we don't know for certain," she begged, trying to make herself heard over his cries. "Until we've established the identity through dental records we can't be sure it's your wife. I just need you to be prepared for the worst."

"Chrissy – oh Chrissy, Chrissy," the man howled. "Please God, not Chrissy."

It had been a tough few days for Vince, and Amanda did feel sorry for him. Not only had his daughter, Ruby, been raped and left for dead, he had since discovered that he might not even be her real father! Plus, Christine had disappeared, and it looked very likely that she had perished in a fire at a rundown stately house out at Amberley. Police had someone in custody for Ruby's rape and attempted murder – the same man who owned the mansion that had burned down.

Dr Craig Donohue was now unconscious and under police guard at St Richards Hospital after having been severely burned in the blaze. He would be questioned the moment he was fit enough to be interviewed. Blood samples had already been taken to ascertain if he was responsible for the girl's attack, as well as a host of murders, current and historic, that bore the same MO. The police were awaiting the results, which were being fast-tracked.

"I can't take any more bad news," Vince confessed, his voice a little calmer. He lifted his head a fraction and peeked up at Amanda. Her face softened at the sight of his wretchedness.

"Look, we don't know – not for sure," she said again, in a vain attempt to give him a smidgeon of hope. She watched as he pulled himself up from the floor before collapsing heavily into an armchair.

"Sorry," he mumbled, apologising for his display of grief. He reached across with a shaky hand to retrieve a packet of cigarettes from the coffee table. "You don't mind if I smoke do you?"

Amanda shook her head, pretending she didn't. It was his house, after all.

"As soon as I know more, I will let you know."

Vince nodded and ignited his fag, drawing in a comforting lungful of nicotine. He turned away slightly and projected a gust of smoke towards the wall. Then he sniffed and ran his fingers through his wavy black hair, messing it up further.

"There's something else I need to know," he said quietly, pinning Amanda with an intense stare. Suddenly he was very calm, his eyes dark and his lips pressed firmly together. Gone was the emotional wreck of a few minutes earlier.

"And what's that?" she asked carefully, feeling a prickle of unease as a hint of danger hung in the air between them.

"I need you to find out something," he whispered, tapping the side of his cigarette packet with his index finger. "If Ruby isn't my child, then what happened to my real baby? Dead or alive – what did they do with her?"

CHAPTER ELEVEN

"Wh-what did you say?" Sophie gasped, her eyes darting frantically back and forth between Rosemary and the female police officer. Even though the string of words had entered her brain, she didn't want to believe the damning sentence they had created. It couldn't be true, please God! But grim reality stared her in the face. Her stepmother looked devastated – her appearance so dishevelled that Sophie was sure she wouldn't recognise her if she saw her on the street.

Rosemary sank into a nearby chair and buried her face in her hands. Then she broke down and cried – pitiful heart-rending noises. Sophie stared down hard at her, unable to move – her expression frozen in shock. PC Sue Llewellyn, who stood awkwardly to one side, also seemed bewildered by the turn of events. That suggested to Sophie that what Rosemary had just told her must be true.

But Adam's daughter needed to get things straight, so she repeated her question.

"What did you say?"

Her throat was tight. There was no way that she could disguise the rising hysteria in her voice. Rosemary continued to sob. Sue reached out and gently patted her shoulder, as if she were petting the family dog, whilst waiting for the distraught woman to answer the child. But Rosemary seemed unable to stop crying long enough to explain what had happened, so Sue realised she had to. She couldn't help but feel the utmost pity for this family. Adam Kent was just as much a part of her family as well, professionally, of course.

"I'm sorry, but your dad's been arrested," she said carefully. Rosemary wailed loudly from behind her hands. Sophie frowned and blinked. Yes, she had heard right, but it still didn't add up.

"No, that can't be true. Dad can't be arrested. He's a policeman, like you," she pointed out, her brain desperately trying to form some logic. "He arrests other people."

Sue's face softened. She was close to tears herself.

Sophie swayed from side to side and looked as if she were about to topple over. She fell into a chair and wrapped her arms around her torso, staring down at her feet, distractedly noticing that her toe nails needed repainting. Her brow furrowed in thought as her adolescent mind tried to work through this gravest of adult situations.

"What for?" she eventually murmured, her voice barely audible above Rosemary's cries. Sophie raised her head, locking defiant eyes with Sue. Right now, this uniformed lady, with all her horrible stories, represented the enemy. Sophie clenched her jaw before switching her attention to her stepmother.

"What for?" she demanded, a little louder, indignantly. She needed to know the truth, and she needed Rosemary to be the one to give it to her, not this stranger.

Very slowly, Rosemary's grief-ravaged face emerged shyly from the protection of her hands. She hitched a staccato breath to help control her sobs and swallowed, biding her time. The moment she had been dreading had arrived, and she kept her eyes cast downwards, unable to meet the teenager's uncompromising stare.

Sue frowned as she studied the distraught woman, watching the colour flare on her cheeks. Was that shame she read on Mrs Kent's face?

"For mur-der," Rosemary rasped with difficulty before, once again, hanging her head and seeking sanctuary behind her closed fingers.

Bile formed in the back of Sophie's throat, burning her windpipe, but she forced it down. It was ridiculous what they were saying. Nothing made sense. She stared helplessly at Sue, waiting for her to elaborate, as she obviously wasn't going to get any further information from her stepmother.

"He didn't fucking kill anyone," Sophie argued, not caring if she was chastised for using bad language. "He wouldn't do such a thing." God, could this day get any worse? Sue instinctively held out her hands to placate the angry teenager, whose angelic features were contorted in rage and denial. The time had now come for her professionalism to kick in.

"I'm afraid it is true," she said gently but firmly. "Your dad has been arrested for murder."

Rosemary continued to weep. Sophie shook her head, her eyes wide with disbelief.

"And who's he supposed to have killed?" she spat, challenging the voice of authority.

"A man by the name of Jason Sadler, so I've been told," Sue stated, once again peering down at Rosemary for confirmation.

Sophie suddenly felt icy cold. She could no longer feel her hands or her feet. Her teeth began to chatter, and inwardly she screamed as a crippling panic took hold. *Jason!* Dad's killed Jason! No. No. The words spun around in her brain like a swarm of angry bees. Yes, she knew her stepfather was dead; she remembered the evening her father had told her the news. Sophie could also recall how glad and relieved she was that the man would never again be able to hurt her. But never, *never* in a million years, would she have suspected her dad to be capable of doing something like this.

"There must be some mistake. Dad's a policeman – like you," she murmured, pointing rudely at Sue. "He wouldn't do that!" But even as she protested his innocence, elements of doubt formed a troubling picture in her mind. *Would he?*

Sue glanced down at Rosemary, who was sat hunched over like an old woman. She was conscious of the awkward distance between these females. Despite their grief, it appeared as if they

43

were far from united, as if an invisible barrier was separating them when they should be consoling each other. Adam's wife was being of no help whatsoever. Who was the child here? Evidently it would be left to Sue to calm the teenager down.

"Things will become clearer very shortly," Sue stated, trying to keep her own worry for Adam in check. "I really don't know anything more than I've told you. Nothing's been officially confirmed. I was just instructed to drive your stepmother home."

"So there's every chance he might be okay?" Sophie asked, grasping at straws. "It might all be one gigantic mistake."

Sue fixed her eyes on the girl's hopeful face. Rosemary hadn't moved, but seemed to be holding her breath.

"I don't think so," she said carefully. "At least, the arrest part. It's whether your dad had anything to do with Mr Sadler's death, but it seems as if he's confessed, so we'll have to wait and see." Sue knew she was probably saying too much, but these weren't ordinary members of the public – they were part of the police family. As far as she was concerned, they had a right to know what was happening.

"This is your fault," Sophie hissed with hostility. Sue looked up in surprise, assuming the girl had been addressing her, but instead saw that Sophie was directing her wrath at Rosemary. Animosity and pure hatred radiated from her. Sue's earlier suspicion had been correct – Adam's wife and daughter had issues and, much like a scab that had been ripped away to reveal a weeping wound, there was something between these two females that had never been allowed to heal. Rosemary kept her head down. In fact, she appeared to shrink further into her chair as if protecting herself from this vitriolic attack.

"If it wasn't for you, everything would be fine. I told you my secret, and you betrayed me. Now dad's paying the price," Sophie screamed before springing to her feet and running out of the room.

CHAPTER TWELVE

The first thing George Robins did when he arrived home was to make a beeline for the drinks cupboard. His target? An unopened bottle of whisky given to him last Christmas from his aunt and uncle. He made this his number one priority, even putting his craving ahead of kissing his girlfriend, Natasha or patting Claymore, his elderly basset hound. George needed to wipe from his mind what had happened during the past few hours, and he figured the only way to achieve any inner peace was to get thoroughly pissed.

Natasha knew straight away something was amiss. Although George had lately been displaying signs of stress from work, he always made time to remind her how special she was to him the moment he came home. Each time he walked in through the door he would hold her and kiss her whilst asking if she'd had a good day. But something was clearly different. George barely paid her any attention as he barrelled his way through the house consumed by his quest for alcohol.

"What's the matter George?" she cried out in halting English, her Romanian accent strong in her confusion. "Has something happened?"

The dog barked a couple of times and wagged his tail enthusiastically as his master strode past, then slumped down with a huge dejected sigh when George ignored him. Natasha wasn't quite as quick to catch on as she trailed after her boyfriend, demanding an explanation.

"George, talk to me," she nagged, following him into the kitchen. Claymore had returned to his bed in the lounge. George fumbled with the bottle's screw top lid, his hands shaking as he poured a healthy measure of whisky into a tumbler. He put the glass to his lips. So desperate was he to feel the first bite of alcohol that he knocked back the entire contents in one hit. He coughed and wheezed from the burning sensation travelling through his oesophagus before immediately replenishing his glass. Whisky wasn't exactly his favourite tipple, in fact he didn't really like it, but he would never tell his relatives. They had been buying him the same gift for more than a decade, so the time for honesty had long since passed. He had a growing stash of bottles hidden away in the understairs cupboard, gathering dust. But not for much longer, he thought. Judging by the way he was feeling, George took great comfort in their close proximity and was glad he hadn't given any of them away.

"George, please, talk to me," Natasha beseeched, her large hazel eyes wide with bewilderment. He was acting totally out of character, and it was scaring her.

"I don't want to talk about it," George muttered, throwing another mouthful down his throat before taking the bottle and brushing past her on his way out to the hall. Natasha's hand fluttered to her mouth, but she didn't move from the kitchen. She heard his heavy tread on the stairs and closed her eyes tight when the door to the bedroom slammed shut. All that was left in his wake was the unfamiliar tang of whisky hovering in the air.

CHAPTER THIRTEEN

"Hello, this is Peter Jennings from the News of the World. I've just received a tip off that one of your police officers has been arrested for the murder of Jason Sadler. Can you confirm this?"

DI Brian Proctor bristled, his face turning scarlet. He tightened his grip on the phone, throttling it as he imagined he might do to the journalist's throat.

"I don't know where you have got this information," he seethed. "But I have no comment."

"So you're not actually denying its true," challenged the eager journalist. Brian, who could almost picture him salivating with excitement, was still at a loss as to what had touched off the media frenzy. Jennings was the fifth enquiry relating to Adam Kent's arrest. For now, as with the previous calls, he found it easier just to end the call.

"Good day to you," he said bluntly before switching off the phone.

"Another one?" Nick asked, as he watched Brian shove the mobile back into his jacket pocket. Brian nodded glumly, his lips pressed into a thin white line. "Christ! It didn't take them long," Nick added, equally befuddled by the shrewdness of the press. "How could they possibly know so soon?"

"Well, obviously, we have a leak," Brian growled. "One of our officers is clearly untrustworthy and is going to cause all manner of fucking damage. Something as juicy as this is bound to spread like shit. And it could be anyone!" Brian, who never used bad language, was certainly making up for it today.

The interview with Adam had gone relatively well. But the fact that the 'culprit' was one of their own had soured any inclination to be pleased. Adam, an effective and highly respected member of their team who had been on his way up the

47

career ladder, had blown his entire future with this devastating revelation. Moreover, he had been charged and consequently would be spending the night in a police cell. Yes, they could have granted him bail – they knew him and they trusted him to turn up at the Magistrates Court for a bail hearing the following morning. But this was a murder charge – serious enough to keep any member of the public in custody. And as much as Brian hated to do it, he couldn't be seen to grant any special favours. That's why, because of his recommendation, the Custody Sergeant denied bail until the next day.

Adam had accepted the news with good grace. The only difference was that his booking in details hadn't been entered onto the computer system. For a prisoner as sensitive as he, procedures were put in place to use a paper trail so that only those closely involved with the investigation would be party to the contents.

"I hate leaving him there," Nick remarked sadly as he strode alongside his colleague on their way out of the Custody Block. Adam's incarceration was resting heavy on his mind, and he knew he was unlikely to get much, if any, sleep tonight. He had planned to go out to dinner with Amanda, but wasn't in the mood and suspected he wouldn't be much company. He was sure she'd understand, imagining that she might not be feeling any better than he under the circumstance. Instead, he would go home and probably spend most of the evening negotiating, or rather bickering, with his soon-to-be ex-wife, Philippa, over the division of property and custody of their children. Not a very pleasant task, he thought, but his marital problems paled into insignificance when compared to Adam's situation.

"It's out of our hands now," Brian said curtly, referring to Nick's comment about leaving their colleague in the cell block. Names were spinning around in his mind as he considered who might have had the audacity to go to the press. And when he found out who the culprit was, he or she would be out on their ear with their career in tatters – that's *if* he ever found out. But there was one problem to deal with first – something Brian needed to do his utmost to subdue.   When Superintendent Tarring got to hear about this leak, he was going to go 'nuclear', and everyone would suffer. Tarring had been infuriated when he'd been informed of Adam's arrest. The force should have been rejoicing in finding Jason Sadler's killer, but the whole atmosphere was more befitting of a funeral.

CHAPTER FOURTEEN

Superintendent Carl Tarring was in a foul mood. The day had started badly when it turned out his wife had forgotten to buy his favourite cereal. Then his car, a twenty-year-old Jaguar XJS, was making strange clunking noises on the way to work. He'd turned up the volume on the radio in a failed attempt to drown out the sound, and knew that, whatever the problem was, it was going to be an expensive one to fix.

At work, the day had been fraught with complications from above and below. A witness had died in a house fire out at Amberley, and the other was fighting for his life. And just when he thought things couldn't get any worse, he was bowled over by the news of DS Adam Kent. His natural reaction would have been to assume that this was some sort of sick joke, but it had been DI Proctor who had informed him, and he wasn't best known for playing tricks.

Tarring was now waiting for Brian to brief him on how the interview had played out and whether it was really as bad as he feared. In the meantime, he tried to concentrate on an email he was composing to the Assistant Chief Constable but, no matter how many times he jigged the sentence around, it still didn't read right and made him sound like a complete imbecile. The fact was, there was only one word jostling to the surface of his mind – 'fuck' – not exactly a fitting word when one was addressing a superior officer. He read through the message again, just to make sure he hadn't accidentally entered the offensive expletive.

Tarring rested back in his seat and stared intently at his phone, willing it to ring. The suspense was killing him. He'd had such high hopes for Adam Kent – how could this officer have done such a thing? If he even had! For fuck's sake, Brian, hurry up and call!

His wish was granted. The phone shrilled loudly and, even though he was expecting the call, the noise made him jump. He snatched up the handset, trying to calm his racing heartbeat. DI Proctor's dulcet tones filled his ears.

"Well?" Tarring didn't even try to disguise his impatience.

"He's confessed, sir," Brian replied soberly. "There is no doubt."

"I see," Tarring said quietly as a thousand and one problems galloped through his mind. Adam Kent had been his recommendation for the Inspector Boards. Now he was going to look like an arse. Was there a suitable candidate to take his place? No. It was much too late.

"Sir, I'm afraid it gets worse," Brian added, interrupting Tarring's chain of thought.

"How could it possibly get any worse, Inspector?" he barked. "This is a black day for Sussex Police. Adam Kent has let me down – let us all down."

"And the press already know about it," Brian said, delivering the final blow.

CHAPTER FIFTEEN

Sir Robert Sinclair had never considered himself a bad person. He'd worked hard all his life, paid his taxes on time and built his company to be one of the most respected names in the world of pharmaceuticals. He was also one of the oldest men in his line of business, and his reputation as a fair and caring employer had earned him the affectionate nickname 'grandfather'. Even though he had recently suffered a stroke, Sir Robert had no intention of ever giving up work – well, not completely. There was no way he was ready to let his son, Oliver, take over the reins of the company, but that was another matter entirely. In short, there were no dark corners in Sir Robert's professional world. It was his personal life that gave him sleepless nights.

There were two things of which he wasn't proud. The first occurred seventeen years ago. His younger son, Lawrence, who was eighteen, raped the eleven-year-old granddaughter of his then housekeeper. The result was a pregnancy that was so far along when it was discovered that an abortion was out of the question. So Sir Robert did what any father in his financial position would have done – he paid off the aggrieved family and made the baby disappear. He and his wife, Lucinda, regularly graced the pages of society magazines and he didn't need the bad press.

Lawrence had been a problem child since the word 'go' and was a constant ticking time bomb – nobody knew what he would do next. Therefore, it was felt best that he be cut loose from the family and any connection to his birth right severed. It was either that or face prosecution, which neither man wanted. So, much like his offspring, Lawrence also disappeared off the radar, reinvented himself as Jason Sadler and made his own warped way in the world.

Seventeen years later, the legacy of Sir Robert's past actions had come back to bite him. Lawrence Sinclair, or Jason Sadler as he was now known, had been murdered. The police were digging into his past, shining unwanted light into all his family's secrets and dragging skeletons out of long-closed cupboards. They'd been discreet – Sir Robert couldn't fault them there. And the press hadn't gotten wind of Sir Robert's past indiscretions, nor made the connection between the dead man, Jason Sadler, and his estranged son, Lawrence. If they ever did, Sir Robert was certain his fall from grace would be devastating. He would be hounded by the media and his knighthood revoked. No, he could never allow that to happen. From now on, things would have to be handled very carefully, especially since he had recently been reunited with his long lost granddaughter, Ruby – the baby he'd given away.

Although it was probably advisable to leave her where she was and not bring attention to her, Sir Robert couldn't help himself. Despite his nickname, he had no other grandchildren. He seriously questioned Oliver's sexuality, and Lawrence had been a deviant – both of them a source of constant disappointment. Ruby, on the other hand, was the only good to come out of all this – the one pure thing Lawrence had created, even if she was born of a rape. Her grandmother, Lucinda, was excited about meeting her and was already planning to take her on extensive shopping trips. Oliver had expressed concerns about introducing the girl into their lives, but Sir Robert needed to make things right.

Ruby had grown up in a mediocre working-class family when she should have been cushioned by all the luxuries money could buy. She was beautiful, inquisitive and displayed none of the characteristics of her natural father – thank goodness! Her birth mother, Sir Robert seemed to remember, was of Italian origin, so Ruby had been blessed with luscious locks of black hair and a smooth olive complexion. He likened her sharp intelligence to his own and knew that, with the right nurturing, she could go far. Maybe one day, even run his empire.

But Ruby had suffered, not only at the hands of an abusive boyfriend named Simon who, along with his brother, Leo, had manipulated her to do all manner of degrading things before setting out to blackmail her by way of a damning sex recording but she had also been brutally raped and left for dead. Now Sir Robert intended to compensate for all the ill that had befallen her.

Had he handled things differently back then and reported Lawrence for his crime, none of this would have happened. Sure, it would have been a scandal, but Sir Robert was now certain that, as parents, he and Lucinda would have come out blameless. But by having protected their guilty son, a twisted sequence of events had unfurled. With one lie came many others – and still Sir Robert was unable to stop!

As far as Ruby's so-called father was concerned, his greatest fear was that Vincent Taylor was not going to let the subject drop. Nor could he be bought off. Money wasn't always the answer. Yes, the man was unhinged. He had a violent temperament and was infuriated at the suggestion that Ruby wasn't his flesh and blood. Taylor was your typical Neanderthal brute, but he was no fool. As much as Sir Robert dearly wanted him to believe that Ruby had accidentally been handed over to the wrong parents because of a hospital blunder, he guessed that Taylor would see through the whole fabrication.

Unbeknownst to Vince and his wife, Christine, their child had been stillborn. But the nurse in charge, who had been paid to abandon Ruby at an orphanage, thought on her feet and switched the babies. She genuinely believed she was doing her best for everyone involved, and Sir Robert tended to agree. Her smart actions had saved the Taylors' insurmountable heartache. Then. But now Sir Robert wanted Ruby back and it was because of this desire to atone for the past, he had been forced to do another thing he wasn't proud of – arranging the execution of Ruby's boyfriend, along with his equally fetid brother.

If Ruby were ever going to be introduced into society as his long-lost granddaughter, there was no way these scumbags could be allowed to hold such damning video footage over her future. So Sir Robert had enlisted the help of a professional, the recording had been seized and the lowlifes would never give Ruby any trouble again. It didn't rest easy with Sir Robert, having their blood on his hands, but he could see no option. People like Simon and Leo Richards would always be in the background, applying pressure and threatening the status quo. In Sir Robert's mind, it was easier to compare them to other irritants such as wasps, flies and mosquitos – all a bane to mankind. Of course his moral self-justifications only thinly disguised the fact that he had, once again, danced with the Devil.

* * *

Sir Robert was on his way back to the hospital for the second time that day. He was exhausted, but Ruby's doctor had rung, saying there was something he needed to discuss with him face to face and that it couldn't wait. He was mystified. Because of her youthful resilience, she had recovered by leaps and bounds and would soon be discharged. Sir Robert envied her. Because of his stroke, he tired quickly, and since ordering the executions, hadn't been able to focus on much else. Images of two dead bodies constantly danced behind his eyes.

He was seated in the rear of his Mercedes Pullman, being chauffeured to The Primrose Private Hospital. He stared blankly out of the window, lost in a whirlwind of anxieties. It was a muggy day. Storm clouds were approaching and gathering pace. Any minute, the heavens would open and offer a bit of relief. People moved quickly to find shelter before the rain started. Sir Robert watched them but his thoughts lay elsewhere. He wondered how long it would be before Simon and Leo's bodies were discovered and whether the police would make the connection? Beads of sweat formed on his brow and upper lip. He grappled with his good hand for a silk handkerchief and dabbed the offending moisture away.

55

The doctors were allowing Ruby to leave soon. She was very excited about coming to live with her grandparents. Sir Robert was amazed at her inner strength and tenacity but one thing seemed a bit off. He was puzzled by how she seemed to have written Vince and Christine Taylor out of her life. Ruby had been brought up by them and knew nothing else. He would have expected there to have been a little regret or sentimentality, but the girl appeared to have shed her past like an outer skin and was eager to embrace her newly found wealth. In one way, this was very positive. She was happy to turn her back on her old life and had clearly dismissed the man she had once considered her father. If only Vince Taylor would take the hint and accept Sir Robert's story that the whole regrettable situation should never have happened, everything would work out fine. As it was, he feared Vince could become a pest, but what disturbed him more than anything was what he would be prepared to do to lessen the potential damage. Right now Taylor was the one weak link in Sir Robert's string of lies. The world would happily accept the heart-rending story of the hospital blunder, but would Vince and Christine? Sir Robert was certain the man would continue to dig and dig, and he couldn't allow that to happen. If Taylor wouldn't go away of his own accord, then there was only one solution.

His telephone rang, dragging him away from a place he didn't want to be. Happy to be interrupted, Sir Robert accepted the call. It was Detective Inspector Proctor – the man heading up the investigation into Lawrence's murder.

"Sir Robert?"

"Yes, speaking," Sir Robert replied, trying to project his usual upbeat, no-nonsense tone of voice.

"I just wanted to inform you that we now have somebody in custody for your son's murder."

How peculiar, Sir Robert thought as he ended the call. Proctor didn't sound at all pleased by his own news but rather flat – depressed even. Sir Robert hadn't enquired about the identity of the suspect. In truth, he wasn't interested. Lawrence had been dead to him for years. All he wanted was to keep the secret of his perverse degenerate son away from the ears and eyes of the press. A man named Jason Sadler was the victim, and he had absolutely no connection with the Sinclairs.

The Mercedes drew to a halt outside the hospital. Sir Robert waited for his chauffeur to collect the wheelchair from the boot and unfold it before he opened the door. Briers had been doing this for several months now and had become quite proficient. Within minutes, Sir Robert was being steered through the double doors into the cool reception. He was greeted warmly by the receptionist who immediately picked up the phone to announce his arrival.

Generally, Sir Robert didn't like to be kept waiting. He wondered what on earth the doctor needed to see him about that was so urgent. Even though only a short amount of time had passed, he was becoming rather agitated as his mind spun with a host of possibilities. Briers stood dutifully to one side, looming over him as they both stared down the corridor that led to Ruby's room. The scent of freesias filled the air. Sir Robert closed his eyes briefly and thought back to the doctor's phone call. It was something that needed to be discussed in person but away from his granddaughter's ears. Had she suffered brain damage? Was that the problem? After all, she had been left for dead. If that were the case, did he really want a brain damaged teenager on his hands? Perhaps she would be better off back with Vince and Christine. Robert shook these speculations from his mind. Ruby seemed fine, alert. There was nothing to suggest that she was in any way impaired.

He heard a brush of footsteps and saw Dr Pasha walking towards him, white coat fanning behind like the cape of a superhero. He was a tall, dark-skinned gentleman of slight build with cropped salt and pepper hair.

"Sir Robert," he said respectfully, with a slight bow of his head. "Please come into my office."

Briers pushed the wheelchair forward and all three men entered an average-sized room lavishly appointed with highly polished walnut furniture. Dr Pasha slipped in behind his desk and made a concerted attempt to smile, although his soulful chestnut-brown eyes betrayed concern. Sir Robert's gaze swept the room and quickly took in the finer details of his surroundings. An abundance of medical encyclopaedias and reference books lined the shelves. There were luscious green-leafed plants set upon the desk and in the far corner of the room. Sir Robert was unable to tell if they were real or fake but because of the proximity of the building next door and therefore, the lack of natural light, thought probably the latter. Dr Pasha had clearly made this office his home from home. Several silver photo frames adorned the desk and were turned discreetly away from his guests. Pictures of his wife and children? Or his mistress? His homosexual lover? Who knows?

"What did you want to discuss?" Sir Robert asked, unable to disguise his irritation. He considered what time it was and how bad the traffic would be for his journey home.

Dr Pasha opened his mouth and glanced swiftly at Briers before settling his gaze once again on the man in the wheelchair. He nervously cleared his throat.

"What I have to say is extremely sensitive. I don't know if you would, perhaps, wish for us to be alone."

"Rubbish," Sir Robert snapped. "Briers is my right-hand man. I have no secrets from him. I'd like him to stay."

"Very well," said the doctor, resting his elbows on the desk and steepling his fingers. He pursed his lips.

"It's about Ruby," he began.

"Well of course," Sir Robert sighed. "Who else would it be about?"

58

"As you know, she was raped but before she was brought here we were led to believe the hospital in Chichester would have taken swabs."

"I would have hoped."

"We've carried out another test, just to be on the safe side, and it was because of this result that I felt I needed to speak to you face to face."

Sir Robert had no idea where this was going so he just stared blankly at the man. He was so tired and he couldn't trust himself to be civil. Dr Pasha took his silence as an invitation to continue.

"The thing is," he paused, once again looking a little uncomfortable. "The thing is – the test came back positive. There is no doubt. I'm afraid Ruby is pregnant."

CHAPTER SIXTEEN

"GET IT OUT OF ME! GET IT OUT OF ME!"

Sir Robert Sinclair watched in horror as the doctor and nurse tried to calm Ruby down. The teenager was thrashing around, clawing at her stomach. He had never witnessed such madness. He'd expected her to be upset by the news of her pregnancy but not so dramatically. Her nightgown was splattered in blood as she stabbed her soft flesh with her nails, trying to dislodge the life growing inside her.

"It's okay Ruby; it can be dealt with," he shouted above her screams, not for the first time today wondering what he had let himself in for. He mopped his brow again with his handkerchief, feeling his blood pressure soar.

Dr Pasha and the nurse fought to capture Ruby´s wrists as she writhed on the mattress – legs akimbo, the bedding no longer offering her any modesty. Both Briers and Sir Robert averted their eyes. Eventually, Ruby's strength faltered and her flailing ceased. She began to cry.

"Get it out of me, please," she sobbed, her head buried deep in the pillow beneath a cloud of long, black hair.

"We will," Dr Pasha assured her, nodding at the nurse before they carefully released their grip on her wrists. Ruby curled herself into a ball, dragging the sheet over her naked legs. Now that she was no longer behaving like a dangerous wild animal, Sir Robert signalled to Briers to push him closer.

"Ruby, my darling," he crooned. "It will be okay. They can do the procedure and you'll be as right as rain, I promise."

"When? When will they get this bastard out of me?" she hissed, raising her head and fixing wild grey eyes on her grandfather. His breath caught in his throat. He was completely taken aback. He had never seen this side to Ruby. For all her beauty, the angry set of her jaw reminded him of someone from the past. It was the face of someone he longed to forget, his dead son Lawrence. Sir Robert blinked and hesitated as a shiver ran through him.

CHAPTER SEVENTEEN

Adam would have given anything to sleep – just for an hour, one tranquil hour. He'd spent the night in the cell block, staring into space and listening to the other prisoners complaining. Doors opened and closed up and down the corridor, footsteps went back and forth past his door and, occasionally, someone would stop and slide back the viewing window to check on him. It seemed his neighbour, 'Hooray Henry', had long since been interviewed and bailed. No doubt he was now at home, enjoying a good meal with his family. But, then again, he hadn't been charged with murder.

Despite the pleasant temperature, Adam felt chilly, and the custody assistant had kindly given him an extra couple of blankets. But he couldn't bring himself to lie down – not on that plastic-covered mattress and pillow upon which hundreds of other heads had lain. Instead, he pulled the blankets around his shoulders like a cloak and rested back against the wall, wishing the morning would arrive.

After the interview, he had been allowed to shower and was asked if there was anybody he wished to call. Adam's natural choice was his wife, but he changed his mind at the last minute and rang his parents. By the end of the short conversation his father was speechless and his mother hysterical. So he'd spent the remainder of the night wondering if he could have made it easier on them by saying something different. Foolish idea, that. How could he sugar-coat the fact that he'd confessed to a murder and destroyed his career in one fell swoop?

The morning had passed by in a haze. Once again, after a small bowl of cornflakes, Adam was allowed to take a shower. The water was lukewarm and the water pressure pretty pathetic. One of the officers had collected his suit from home and this was brought directly to his cell by the Custody Inspector.

"Best to try and make a good impression, mate," the man had said, a sympathetic smile on his familiar face. Adam didn't know his name, but he nodded a thank you.

The worst thing, so far, were the handcuffs. "It's procedure," they told him. "We're sorry; we know you wouldn't try to make a run for it." Even so, the weight of cold hard steel being snapped around his wrists was a brutal reminder that this was no dream. He automatically strained against them, panicking. Right then, Adam desperately wanted to run – more than they could ever imagine.

Two security officers then escorted him to a van parked in a secure undercover bay. As Adam passed by the Bridge, conversation was temporarily suspended, but he could feel the heat from dozens of pairs of eyes watching his progress. He kept his head down, concealing his shame, the cuffs visible to all and sundry. He knew the moment he was out of ear shot, his crime and fate would be discussed for weeks to come. Colleagues and people who he'd classed as friends would undoubtedly turn against him. Adam knew he was an outcast, and it was only because he was still anaesthetised by shock that he wasn't falling apart.

Luckily, he was the only prisoner to occupy the rear of the van. He guessed the custody staff had deliberately orchestrated this – keeping him segregated from others who might also be scheduled for a bail hearing. There was every chance he would be recognised. Adam had worked out of Chichester Police Station throughout his entire career and undoubtedly made a few enemies along the way. He was thankful for this small mercy.

As the large security gates opened, the van shunted forward. Adam sat behind a toughened Perspex barrier. His escorts refrained from speaking to him. One was discussing a football match and teasing his colleague about his team. Adam was beginning to feel really afraid now. He licked his lips, but his mouth was dry. He tried to switch off from the security guards' chatter whilst speculating how the next couple of hours would pan out. It was a wasted exercise – his thoughts were jumbled and made no sense whatsoever. Instead, he peered through the gap between the officers' heads to stare longingly out of the front windscreen, watching a familiar world turn around him. A flash of a camera made him blink in surprise.

"I don't believe it. The fucking press are here already," the driver muttered as they exited the grounds. Adam was too spaced out to grasp the significance of their presence. The journey was brief. Chichester Magistrates Court was literally just around the block.

Before he realised it, he was in the courtroom, trying to keep his eyes open. As strange as it might seem, given his surroundings and the seriousness of his predicament, Adam desperately craved sleep. Just for an hour; let me sleep for an hour, he silently prayed. Terry Brown sat alongside him. To their left was the Prosecution. It felt weird to be seated in this half of the room. He stared blankly straight ahead – the Magistrates Bench dominating his line of sight. He refrained from making eye contact with anyone and yet he knew Rosemary was there. He sensed her presence, although he didn't seek her out. Every time he pictured his wife, he saw her half-naked in their bedroom with Guy Kane. Her betrayal had, without doubt, expedited this moment.

Somebody close by was sucking on an Olbas pastille – its distinctive mucus-busting odour sailed past his nostrils. Adam could hear his solicitor, Terry Brown arguing his case in an attempt to achieve bail. The Prosecution were strongly contesting it.

"Your Worship, my client has readily come forward. He is definitely not a flight risk. I have no concerns that he will honour his commitments."

Adam was vaguely aware of the authority he was up against. The magistrate that morning was not one of his favourites – a man named Porter. Ever since Adam had been a young probationer, it seemed Porter had taken an instant dislike to him, calling him a 'cocky young copper'. He sincerely hoped that, for once, he would put aside his personal feelings and take on board what Terry was telling him.

"A police officer on a murder charge! Disgraceful!" the magistrate sneered nastily from the bench. "I would suggest he has a great deal to lose and, therefore, every reason to take flight. No, bail is denied. The prisoner will be remanded in custody until the preliminary hearing at Lewes Crown Court."

A rumble of astonished voices from his family broke free. Adam could hear sounds of weeping. He glanced over his shoulder, his eyes sweeping the room. He noticed Rosemary and his mother consoling each other. He quickly looked away to stare miserably up at Porter, catching the malicious glee on the man's face.

"I'm sorry," Terry muttered in his ear, as he gathered his notes. "I'll need to speak to you as soon as possible. We have to discuss your plea."

Terry rose and Adam was encouraged to stand. His legs felt like rubber. The small court room was suddenly filled with the buzz of conversation. With his heart hammering against his rib cage, Adam was led away by a security officer. The crying in that section of the room intensified. As he passed by, he risked a glance towards its source, intentionally dismissing his wife to instead lock eyes with his parents. Both appeared shell-shocked as they huddled together. He had never seen his mum and dad looking so small.

"I'm sorry," he mouthed silently to them before being escorted from the room.

CHAPTER EIGHTEEN

The postman never knocked. There was never any reason to. So as Gavin was encouraging Adrian and William towards the front door to head for school, they were surprised to hear a couple of heavy raps on the knocker. Gavin could see a wide-shouldered man in an orange jacket standing on the other side of the glass panel. He brushed past the kids to open the door.

"This won't fit through the slot," the postman muttered, thrusting a large box against his chest. Gavin struggled to grab it with his one good hand. A pile of junk mail was stacked on top.

"Do I have to sign for it?" Gavin enquired, placing the box on the floor between his legs. Adrian and William automatically fell to their knees and started shaking it, scattering the remainder of the post in the process.

"No," the man replied before turning around to continue on his rounds.

"Don't shake it. It might be fragile," Gavin chastised the boys as he struggled to pick the parcel up off the floor. He had no idea what was in it, but it wasn't particularly heavy. He closed the front door and wandered into the lounge, placing the box carefully on the settee.

"What is it, Daddy?" William asked, plonking himself down beside it, eager to see inside.

Gavin frowned and glanced at the postmark. It was local. He hadn't ordered anything in a long time. Money was tight now. He studied the packaging. It was addressed solely to him in handwriting that looked strangely familiar. Gavin felt a prickle of unease. Something told him he needed to be alone. Without further ado, he instructed the boys to get on their way to school. Whining and remonstrations followed, but the noise ceased immediately the front door slammed behind them. Gavin was left in silence – just him and the box.

He now realised it was from Jenny, his ex-mistress. Just lately, she had made his life a misery – illegally entering his house, keying his car, confronting his wife in prison. What could she have possibly sent him? Something dead? He was almost afraid to look. He nervously plucked at the tape with his good hand. Would it explode in his face? Gavin pressed his ear to the cardboard – nothing appeared to be ticking. It had to be said Jenny made *Glenn Close's* character in *Fatal Attraction* come across as almost reasonable.

"Fuck," he whispered as he tore at the packaging, preparing for the worst. He had to know what was inside.

* * *

There was no dead rabbit or any other deceased animal, come to that. Instead, Gavin encountered wads of ivory-coloured fabric. He grasped a handful and pulled it out. The material expanded, billowing like a huge puffy cloud. As it broke free from its restraints, several glossy square objects also fluttered to the floor. Gavin's eyes widened in surprise as what appeared to be a wedding dress tumbled forth. *Used to be a wedding dress,* more like. Now out of the box, he could clearly see that it had been slashed down the front, with the bodice hanging in ribbons. He dropped the garment as if it were contaminated, only then noticing photographs scattered around the lounge carpet. With quivering fingers, Gavin picked one up. He gasped. It was a picture of him and Jenny, but where his face remained intact, hers had been scored out by something sharp. He reached for another – a different photo, a different background, but vandalised in the same way. Jenny's face had literally been obliterated. There were ten photos in total. All had been damaged. Hazy pleasant memories of their time together came flooding back into his mind.

"What's this all about, Jen?" he asked himself. "Another cry for attention?"

He kicked the empty box across the room. What a creepy thing to do! It was only then that he remembered what she had said during their last phone call – less than twenty-four hours ago. Her words returned to haunt him.

"I've done something. I've taken some pills. I think I need an ambulance."

Gavin sprang from the settee and rubbed some life into his face. His hand hovered over the phone as he pondered on what to do. He had been angry with her. She had gone to Granville Prison and told Tracy all manner of lies. With her mind warped about some imaginary future with him, Jenny must have sounded very convincing – enough to make his wife believe that he was staying with her purely out of sufferance. That was why Tracy wanted a divorce. Jenny had well and truly destroyed his marriage, which was the primary reason he hadn't listened to her.

Was this just another ploy to play him, or had she done something terrible to herself? Gavin suddenly felt very sick. Whether or not he ended up dancing to her tune, he needed to check. Fuck Jenny, this had better not be a game, he thought as he picked up the phone and dialled her number.

CHAPTER NINETEEN

The bedroom reeked of alcohol. Natasha was convinced that if she were to strike a match, the entire house would explode from all the noxious fumes being emitted from his mouth. George was snoring loudly, the noise resonating off the walls. The alarm had sounded, but he hadn't noticed. Every time she tried to wake him, he swore at her. In desperation, she had gone downstairs last night to lie on the settee but couldn't sleep there either. The other male in the house, namely Claymore, had snuffled and licked himself periodically until the break of dawn.

Gritty-eyed and at a complete loss, Natasha tried once again to revive her boyfriend. He was acting very un-George-like. The love of her life had left the house yesterday morning and somehow returned home a stranger. He still wouldn't speak to her.

"George, you're going to be late," she called from the bedroom door.

He groaned and turned over. Lifting his head slightly, he winced in pain and opened one bloodshot eye to glance at the clock.

"Fuck," he said and fell back heavily against the pillow.

"I have to go to work now. Do you want coffee?"

He laughed mirthlessly and flung his arm across his face but didn't answer. Afraid that he would shout at her, Natasha closed the bedroom door and tiptoed downstairs. Usually, George would feed and walk Claymore but she felt it best if she saw to the dog's needs. She didn't have time to walk him though. Claymore, being a Basset Hound, never hurried himself when he took the morning air. So she emptied a tin of food into his bowl and opened the back door.

"No walk today," she informed him. "Go out in garden for poo."

Claymore threw her a disdainful look before padding slowly over to inspect his dish. He sniffed at the contents and then slumped down with a huge dejected sigh.

"I'm sorry, Claymore," Natasha said, feeling guilty as she headed for the front door.

CHAPTER TWENTY

"It is with deep regret that I have to inform you, although most of you probably already know, that your colleague, Detective Sergeant Adam Kent, was charged last night with the murder of Jason Sadler."

Nick Marshall scanned the sorrowful faces that occupied the room. They looked everywhere but at him, each lost in their own depressed world. Some stared blankly out of the window, others at the floor. Nick's eyes rested briefly on Amanda Black, who had evidently been crying and was wiping her nose on a tissue. Nick made a mental note to talk to her after the briefing. They were supposed to have gone out to dinner last night but, with everything that had transpired, neither of them was in the mood to cultivate their budding romance.

Instead, as predicted, he'd spent much of the evening arguing with his wife, Philippa. Despite her being the guilty party, she wanted him out of the cottage. Bloody cheek! His brain had been bombarded with her constant jibes. Since he had shown he wasn't interested in a reconciliation, she had turned nasty. But Nick had more important things to worry about – most singularly what was happening to his friend.

DI Brian Proctor had been to the Magistrates that morning and given evidence. He had called Nick directly with an update. Adam had looked completely zoned out, as if he were up to his eyeballs on Valium.

"He didn't get bail," Brian had told him soberly. "He's going to Marden."

Nick felt a gut wrenching sensation whenever he thought of *that* prison. It was one of the worst – if not *the* worst in the UK. Likened to some of the hell holes abroad, they had major *major* problems. Even hard time cons found it tough to settle in. It wasn't the place to send a copper on remand. Why not Lewes? Why hadn't they sent him there? Someone in the Prison Service needed shooting. Nick knew of two other people who had gone there quite recently – Reginald and Albert Samuels – for armed robbery of post offices. Reginald had been convicted and, like Adam, Albert was on remand awaiting trial. Nick didn't cry often, but he could definitely shed a tear right now for his friend's bleak future. They'd kill him in there, if they ever found out who he was, which reminded him of another important issue.

"What is extremely unsettling is that the press were informed of Adam's arrest long before he was charged which puts them streets ahead of the game. We don't know where the leak originated but when we do find out, that person's life won't be worth living," Nick informed them sternly. "You may have noticed people milling around the front of the building, asking questions. I beseech you, do *not* talk to them. If you care anything about your colleague, it's imperative for his safety and wellbeing that idle talk and speculation is kept out of the papers."

Nobody spoke. The atmosphere was tense, just the odd sniff and clearing of the throat. Nick scrutinised each familiar face. Would anyone here have alerted the press? He sincerely hoped not. He sat up straighter in his chair. Despite the sombre mood, they had to crack on. There was a charred body lying in the mortuary and a badly burned suspect unconscious in hospital.

"Now then, where are we with DNA samples from Craig Donohue for the rape and attempted murder of Ruby Taylor?"

Amanda wiped her eyes and raised a finger.

"They have been fast-tracked. I'll give the lab a buzz today and follow up," she croaked.

"And the suspect himself? Someone told me he nearly died."

DC Aaron Hawker nodded.

"Yes, Guv, but they managed to stabilise him. I'll contact the hospital and find out what his condition is."

Nick nodded.

"Good. He needs to be questioned as soon as he wakes up. I don't have to remind you, this man may be responsible for a great number of deaths over the years. Adam was working on it, he would know..." Nick tailed off. God, where is my right-hand man when I need him? He shook himself from his reverie. There was nothing he could do except perhaps extract some of Adam's notes from his desk, that's if he could read them. Adam's handwriting was fairly neat, but full of a strange kind of shorthand which only he could decipher.

"I'm also expecting to receive the dental records of the fire victim," Amanda added. "To prepare him for the worst, I have informed Vince Taylor that a body was recovered which may or may not be his missing wife, Christine. Adam seemed to think it could be." She swallowed hard, her eyes welling up again.

Nick looked away. The case was in its final stages – just a few results pending. Once he was in possession of these facts, he would call his Hampshire colleague, DI Miles Button, and brief him. It would help to finalise some of their outstanding murders as well. If Donohue was their man, he had been active since the Eighties, perhaps even earlier.

"Just one thing," Amanda said, forcing herself to be strong. Nick and the rest of the team turned her way. "Mr Taylor is focusing on another issue."

"Go on."

She cleared her throat.

"It's to do with his daughter, Ruby – the latest rape victim. As we know, there is some discrepancy over her identity. Mr Taylor now suspects the worst – that she was switched with their real daughter on the night she was born. He wants to know what happened to his child."

Nick huffed loudly and shook his head.

"That's a completely separate matter. Let's not get sidetracked. Operation Crossword is currently dealing with the Sinclairs who, I am led to believe, have put this suggestion forward about Ruby. Our task is to interview Craig Donohue and, with luck, charge him with multiple rapes and murders, as well as to find out the identity of the fire victim. We need to lay this thing to rest people before we muddy the waters with further crimes."

Amanda nodded and turned away, clearly disappointed. By the set of her narrow shoulders, Nick sensed her displeasure and wondered how he could make it up to her. Maybe it was going to be a problem, dating one of his team but he was so attracted to her, he couldn't help himself.

CHAPTER TWENTY ONE

"Be careful what you wish for." That's what his mother always told him. Today, her warning had never seemed so poignant.

DI Brian Proctor had arrived at the conclusion of his briefing and, apart from a few loose ends, Operation Crossword had been solved and his time as a police officer was also drawing to a close. Never in his career had Brian experienced such a depressing outcome to a case. He cast his eyes around the incident room and the people gathered there. DS George Robins was still a no-show, having already failed to attend court for Adam Kent's bail hearing. Brian wasn't in the least bit surprised – ever since Adam had pressured George into arresting him, the man had been a total mess. Even so, Brian was a bit miffed that George hadn't had the decency to call in sick.

Apart from DC Guy Kane, slouched as usual in a chair at the back of the room with his arms folded, Brian could see his own sombre mood reflected in his team's eyes. Kane, on the other hand, had a smug self-satisfied expression on his face. Brian swallowed his temper. Thank God he wouldn't have to deal with that man for much longer.

Very soon, all the crime photographs and various charts relating to Jason Sadler's last-known whereabouts would be taken down from the wall. Piece by piece, evidence would be stripped away, leaving a bare canvas, ready for the next major incident. The telephones, which used to provide a constant background noise, had fallen silent.

It was over. Jason Sadler's killer was on remand, awaiting trial at Lewes Crown Court, leaving Brian with nothing but the bitter taste of regret in his mouth.

Just as Nick Marshall had done, Brian stressed the importance of not consorting with the media, whilst at the same time wondering whether any of the people seated here had anything to do with alerting them in the first place. His eyes instinctively fell on Guy Kane. He had his suspicions, but that was all. Kane was hardly going to admit to doing such a thing, and Brian unfortunately had no grounds to interrogate him.

CHAPTER TWENTY TWO

Sophie had barely moved all morning from her spot by the lounge window, nor had she uttered one syllable to Rosemary's parents since they had arrived with Paige and Luke. They had agreed to stay and babysit until their daughter returned from court, hopefully with their son-in-law.   Everyone was on tenterhooks.

From his seat in the armchair, Patrick would surreptitiously watch the teenager from behind his newspaper.   She sat kneeling on the settee as she stared out at the street, waiting for her dad. Her pain and confusion were palpable.   Every time a car drove by she would snap to attention, noting its make and model before slumping back down.   All the while Patrick's brain was on overdrive as he tried to come to terms with what Adam confessed to having done.   He still couldn't believe it – *wouldn't* believe it.   Rosemary's husband was the most upstanding person he had ever met, and he was proud to call him his son. He didn't know all the facts, but he strongly believed this had to be some kind of terrible misunderstanding.

Carol, meanwhile, was jittery and unable to sit still.   She was constantly up and down out of her chair.   She'd made gallons of tea which, more often than not, was left to grow cold. Occasionally, she would lose control and succumb to her emotions – desperate to talk through the catastrophic situation. That left Patrick no choice but to ask her to be quiet, especially given that she was within earshot of two very fragile little children.

Despite their grandfather's efforts, Luke and Paige had picked up on these vibes and were sat cross-legged on the living room floor, quietly playing Snakes and Ladders.   They knew something was amiss but were far too young to comprehend just how precarious the next few hours would be for their father. They guessed they were waiting for something to happen.   It was hard to ignore the air of expectancy clinging to the house, but they didn't know whether to be excited or afraid.

"What if they don't give him bail?" Carol whispered feverishly in Patrick's ear. He instinctively turned his worried eyes to Sophie and, noticing the stiffening of the girl's shoulders, pressed his finger to his lips. His wife, who was a born worrier, sat chewing her thumb nail. She was now staring intently at him, as if he possessed all the answers.

"He's no risk," he murmured softly, trying to think things through logically. "I can't think why this has happened." Clutching at straws, he added: "It's probably just a bloody mistake – I hope."

"Why hasn't she rung?" Carol asked. "We should have heard something by now."

"No news is good news," her husband replied with forced joviality as he patted her knee.

Carol released a shaky breath and wrapped her fingers around her mug of tea. She took a sip and grimaced. Another one gone cold. She stared at the clock, trying to work out what Rosemary and Adam would be doing now. With luck, they'd be home shortly and not a moment too soon, she thought. This waiting around lark was doing her head in.

"They'll lose the house," she murmured quietly, her mind all over the place, buzzing from one hellish scenario to the next. "If he's sacked and goes to prison, they'll lose this house."

"Carol!" Patrick shot a warning glance her way.

"I see the car," Sophie suddenly blurted out. She pressed her face closer to the glass, trying to see whether there was more than one person inside Rosemary's Beetle. The car approached the house and turned sharply into the drive. In a flash, Sophie was at the front door, flinging it wide open, with Carol and Patrick hot on her heels.

"Where is he?" Sophie whispered to herself as she watched her stepmother alight from the vehicle. Patrick rested a firm hand on the girl's shoulders. He could feel her body trembling

78

beneath his touch. By the haunted expression on his daughter's face, the outcome wasn't good. There was no passenger. Rosemary was alone, and she looked devastated.

"Oh my God," Carol cried from behind him.

"Where is he?" Sophie sobbed. "Where's my dad?"

Patrick pulled Sophie back inside. The last thing they needed was to draw attention to the situation by alerting any nosy neighbours. Rosemary followed them in and closed the door, shutting out the world. Only then did she let go.

For a moment she was unable to speak. She pushed herself into her father's arms and then fell apart. Sophie stood off to one side, visibly shaking, watching her stepmother through wide astonished eyes. Carol was talking to Paige and Luke. Patrick couldn't hear exactly what she was telling them – something about being good and strong for their mum.

"He-he's – they're sending him to prison – until – the trial," Rosemary managed to stammer through an explanation.

"No!" Patrick breathed. "Oh God, no."

He shifted his gaze to Sophie and held out his other arm.

"Come here," he beckoned, inviting the teenager to come forward for a hug. Despite her desperate need of comfort, she didn't budge but just stood pressed up against the wall. She was breathing rapidly like a raging bull about to charge, slowly working herself up to a frenzy. For a moment, Patrick was afraid she was going to hyperventilate.

"Sophie, darling," he crooned as his own daughter sobbed against his chest. "Come on." The girl's face hardened and then contorted in disgust.

"No," she hissed, jabbing her finger at Rosemary. "It's all *her* fault. I don't want to go anywhere near *her.*"

"Come on. What do you mean?" Patrick was stunned by the vehemence in Sophie's eyes. She bared her teeth at him, her pretty features twisted in hate. He couldn't understand her reaction. Under these circumstances, they should all pull together as a family, but it seemed as if Adam's child despised his daughter. Why on earth would she hate Rosemary?

"She knows what I mean," she sneered. Patrick felt Rosemary stiffen. "If my dad goes to prison, it's because of *her*. And then I want to go and live with my grandparents – my *real* grandparents," she added nastily, instantly dismissing Rosemary's mother and father from her life.

"What's going on?" Carol's worried face appeared from around the corner.

"Just keep Luke and Paige away from this," Patrick warned, his wary eyes locked hard and fast on the spiteful teenager. It was as if Sophie was possessed. Patrick was stunned by the degree of hatred emanating from her. She was spitting venom like a cobra. It was natural for her to be upset and confused, but this reaction went far deeper. Seized by a sudden urge to protect his own daughter, he pulled Rosemary into a tighter embrace, all the while focusing on the little ball of hostility standing before him.

"Why not tell them the truth?" Sophie screamed, levering herself away from the wall and storming angrily into the lounge, almost knocking Carol over in the process. Luke and Paige gazed up at her, confused and frightened. They had never witnessed anything quite like this and Paige, being the youngest, began to grizzle.

"Plenty more crying where that came from," Sophie teased cruelly. "Daddy isn't coming home. Daddy is going to prison, and all because your mother couldn't keep her big fucking mouth shut."

CHAPTER TWENTY THREE

There are some places that seem locked in a time warp and HMP Marden was one of them. The first time Adam saw the place, he compared it to a Charles Dickens creation crossed with a Hammer House of Horror production set. It was fair to say this intimidating Gothic structure was a thing of nightmares. Built in the early 1800s on a foundation of clay soil just beyond the Surrey border, Marden was renowned for being constantly shrouded in fog. It didn't matter what time of year either – the mist clung to the exterior like a fine grey veil, adding to its already spooky aura. The notoriety of the one-time 'asylum for the insane' had seeped into the present where, as a prison, it was said to be out of control, and even the most hardened prisoners would quake at the prospect of being sent there. Adam had heard of its infamy through a number of colleagues, but had never had the occasion to visit it. The only inmates he'd ever interviewed were held either in Lewes or The Isle of Wight.

He was still reeling with the knowledge that he would now be making the acquaintance of Marden under the most terrifying of circumstances and that he wouldn't be able to just up and leave. And, to make matters worse, the journey there was passing by a lot quicker than he'd hoped. Sod's law meant that today, of all days, the traffic was light.

Adam sat quietly in the rear of the prison van, staring blankly at his manacled wrists and contemplating his grim future. Looking at him, one might be tempted to imagine that he was calmly accepting of his fate, but his head was filled with a maelstrom of disturbing images. In particular, he remembered the devastated look on his parents' faces in court. He was their only child, so he could only imagine that his dramatic fall from grace must be causing them something akin to bereavement. And then there was his wife. Adam hadn't seen that one coming – that Rosemary would feel the need to sleep with another man! There was no doubt about it – her indiscretion had broken his heart. Of course, she had tried to wriggle out of the blame but it was all so cliché – him walking in on the scene and catching them in flagrante delicto. So what was it about Guy Kane and his uncanny success with women? Adam mused absentmindedly. The man wasn't exactly God's gift but somehow managed to worm his way into the most solid of marriages. Yet Adam still couldn't believe that Rosemary could do this to him.

In a bid to block out the vision of Guy's smug expression, he buried his face in his hands, feeling the vibration of the road beneath. How much longer now? whispered his inner voice as it tore through his reverie. He lifted his head to look around the drab functional interior of the van as if seeking an answer. Without his watch, he had no idea what time it was, but they had been travelling for quite awhile. Oh my God, I'm going to prison, he thought as reality hit him square on for the hundredth time since court. It was far too horrifying to contemplate but, when an image of the Magistrate's mocking face floated into his mind, he was cruelly reminded that this was no nightmare. This was actually happening. He had murdered someone and must now face the consequences. If he had just taken a moment to think it through back then, instead of giving in to his rage, things would have been so much different, and Jason Sadler would have been the one going to prison. Adam's moment of madness had cost him dearly.

Not for the first time today, a wave of panic crashed through his body, leaving him breathless. He doubled over, gasping for air. He was trapped in a van, being driven to Hell and there was nothing he could do to stop it. My life is over, a voice screamed in his head like a raging banshee. Adam sniffed and blinked rapidly, desperately trying to keep the tears at bay. Mustn't cry, mustn't give in to self-pity, he kept telling himself. From this moment on, weakness was not an option. If he wanted to survive another hour – not to mention a day, a month or a year – there was no way he could turn up at Marden puffy-eyed from crying. It was imperative for him to remain calm. With this thought in mind, he tried to concentrate on breathing – slowly inhaling and exhaling – gradually bringing his racing heart beat to a sensible level.

Adam's attempt to relax was very short lived. The van began to decelerate. It lurched slightly, throwing him a little off balance. Needles of fear spiked through him. They were getting close now. He could sense it.

The vehicle slowed even further and turned right. Just recovering from the last panic attack, Adam felt another impending when he caught a fleeting glimpse of the legendary Victorian monstrosity. The van then negotiated a tight left-hand turn into the grounds and HMP Marden reared up through the mist like a nightmare intent on devouring him. In perfect harmony with the rumbling of the engine, Adam's stomach rolled and twisted as the vehicle finally shuddered to a halt.

The next thing he heard was the driver talking to someone, followed by the opening and slamming of a door. Somewhere, a dog was barking. Adam's mouth went completely dry as he waited. The voices were discussing him, he was sure. Would they say anything to the guards about him being a police officer?

Eventually the door was yanked open and he turned and blinked as his eyes adjusted to the sudden change of light. Three figures stood in silhouette against the foggy backdrop – all looked to be male, the tallest of whom was holding a gigantic German Shepherd by a short leash.

"Come on lad," said the voice of his driver, encouraging him to leave the confines of the van. Reluctantly, Adam rose from his seat and shuffled on wobbly legs towards the exit. As he stepped down onto solid ground, he began to stumble, but several pairs of hands reached out to steady him. The dog growled and strained at its leash – its fangs snapping at him. Adam jolted away from its barbed jaw, catching the eye of the beast's handler – a tall gangly man with a pock-marked face. He wore a navy blue jumper with epaulettes on each shoulder and HMP Marden embroidered in yellow on the left-hand side of his chest. Adam couldn't help but notice the sardonic twist of the guard's mouth as he eventually stepped backwards, dragging the salivating animal away to a safe distance and allowing his prisoner room to move.

Adam was then led towards the prison. In the muffled silence created by the fog, the crunch of the gravel beneath their shoes was loud and intrusive. Whilst the guards chatted amongst themselves, he lifted his head and took a moment to gaze up at the imposing façade towering above him. It still didn't seem real that this place could be his future – would undoubtedly be his future once he was convicted. They were now standing within a semi-circular courtyard blighted with weeds and pockets of moss. From here, Adam could make out the basic configuration of the building. It had been constructed in a simple H shape, the central part of which was directly in front with what he presumed to be the detention wings jutting out each side. There were hundreds of windows, not much wider than arrow slits. Even though no human being would ever be thin enough to slip through, these windows had been fitted with bars The grey stonework was blackened with age.

Adam noticed another van parked off to one side, its back doors left open. The vehicle was empty, and he assumed it must have arrived with another prisoner or prisoners just minutes before. Once again, a spasm of fear shot through him. Without thinking, Adam turned one hundred and eighty degrees to stare helplessly at a set of double gates at least fifteen feet high. Straight away, one of the guards placed a cautionary hand on his shoulder, which was a pointless exercise, considering there was nowhere he could run, especially when still wearing handcuffs.

There was a sentry box, complete with a guard, who was in charge of operating the gates, which appeared to be the only way in and out. Rolls of barbed wire, threatening to impale anyone attempting to climb over, had been secured to the top. The wire stretched all along the drab stone walls that enclosed the facility, challenging any hope of escape.

Adam heard the lazy caw of a crow and looked up towards a cluster of broad-leafed trees which loomed in the fog like ghostly shadows just beyond the prison boundaries. The guards were still talking. A whiff of nicotine sailed past his nostrils as he breathed in the damp air. How long would it be before he would stand outside again?

Still focusing on the austere environment, Adam strained his ears, listening for sounds from within. He'd half expected to hear raucous voices from the other inmates but perhaps this mist was acting as a muffler, reducing the noise of the jungle that lay in wait. He was petrified. Very shortly, he'd be rubbing shoulders with some of the nastiest criminals in the country and would no longer have the protection of his job to keep him safe. In fact, it would be a downright liability if the people banged up in there were to learn of his history. He would have to rely on the prison staff to keep him out of harm's way. One of the guards carelessly flicked his cigarette onto the ground and squashed it beneath his boot. Only then was Adam encouraged to walk through a grey metal doorway into a living nightmare.

CHAPTER TWENTY FOUR

It was almost as Adam had pictured. Like most government facilities, especially ones of this proportion, Marden was in need of extensive renovations. The grey speckled linoleum leading to the reception area had ripped in several places and been temporarily repaired with black tape. The décor, yellowed with age, was flaky and dull. Directly opposite the desk was a bench, the wall behind it shiny with grease from the thousands of heads that had rested up against it. Two men dressed in smartish shirt and trousers were sitting there, waiting to be processed into the system.

One of them had a completely shaven head, with tattoos climbing up his neck like a nasty skin infection. Adam could tell by the muscles straining beneath his clothing that he was a fitness fanatic. He had the clichéd LOVE and HATE inked above the knuckles of his hands. The other prisoner was small in stature with a thin wiry frame. With brown hair cut close to his skull, his piggy eyes were constantly on the move. At the same time, he kept licking his lips like a snake in search of its next meal. His behaviour was decidedly agitated, and Adam wondered if he were an addict.

The moment he entered the building, both prisoners raised their heads to scrutinise him, brazenly looking him up and down. After removing the handcuffs, one of the guards nudged him in the small of the back towards the bench, leaving Adam no choice but to put one foot in front of the other. All the while, he tried to project an air of nonchalance. There was no way he could afford to show fear. Slowly he sank down next to 'addict man'.

"All right mate?" said his neighbour. His breath reeked of tobacco. Adam managed a weak smile and grunted a response. The big guy leaned slightly forward, narrowing his eyes in an attempt to intimidate the newcomer. Adam stared directly ahead, pretending he hadn't noticed. Neither man knew him, so had no concept of his inner turmoil. He swallowed and continued to adopt what he hoped was an expression of sheer boredom, suggesting that he too knew the drill and didn't give a toss. He focused his attention on what the guards were doing and the big man eventually got the message and gave up trying to threaten him.

Adam could see a familiar holdall being placed upon the counter and recognised it as one from home. Rosemary must have packed it just in case, and the driver had brought it in. Remand prisoners were allowed to wear their own clothing. He could only hazard a guess as to what was inside. He was still wearing his suit.

A guard who was as large in girth as he was in height was searching through Adam's bag. Despite the hostile working environment, he had an open and friendly face. With his hands clad in blue Latex gloves, he dove into the depths of the holdall, dragging out Adam's personal possessions for all to see. The guard who had been the dog handler, was now making notes. He sneered every time an item of clothing was pulled free. Adam had no idea why. Perhaps to intimidate? He watched as, one by one, his possessions were removed and counted – two pairs of tracky bottoms, several items of underwear, three sweatshirts, four tee shirts, some trainers and one pair of pyjamas. Besides the garments, there was a wash kit. Rosemary had done well under the circumstances. The gangly guard made a grab for Adam's bottle of Paco Rabanne aftershave. He unscrewed the lid and inhaled its scent, then sniggered before addressing its owner.

"I'd think again if you don't want to end up being someone's bitch."

His colleague and the prisoners cackled. Adam caught the eye of the driver who had delivered him to Marden and was relieved to discover that he and his mate weren't sharing the joke. In fact, he could see pity in their eyes. A handful of paperwork was passed over. The larger guard scanned the contents, his eyebrows rising several notches at what he read. He glanced fleetingly towards Adam.

"Let's get Hunt and Bannerman booked in first," he said to his colleague, surreptitiously placing the bundle of documents beneath the counter. Adam stayed put as the other prisoners rose from the bench and ambled forward. Both were compliant and seemed to know exactly what was expected of them. Within less than ten minutes, they were out of sight. Shortly afterwards, Adam's escorts had also vacated the premises.

"So you're a copper," the large guard said in a low voice. Adam swallowed and nodded.

The guard shook his head.

"Someone doesn't like you very much," he added thoughtfully.

* * *

Officer Thomas Hennessy took time to carefully explain the basic procedures, promising that tomorrow's induction with the Governor would outline things in much more detail. Adam was allowed to keep all his possessions. There was no need for anything to be confiscated especially as he didn't smoke, take drugs or drink excessively.

"You're a regular boy scout," Thomas muttered with a hint of a smile as he ticked off the various boxes. "Apart from being on remand for murder, that is." Adam was quite a good judge of character and immediately liked this man. Though meticulous with the paperwork, Thomas came across as pretty easy going and not afraid to share a joke. He guessed he would play fair and even seemed sensitive to the trauma that was undoubtedly raging inside his prisoner. Adam only hoped that the other guards would be of the same calibre.

"Right, your prison number is MN671," Thomas finally said, entering the sequence of numbers and letters on top of the form. He paused and frowned, sitting back in his chair and studying

Adam for a moment or two before continuing. "My first thoughts were to place you straight into segregation – for your own protection. But I also don't want to draw attention to you. If they think we're deliberately hiding something, they'll keep on until they know the truth, and then the bastards will definitely kick off."

By 'they', Adam assumed Thomas was talking about the other inmates. His heart dropped the moment he was informed he wouldn't be placed out of harm's way but would be right in the thick of it. The officer, reading the alarmed expression on his face, smiled sympathetically.

"Trust me. I'm not going to put you in a cell with some kind of loony. I have just the right person – a nice guy. But even so, it is imperative that nobody, however friendly they appear, know anything about your profession." Thomas's face had darkened with the severity of his message. Adam shivered when he considered the implications. "Just drip feed them snippets of relevant information, enough to keep them satisfied. But I cannot stress to you enough – don't trust anyone," Thomas continued, adding to the drama.

"But what about outside influences – television, visitors, internet and so on? Surely, it's only a matter of time before they know about me?"

Thomas grinned.

"Luckily for you, we don't have a television in the common room. The little fuckers keep breaking them, and the Governor refuses to buy a new one. As far as the other stuff is concerned, we'll have to make a judgment call when the time comes."

Great! That might be too late!

"When can I see my solicitor?" Adam asked, desperate to talk to Terry about his immediate future. He needed a plan and quick. Life inside was going to be like walking a tightrope.

What were the chances that his secret would remain undisclosed indefinitely? Minimal.

"Mr Terry Brown?"

Adam nodded.

Thomas referred to his sheet of paper.

"He's due to see you tomorrow morning. Now, is there anybody you'd like to call?"

Adam's first thought was Rosemary. She would have been his natural choice, but the past few hours had knocked the stuffing out of him. He was too raw to speak to her. And he couldn't handle talking to his parents either. They were far too wounded by what had transpired. He shook his head, feeling a crushing wave of despondency.

"No, thank you. Not right now."

Thomas regarded him curiously and sighed.

"Would you like a shower? I'd advise changing out of that suit and putting on something more comfortable."

Adam nodded. A shower would be good. He didn't relish the future – sharing the washing facilities with dozens of naked men. Hopefully, he would be alone this time.

"Yes please," he replied.

CHAPTER TWENTY FIVE

Feeling marginally fresher after another inadequate shower and now dressed in tracky bottoms and a tee-shirt, Adam followed Officer Hennessy into the core of the building. When he had removed his suit, Hennessy had taken the time to fold it neatly away into a carrier bag. Adam guessed it was probably because of who he was.

The noise inside the block was deafening, made ten times worse by the way it echoed off the walls. Faces were pressed against the small viewing hatches like animals in a zoo – hands reaching out through the gaps. It was as if they could smell the fear of a new inmate. The moment they laid eyes on him, they bombarded Adam with a series of wolf whistles and kissing sounds that made his blood run cold. His clean-cut good looks could also prove a disadvantage. Once again, he considered that he would probably be better off locked up, out of the way. Not that he had a choice in the matter.

Hennessy refrained from speaking as he escorted him further inside. He didn't appear to hear the barrage of intimidation, just took everything in his stride. But there again, he wasn't a prisoner, and these threats, sexual or otherwise, weren't directed at him. Officer Hennessy would be going home tonight.

Adam stared in awe at the cavernous space surrounding him, the ceiling of which seemed to rise miles above. During the booking in procedure, Officer Hennessy had explained that both convicted prisoners and those on remand inhabited this part of the prison.

"There's the hospital wing, which also houses those undergoing drug rehabilitation," he told him. "And then there's a section for the most dangerous, bordering on lunatic."

The interior of this wing was much like any other standard prison – metal doors fronted each cell, complete with small viewing hatches. Some were slid closed, while others had been left open. A series of metallic stairways crisscrossed their way towards the upper floor leading to walkways, again constructed of metal, which circumnavigated another collection of cells. Safety netting had been strung up in between, just in case anyone was unfortunate enough to fall, or perhaps get pushed, over the side. Adam refrained from making eye contact with the other prisoners as he took one leaden step after another towards his fate. If they ever found out who he was, he would be in grave danger. Every minute inside this hellhole was going to be a game of survival.

Eventually, Officer Hennessy came to an abrupt halt outside a cell, half way along.

"Stand away from the door," he bellowed before bending slightly forward to peer in through the viewing window. Satisfied that he wasn't about to be jumped, he removed a hefty bunch of keys from his belt and inserted one in the lock. He then pushed the door open.

"In you go," he said, swinging the keys backwards and forwards on his stubby right index finger. Adam took a deep breath to steady his nerves and shuffled forward.

The cell was approximately eight feet by eight. To the left, bunk beds were pushed hard up against the wall. There was a metal toilet with no lid and a metal sink. A number of personal possessions were stacked upon a small table that had been set off to one side. Seated on the top bunk was a male in his mid-twenties, who was tall and of average build. He was nice looking, with a flop of dark hair.

"This is Azz. He'll be your cellmate. Azz this is Adam. Time to make room, Bud. I hope you'll be very happy together," Thomas said cheerily.

Azz slid off his bed, landing firmly on the floor and enthusiastically approached Adam with his hand extended in polite greeting.

"Good to meet you," he said, his face creasing in a genuine smile. Adam clasped his hand and they shook like two businessmen completing a deal. It was all very civilised and most unexpected, given where they were. Adam turned to Thomas and raised his eyebrows in relief. The guard winked back at him as if to say, "See, I told you so. You'll not have any problems with this guy."

"How long 'til grub break, boss?" Azz asked conversationally.

Hennessy consulted his watch.

"Not long now, mate. You'll keep your eye on this one for me?" he said gesturing towards Adam.

Azz smiled good-naturedly and nodded, flashing a cheeky wink. Just then, Adam saw something that made his insides curdle in fear. Hennessy, now satisfied, began to back away and, within seconds, had closed the door behind him. Adam stared in desperation at the exit and winced when he heard the turn of the lock. He then felt a hard slap across his shoulder blades.

"Come on, you're on the bottom bunk," Azz said. "It's your first time inside I take it?"

Adam swallowed and nodded. He attempted a smile. On the whole, the lad was friendly and seemed perfectly normal although what was unsettling him was the fact he looked strangely familiar.

"Well, don't you worry. You'll be having the sugar-coated induction crap from the Governor tomorrow morning, but just listen to me if you want to know the real score. I'll keep you updated as to who you should stay clear of and, believe me, there are plenty of them. By the way, do you want some tea?"

Adam cleared his throat and tried to relax. The lad was making an effort to be nice. He nodded.

"Yes, please," he murmured. Azz smiled again and turned towards a sink. There was a small travel kettle set upon the table in the corner of the room.

"I didn't think we'd be allowed anything like that," Adam said, all the while trying to think where he had seen Azz before.

"Well, you have to work your way up to this. Earn the right. It's all down to privileges. You're lucky to be in here with me. I'll explain everything to you after lunch – how it all works and crap."

The kettle boiled and Azz dumped a tea bag into a plastic beaker before drowning it in water. He filled another beaker with hot water and then set about sharing the precious teabag between each cup. After about a minute or so, he turned towards Adam and handed him the tea.

"Thank you," Adam said.

It looked revolting. There was no milk for one thing, but beggars couldn't be choosers. He took a sip. Azz carried on talking although Adam was barely listening. He was having trouble coming to terms with everything that had happened to him – that he was sharing a cell with a convict. It was only when he realised his cellmate had gone quiet that he glanced his way. Azz was staring directly at him, a puzzled expression on his handsome face.

"What is it?" Adam asked, suddenly alarmed.

Azz shrugged nonchalantly, which was at odds with the way he continued to scrutinise him.

"I don't know," he murmured thoughtfully and frowning. "It's just that, I think I've seen you somewhere before."

CHAPTER TWENTY SIX

"You've missed a spot," the man said lightly, almost cheekily, as Tracy stopped for a breather and leaned on the mop she had been pushing. Her head snapped round to discover Prison Officer Mark Bowson standing a few feet away. The everyday racket of prison life had masked his approach and caught her off guard. He was now smiling down at her, his green eyes sparkling with amusement. Too shocked to think of a witty retort, Tracy just stood there dumbly, her cheeks burning crimson. Bloody Charlotte. It was all her fault!

Tracy had been excused from doing anything strenuous whilst recuperating from her operation, but had begged the powers-that-be for some lighter duties – anything to stave off the boredom. It was probably because she was an ex-nurse and qualified to assess her own level of fitness that they eventually agreed. Hence she was now pushing a mop, soaked in a mild cleaning fluid, around the floors of her prison wing. Tracy didn't belabour the point that doctors and nurses made the worst patients – she was just grateful to be doing something to help take her mind off Gavin's recent visit. Charlotte was a little way off in front, busy unfolding and placing warning signs about slippery floors. If she were to suddenly turn and see Mark chatting to Tracy, her suspicions would be confirmed.

* * *

Mark had only just left their cell earlier in the day when Charlotte started prattling on that he fancied her. Tracy was blind to this suggestion. Not only was he a prison officer and she an inmate, but he was also several years younger. Still jittery from the altercation with her husband, the fleeting surge of courage that had given Tracy the strength to demand a divorce was now in danger of waning. The crux of the matter was that Gavin was all she knew and that, warts and all, perhaps she should reconsider. And they weren't the only ones in this equation – Adrian and William's welfare had to be addressed as well. Their parents divorcing would devastate them.

But Charlotte's whimsical idea was not to be easily dismissed – nothing wrong with a bit of innocent fantasy to lift her from the monotony of her own existence. As soon as Mark Bowson retreated from their cell, Charlotte had sprung from the chair across the room and scuttled over to Tracy's bunk, her face beaming with excitement as she stated her observations.

"It's so bloody obvious, Trace," she whispered feverishly. "He watches you *all* the time. Maybe you don't see it, but I watch him and he's always looking at you."

"Don't be ridiculous," Tracy argued. Her self-esteem was at rock bottom. Even if she were feeling good about herself, which was certainly not going to happen being stuck in here, it didn't alter the fact that he wouldn't look twice at a prisoner.

"I'm not," Charlotte retorted, refusing to drop the subject. "Just now, he was focusing solely on you. He didn't have to stop by."

"He was concerned. That's his job. He'd witnessed the scene in the visitors' room with Gavin. He was just making sure I was okay."

Charlotte didn't reply but continued to wear the same annoying, all-knowing smirk. She returned to her chair, pleased that she had at least planted the seed.

Since Gavin's visit, Tracy had endeavoured to push away any romantic thoughts of Mark. There was no point even dwelling on this idea, however pleasant it might be to think that somebody fancied her despite her lack of grooming and no make-up. The idea was ludicrous. Yet here he was, taking time to strike up conversation. Could Charlotte's suspicions be correct? Hell, Tracy was so out of practice when it came to interpreting the subtle signs of the mating ritual.

* * *

"I'm sorry, but I'm going to have to step on your clean floor," Mark continued, gently placing the sole of one immaculate boot onto the wet surface.

"That's okay," Tracy mumbled gruffly, aware of the heat rising on her face. *Bloody Charlotte!* She stood aside, mop in hand, as she allowed him to pass. Just as Mark drew level, he smiled again and winked at her. The wink was so fleeting, Tracy almost missed it. In fact, she wondered if she'd imagined it. She stood watching him move away, stopping once or twice to chat to the other inmates. He didn't look back.

Tracy released a deep sigh. She hadn't breathed properly the whole time he was standing there. She caught Charlotte's eye and the girl grinned, giving her a thumbs up. But Tracy still wasn't convinced. Even if he had winked, it didn't necessarily mean anything. He probably did that as a matter of course. She could see by the way he engaged with the other women that he was pleasant to everyone. So Mark Bowson was a nice guy who treated prisoners like human beings – *all* prisoners, not just her. No, Charlotte was mistaken, and she wished her friend hadn't said anything in the first place. For all Charlotte's good intentions and wild imagination, Tracy's already low self-esteem had just taken a rapid nose dive.

* * *

Mark resisted the urge to look back. He wondered if Tracy was watching him. He hoped so. *What the hell am I thinking?* he said to himself as he continued on his rounds. Nothing would ever come of it! He tried to focus on his job and not the pretty prisoner behind him. It would be unethical to strike up an affair in here – occupational suicide. It was just that Tracy Peterson didn't belong among this rabble of convicts. She was elegant, attractive and vulnerable – his perfect woman. His mother was always on at him to find a nice girl and settle down, but he guessed that a divorced ex-con wouldn't be her idea of a suitable daughter-in-law. He really had to get a grip.

97

Mark stopped once or twice to answer a couple of questions. They were always the same, and he rattled off the answers almost parrot fashion. The women in here were cheeky, sex starved and they weren't shy about making their feelings known. He spoke to several of them, trying to balance friendliness with professionalism. It was tough being a youngish bloke in here. He knew most of them fancied him sexually, so felt an affiliation with women being constantly ogled by men.

He had a date tonight – an old school friend. Perhaps he just needed to get laid – anything to take his mind off someone so unattainable. There was no way he could even tell anyone how he felt. No one he would dare trust.

CHAPTER TWENTY SEVEN

"Craig, can you hear me?"

Alex?

"Craig. If you can hear me, move your fingers."

The beguiling voice sounded closer now. He had heard it before but it had been far-off – like a distant dream. Now as the barriers to his dormant mind began to fall away, Craig Donohue was waking up.

"Craig, can you move your fingers?"

Alex?

It didn't sound like his friend, but he couldn't be sure. The request was simple. *Move my fingers.* Why was it so difficult?

The voice moved away.

"I'm sorry, there's still no response," he said. "Maybe we'll have better luck tomorrow."

Oh no, Alex. Please don't go. I'll do what you want. I'll try to move my fingers. Wait!

* * *

DS Amanda Black did everything in her power to conceal her frustration. She needed answers. *They* needed answers. She was trying to keep a man from going out of his mind wondering what had happened to his wife, and Donohue held the key to this mystery. She glanced over the doctor's shoulder at the motionless patient – her suspect. One side of his face was swathed in bandages from the burns he had sustained in the fire at Rosalind Hall. Although he was hooked up to all kinds of contraptions, which monitored his heartbeat and kept him hydrated, Craig Donohue could breathe on his own. He had been unconscious since being rescued from the devastating situation he had created. Unfortunately, the woman with him in the house was not so lucky and had been burned beyond recognition. Police suspected that she was Christine Taylor, the missing wife, but they couldn't confirm that until they received her dental records. If they could only interview Donohue, he would be able to identify the deceased and put an end to their painful speculation.

Amanda turned to the doctor – a middle-aged man whose shiny bald head protruded from a halo of wispy grey hair. His smooth pudgy fingers made her skin crawl and his breath reeked of garlic. She searched around the depths of her bag for a business card. Amanda was losing count of how many she had handed out to medical staff since Donohue had been admitted. It seemed as if there was a different doctor present every time she came here.

"If and when he wakes up, please call this number," she said, pressing the card into his hand. The doctor studied it and slipped it into his coat pocket. Amanda wondered if it would just remain there – forgotten until the garment was eventually laundered.

"Will do, and it's not a case of if, it's a case of when. He's stable now, although we did nearly lose him."

"I know," Amanda said, shifting her gaze to the patient. She took a step forward and stood at the foot of Donohue's bed, watching the steady peaks and troughs on the monitor before staring down at the exposed side of his face. He had been very nice looking before the fire – strong jaw, dark lashes. Just wake up, you bastard, she thought. From the evidence they had so far, this man was responsible for a series of rapes and murders and heaven knows what else. All should become clear once they had a chance to talk to him, and that shouldn't be too much longer.

Right now, she had to give Nick Marshall an update and see what she could do about Vince Taylor, Christine's husband. He had a bee in his bonnet regarding his daughter and Amanda feared he was close to losing his sanity. And after all he'd been through, who could blame him? She was annoyed and frustrated when Nick dismissed her concerns during the briefing, although she reluctantly agreed as to his reasons why. It was just that he had been so blunt about it – showing her up in front of their colleagues. But then again, like her, he was upset about Adam. Everyone was. Emotions were running high. This case was Adam's baby. No one knew it better than he, and now he was out of the equation. How the hell are you coping, Adam? she thought gloomily, suddenly feeling choked up. She turned from Donohue.

The doctor, sensing Amanda's sombre mood, smiled apprehensively and stood off to one side to allow her sufficient room to pass.

"I'll be in touch," he promised as they both exited the ward. She sniffed and nodded, fighting for composure. He probably misread the whole thing and thought she was upset about Donohue. Tonight, she and Nick would go out to dinner – conversation almost certainly centring on this case and on Adam's predicament. How could these subjects possibly be avoided? And instead of what was supposed to be a romantic meal, it would end up feeling like work.

* * *

The voice was gone but Craig was now awake. He didn't know where he was or what had happened. He just knew he was lying down and that his throat was raw. The surrounding noises penetrated his consciousness. They sounded strangely familiar. Bleeping – steady rhythmic bleeping. Was he in hospital? It smelt like a hospital. It smelt like work. He felt pain in his face – pain in his hand. It wasn't extreme but it was mildly unpleasant. Moving his fingers was easy now. Where was Alex? Was he watching over him, keeping him safe? Craig Donohue opened his eyes and stared around. The room was empty.

"Alex?" he croaked hoarsely.

101

But nobody replied.

CHAPTER TWENTY EIGHT

After a number of discreet sideways glances at Adam, Azz was still unable to place where he had met his cellmate. But Adam finally did remember, and the memory flooded him with renewed dread. Struggling to keep his features impassive, he prayed that Azz hadn't notice anything untoward. He had to remain cool and unflustered. There was only one way he was going to survive Marden and that was to keep his profession under wraps. It was important to behave naturally. Sure, he was entitled to be scared – it was his first time in prison – but he had to behave as if he had nothing to hide.

The problem was, Adam had actually arrested his cellmate. It had been many years ago granted, but Azz's memory was bound to kick in sooner or later. To be fair, Adam wasn't responsible for him having been put in here; that had come later, at the hands of another officer. But would he still awaken one night to find a crudely fashioned knife at his throat? He was walking a thin line and knew that if he let his guard down, for even a second, his predicament would turn drastically worse.

He had been a probationer, and Azz was just thirteen. He had caught the lad red-handed stealing a car – the first of many similar offences in his young life. Adam knew him as Aaron Secrett – a cocky whelp who wasn't without a certain degree of charm. He was always polite to the officers and a model prisoner. Nine times out of ten, he'd get off with a caution. But Azz couldn't help himself. He was addicted, and his passion for the kind of cars he would never be able to afford had propelled him into a life of crime.

After that first arrest, their paths hadn't crossed again, but Adam was aware of the kid and how he was constantly upping his game – his targets becoming more and more desirable and their horsepower more impressive. Not only did he steal the cars, but he would race them around like a maniac. That was mercifully usually after dark when the majority of roads were relatively clear.

Sadly he became unstuck two years ago when somebody died during yet another police pursuit. Azz was used to being chased around Sussex by the law; it was all part of the fun and, this time, he was behind the wheel of a Porsche. He had been tearing through Worthing, enjoying the buzz of flashing blue lights closing in on him. It was gone midnight. The weather was foul and the streets were virtually deserted, so any threat to the public was minimal. Or so thought the officers in pursuit. Sometimes it was considered safer for everyone involved to terminate the chase, and the Ops One at the time had to rely on their updates to decide whether or not to call the whole thing off. The fact that the Porsche was thundering through a quiet leafy suburb at nearly 100 mph was enough to finally issue the order to let him go. The driver was clearly putting himself in danger, and the police, suspecting they knew who he was anyway, would just confirm his identity using CCTV.

Unfortunately, the request to drop back came in a second too late. An elderly lady in a long white nightgown suddenly emerged from a line of parked cars into the path of the speeding Porsche. Azz did his best to swerve but impact was inevitable. The old woman was killed outright when she hit the windscreen and careened over the roof of the stolen vehicle, before landing in a bloodied heap in front of the wheels of the police car. Why she was wandering around in the pouring rain in only her nightclothes, they had no idea. It was assumed she was confused, perhaps suffering from dementia.

That night saw Azz slapped with the weighty charge of Causing Death by Dangerous Driving, along with his usual Aggravated Vehicle Taking. The officers at Worthing Station had dealt with him from start to finish. The boy was good at heart and was desperately remorseful for what had happened, but his reckless actions had cost someone her life, and he was sentenced to ten years in prison. And here he was in Marden, sharing a cell with the man who had first arrested him more than a decade ago.

* * *

They had just finished their tea when the door to their cell clunked opened. Adam turned around in surprise.

"Lunch," Azz simply replied. "Come with me."

They both stepped out onto the landing and, before Adam realised what was happening, he was swept along by a tidal wave of bodies heading in the same direction. He tried to keep Azz in sight whilst grappling with the unfamiliar environment. The sound of feet stomping down the metal stairs and across the upper gangways, combined with the heightened level of chatter, was almost deafening. It was like letting baboons out of their cage at the zoo. Adam wasn't in the least bit hungry. He couldn't imagine ever having an appetite in here – his fear wouldn't allow it. But neither could he hide in his cell indefinitely. This would only generate unwanted curiosity, and he couldn't risk them asking questions. God only knew if any more of his past arrests would suddenly come out of the woodwork. Azz didn't seem to remember him, but he might not be so lucky with the next one. He couldn't afford to become complacent.

Adam continued forward, staring at the back of his cellmate's dark head as it bobbed up and down in the crowd. He kept his lips pressed tightly together and did his best to avoid eye contact with anyone else. Just behave naturally, he kept telling himself.

Eventually, they filtered into a cavernous dining hall, lined with rows and rows of trestle tables and wooden benches, all screwed firmly into the tiled floor. The walls were solid grey stone, and narrow windows, similar to the ones Adam had noticed when standing outside, were set high above. Again he observed bars crisscrossing each one, reminding him of his earlier conclusion that they were pointless. Nobody would be able to scale the wall in the first place, unless he had superpowers, of course.

At one end of the room was a long counter with a cluster of servers standing behind it. Surprisingly, the prisoners had now formed an orderly queue. There were two inmates between him and Azz, but Adam resisted the urge to push forward and join him. As each man approached the counter, he grabbed a tray, behaving just as civilised as anyone would in a canteen. Then the food, which smelt reasonably okay, was slopped unceremoniously onto plastic plates by a man sporting Popeye-sized biceps and a mess of intricate tattoos. When Adam arrived at the counter, he refrained from grimacing. It looked to be some kind of curry but he was unable to detect what sort of meat it was. Something fatty in a watery sauce. His stomach curdled in revulsion, but a ladleful of the bright yellow mixture, topped with clumps of white rice, was still dumped onto his plate. He shuffled forward, staring at his lunch in dismay.

"For fucks sake, what's your problem?" It took Adam only a matter of seconds to realise the server was addressing him. Through his peripheral vision, he noticed the man's aggressive stance and so barely looked his way, afraid of the repercussions eyeing this prisoner would bring.

"Sorry," he mumbled as he retreated from the counter, having no intention of eating anything. He peered almost shyly around the noisy environment, desperately seeking Azz in the sea of unfriendly strangers. The guard he had encountered earlier with the dog was standing off to one side, watching the proceedings through narrowed eyes. There were several other officers present, although Thomas Hennessy wasn't among them. Adam hesitated, just standing there in confusion until someone called his name.

"Over here, Adam," shouted Azz.

He breathed a sigh of relief, pleased that his cell mate had saved him a place. Seated opposite were a number of inmates, two of whom Adam recognised from their photographs but had thankfully never dealt with personally. They were brothers – Albert and Reginald Samuels – inside for armed robbery and handling stolen goods. Adam knew Albert's son, Dale who attended the same school as Sophie. In fact, the kids had been dating until Albert had forced the boy into helping him with his illegal dealings and they'd been caught in the act.

Dale was a sensible lad and had respected Adam's initial reluctance about him seeing Sophie. After his brush with the law, he had pretty much acknowledged that there was no future for him dating a policeman's daughter. Adam guessed Dale would probably do the honourable thing and take a step back, but it was only a guess. Because of recent events, he hadn't had a chance to talk to his daughter, but he suspected she would be heartbroken.

Adam forced aside any thoughts of Sophie or the rest of his family. He really couldn't afford the luxury of thinking about them now. It was more important to get through the next few minutes, surrounded by such unsavoury company. He approached the table.

Sitting beside Albert was the biggest man Adam had ever seen. Even seated, he overshadowed everyone else. With mousy lank hair scraped away from a heavy brow, this giant stared blankly into space, holding a fork, the way a child would, in his left fist. Adam shuffled forward. Try as he might, he couldn't take his eyes off this guy.

He was just about to place his tray on the table when a solid punch came from nowhere, hitting him square on. Adam was sent sprawling to the floor, his tray crashing on top of him. Covered in the sticky yellow mess that used to be his lunch, he barely had a chance to look for his assailant before he was kicked in the gut. The other prisoners began banging their trays against the tables and stamping their feet in excitement. "Fight – fight – fight," they chanted. Clutching his stomach and curling up into a tight ball to protect his head, Adam wondered if he was doing the right thing. Would he be considered a coward and signal to everyone else that he was an easy target if he didn't fight back? The problem was, he hadn't had a chance to get a handle on his attacker or attackers. Where were the guards? Why weren't they stopping this?

The kicks came from all directions, raining down on his body, followed by more and more plates of food being poured over his head. He couldn't stand even if he wanted to. Adam could now feel the burning curry sauce seeping into his eyes – there were grains of rice up his nose. Did they all know his secret? Was that why they were attacking him? Because they'd found out he was a copper? Slipping and sliding over the soiled tiled floor, desperately trying to escape, Adam eventually heard the merciful high pitched sound of a whistle and, as quickly it started, the assault ceased.

"Welcome to Marden," somebody shouted. He could hear the roar of laughter and dared to risk a peek. They were all laughing at him – even Azz. Gingerly, he lifted his head and tried to wipe the curry sauce from his face.

"Come on," said his cellmate, smiling down at him. "You can stand can't you?"

He held out his arm and helped Adam to his feet.

"What was that?" Adam groaned. He hurt all over but knew he wasn't seriously injured. He was unable to stop the trembling and hoped Azz couldn't feel his fear.

"Just the Marden initiation. We all go through it," he replied matter-of-factly.

"Did I pass?" he groaned.

Azz shrugged noncommittally.

"That's up to Reginald," he replied.

"Reginald Samuels?" Adam was amazed that Reginald wielded so much influence.

Azz raised his eyebrows in surprise and looked over towards the table. Reginald was watching them curiously.

"You know him?" Azz whispered.

Adam bit his tongue. How could he make such a colossal mistake so early in the game? Yes, being a police officer, of course he knew of Reginald Samuels. He struggled to compose himself, taking his time to respond and hoped that Azz would interpret this delay as him trying to recover from the attack.

"I come from Chichester. I've heard his name through the grapevine, that's all," he murmured, clearing his throat.

Azz nodded, but he didn't seem convinced.

CHAPTER TWENTY NINE

Gavin Peterson had led a conventional sex life; some might even call it mundane. Here was a 21st century man whose sexual conquests could be counted on one finger – the woman he had married. So it wasn't surprising that, bombarded by all the permissiveness of the times, he was ripe for adventure. The thrill of anticipating sex with a new partner, with the added spice of sneaking around behind his wife's back, was just too seductive for a rather average guy with a mortgage and two kids to ignore.

His brief dabble on a dating website had meant no harm. He had even chosen one for married people, hoping to attract a no-strings-attached liaison. But unfortunately, the female who had piqued his interest hadn't exactly played by the rules and by the time he did find out, it was too late. He was already smitten.

Jenny Wallace didn't have a husband, not even a live-in partner. Why she had signed up on the Secret Rendezvous website was a mystery. When Gavin had first made contact with her, his nerves were all over the place, and he innocently assumed that she was in the same position as he – with a spouse lurking in the background. When he did find out, he felt relief, rather than anger. After all, there was no danger of getting punched out by a jealous husband.

Looking back, Gavin wondered if perhaps that was her plan all along – to ensnare a married man. At least there'd be a certain degree of dependability. After all, they had relinquished their freedom to a woman once before. Maybe Jenny had been the victim of a long line of disastrous relationships and so, had decided to try a different approach. But whatever the reason, her enrolment onto the Secret Rendezvous Dating Site had been the catalyst to all that had gone wrong in the Peterson's lives.

During those heady early days of their relationship, when they had repeatedly tumbled into bed like a couple of rampant teenagers, Gavin believed he had fallen in love with Jenny. So much so, in fact, that he had confessed all to his wife, packed his bags and moved out. Tracy Peterson, who had also only had one love in her life, was completely devastated. She had always imagined their growing old together, and she had no idea how to cope with his betrayal. But in a short space of time, her heartbreak was replaced by a ruthless thirst for revenge, which accidentally led to another cheating husband's death and Tracy being sentenced to five years in Granville Prison.

That had given Gavin the shake up he needed. With the illusion of his fantasy life shattered, he was left feeling dirty and riddled with guilt. He dropped Jenny and returned to his family. Now seeing things much more clearly, Gavin had no doubt how much he loved Tracy and was desperately sorry that his immature selfishness had cost his wife her freedom. And if things had been left at that, they would have pulled through as a couple. Despite her incarceration, Gavin and Tracy were rediscovering their feelings for each other, though they couldn't make love or do anything physical to express them. But as time wore on, the future once again looked bleak. Tracy was being slated by the press, the kids were suffering at school and Gavin soon became lonely.

Now armed with a sense of indifference, Gavin returned to Jenny's bed. He had no intention of ever deserting Tracy but he needed sex and his ex-mistress was a willing participant. He ignored Jenny's passionate declarations of love and, even though it made him uncomfortable knowing he could never reciprocate, that didn't stop him from using her. But when Tracy was brutally attacked in prison, Gavin felt the need to abandon Jenny for a second time. He could no longer handle the guilt of cheating on his wife – whether it be with his body or his heart.

Naturally Jenny was confused. She didn't know what she had done wrong. As far as she was concerned, they were happy, and she grasped hold of their once fleeting talk of getting married with both hands. It didn't seem to matter how nasty or evasive Gavin became. Jenny was so wrapped up in her warm, fluffy, make believe world of togetherness, that she was incapable of acknowledging the truth.

From thereon Jenny became a total pain, her own version of *Fatal Attraction.* Whatever Gavin said to put her straight, however he treated her, nothing seemed to work. Jenny had this cockeyed idea that they were meant to be together, and she was hellbent on marrying him. Seeing the situation as nothing more than a lovers' tiff, she pushed and pushed, her actions becoming more and more inventive. Eventually, failing to soften his hardened heart, she turned nasty and began to punish him. She scratched his car, scoring profanities across the bodywork. The situation was becoming desperate, but Gavin believed that she would eventually run out of steam.

She didn't. She did something completely unforgivable, playing what she believed was her ace card. She went to Granville Prison and confronted Tracy with her warped version of the truth. Gavin was furious. Now Tracy wanted to divorce him. She wasn't willing to accept another betrayal. No matter what promises he made to keep his family together, the cracks in their marriage widened and the foundations began to collapse. There was nothing he could do or say to keep his world intact, only the slim chance that Tracy would eventually calm down and consider their children's welfare before doing anything rash.

The last time Jenny had called him, she mentioned she had taken some pills but Gavin was so angry, he put this comment down to more of her game playing. Then the box of mementoes arrived and after achieving no success in reaching his ex-mistress by phone, he decided to bite the bullet and pay one last visit to her house – just in case.

* * *

The boys were at school, and Gavin was now seated in the rear of a taxi winding its way through the familiar roads leading from his house to Jenny's. His muscles were taut and rigid with anticipation. He had no idea what to expect but, if this turned

112

out to be one of Jenny's games, he would really let her have it. A picture of his hands wrapped around her creamy white throat flashed up in his mind but quickly dispersed the moment the cab turned left into her road.

"Looks like someone's in trouble," the driver commented. Gavin peered over the man's shoulder through the windscreen and saw an ambulance, along with a police car, parked on the right hand side. Both had their blue lights flashing.

Instantly he shivered, as if someone had just walked over his grave. It took less than three-seconds to realise that the emergency vehicles were parked adjacent to Jenny's house. In that short space of time, Gavin could see a number of people moving with purpose in and out of an open doorway. He blinked rapidly, taking in the line of smart square lawns fronting these neat terraced properties. But the focus of all this attention wasn't on some random neighbour's house – the door in question belonged to Jenny!

He noticed a couple of paramedics, both clad in hi-viz jackets and with serious frowns etched on their faces. A slender uniformed police woman stood off to one side, talking into a radio. There was an older lady, dressed in a floral skirt, being comforted by a man, her head buried in his chest as she wept. Goosebumps tingled across Gavin's flesh and the hairs on the back of his neck stood to attention. Another shiver rippled through him. The taxi driver was now indicating and beginning to slow, intending to park just in front of the ambulance. When Gavin realised what he was doing, he was thrown into a complete state of panic.

"Keep going," he squeaked.

The driver glanced in his mirror and frowned.

"It's a cul-de-sac mate," he pointed out. Jenny's house was situated within one of the last blocks on the estate.

"Well, just turn around," Gavin snapped.

The cabbie huffed as they passed by, before performing a three-point turn a little further ahead. Gavin was unable to tear his eyes from the scene. He wondered who the older couple were – Jenny's parents perhaps? He'd never actually met them, even though Jenny had badgered him during the early days to come for tea. He'd always resisted; somehow, meeting potential in-laws made the whole thing feel a bit too real. Looking back, he realised again he wasn't as committed to the relationship as he'd first thought. Never had been.

"Now what?" scowled the driver, awaiting further instruction. He had no time to dither as he had another pick-up in twenty minutes.

A hundred and one questions assaulted Gavin's brain. What had Jenny done – tried to top herself or something? That last phone call must have been a cry for help. God, I hope she's okay, Gavin thought. She was the bane of his life but he'd never wish her harm. They'd shared some good times in the past.

"Now what?" the driver repeated, his voice betraying his growing irritation. The engine continued to tick away, and the cost of the fare was increasing by the second. They were now stationary, ogling the scene like a couple of rubber necks, and it was making him uncomfortable. Plus the police woman had clocked the parked taxi and was watching them with interest. Gavin hardly noticed her. He was too intrigued by the events surrounding Jenny's house. Once again, the paramedics emerged, this time wheeling out a stretcher. Even though he wanted to, he couldn't tear his eyes away. He knew he was holding his breath, and it felt as if he were watching everything like a slow-motion movie clip. It wasn't real. He pressed his fingers to the window, wanting to connect with something solid but could barely feel the coolness of the glass.

He noticed a motionless figure being transported towards the rear of the ambulance, a blanket draped over it. The older woman began to howl and wrestled herself from the man's embrace in an attempt to follow the patient into the ambulance. The police officer dragged her attention away from the cab and moved forward to assist.

This sudden exhibition of grief snapped Gavin back to grim reality. He started to pant softly as the contents of his stomach liquified. He clenched his buttocks hard. Was that Jenny under the blanket? Was she dead? If she was, it would be his fault. They would blame him. Her parents would hold him responsible. Only then did he feel extremely exposed sitting there, gawping at them through the window of the cab. If nothing else, it would look highly suspicious. Instantly Gavin shrank down in his seat in a bid to make himself invisible.

"Take me home," he heard himself saying.

Without another word, the driver put the taxi into gear and moved forward. Gavin stared straight ahead, resisting the urge to look back. His stomach lurched, gurgling unpleasantly, and he knew he was in danger of disgracing himself. A waft of sour wind escaped from beneath him and soiled the air. Gavin's face burned crimson with embarrassment. Thankfully, the driver said nothing and just opened his window.

During the journey home, Gavin tried to collect his thoughts. If Jenny had taken her life, could he really have prevented it? Even if he had gone straight to her house, it would have probably been too late. She was a grown woman, in charge of her own destiny. Yes, she had shown signs of being unbalanced, so that would account for any suicide attempt. She was more than likely that way inclined, long before he'd become involved with her. On reflection, he couldn't really hold himself to blame.

The pain in his gut eased a fraction and Gavin began to breathe normally. He was nearly home and was glad of the ever-increasing distance from the scene. If they looked, what would they find? Jenny had sent him all the souvenirs connected to their relationship, so there should be nothing to link them. The fact she had tried to call him suggested she expected to be found in time, so it was highly unlikely she had left a note. The pressure was off, and Gavin guiltily began to feel a smidgen of relief. If Jenny was gone, he would be in a better position to win Tracy back. It wasn't the nicest scenario, but with his ex-mistress permanently out of the picture, his wife might hopefully relent.

By the time Gavin arrived home, he had pushed any feelings of guilt to one side. He felt liberated. The slate was now clean and he had been given a second chance. It was time to beg forgiveness from Tracy.

CHAPTER THIRTY

"That was the hospital.   He's awake. Finally," Amanda sighed as she ended the call and dropped the phone back into her handbag. "And I'd only just left, apparently," she added, shaking her head in frustration.

Nick smiled, reached for his jacket and slipped it on.   This was good news.   The main suspect for several rapes and murders would soon be available for interview. He was looking forward to putting this particular case to bed.   Since he and Adam had pulled a badly burnt Craig Donohue from the flames that devastated Rosalind Hall, it had been touch and go.   There was a time when Nick truly believed the man wouldn't pull through.   He sighed as he consulted his watch.   Nothing more was going to happen today.   Hopefully they'd have the DNA results in the morning and something concrete with which to challenge the suspect.

"Well, we'll deal with him tomorrow," Nick said decisively. "There's no point tearing round there now.   The man's probably still groggy."

Amanda didn't argue.   She was exhausted, mentally and emotionally.   She zipped up her bag and slung it over her shoulder.   Nick opened the door of the CID office and stood aside, allowing her to pass through into the corridor.   He liked the fact that she wasn't one of those feminist types who complained about even the slightest gesture of chivalry.   Nick believed in good manners and never ceased to be amazed when a woman objected to him being polite.   He glanced briefly around the depleted room and the stacks of files, towering like mini skyscrapers on the surface of each unoccupied desk.   Now dormant, it was impossible to imagine how hectic this place could be during the day.   He smiled at the cleaner as he followed Amanda out.

They had planned to go for a quick bite to eat – an early bird special at some local restaurant.   It wasn't the way he'd envisaged their first date, but it was better than nothing. He had so much been looking forward to spoiling Amanda, but best laid plans and all – the job always came first. Thank God, she was just as committed as he. Philippa would have thrown a complete tantrum.

"What did the doc say about Donohue? Is he compos mentis?"

Amanda opened the back door to the station and stepped out into a grey world. Drizzle coated her face in an instant. She bent her head and hurried towards Nick's car, which was fortunately parked under cover. One of the perks of being a detective inspector was to have a parking bay close to the main building. Poor Amanda's little Corsa was buried somewhere out back amongst the rest of the cars belonging to police and civilian staff.

"Apparently, he's making no sense at all. He keeps calling out for someone named Alex. He could be putting it on I suppose," she said sceptically, sliding into the passenger seat of the Mercedes the moment Nick unlocked the car. Nick pursed his lips and climbed in behind the wheel. He too could be quite mistrustful but, where Craig Donohue was concerned, he wasn't so sure.

"Perhaps it's best to get the old trick cyclist to assess him."

'Trick cyclist' was a term fondly used by Chichester police for a psychiatrist.

"Adam thought there was something seriously disturbed about Donohue," he added, turning the ignition key. "Other than the fact that he's an alleged murderer and rapist."

Amanda didn't reply and, for a second or two, both were lost in their own thoughts about their colleague – each wondering how he was faring.

"I may need to see Adam," Nick announced as he backed the car out of the bay. Amanda peered across at him, noticing the

118

clench of his jaw and his lips pressed firmly together, as if anticipating a negative reaction from her. She had seen this look before – it showed determination with a degree of stubbornness. Whenever he was working on a case, if there was something he disagreed with, Nick Marshall would dig in his heels. It was funny how well she knew him – how she could read all the signs. As far as a relationship with him was concerned, she was already several steps ahead. Amanda chose to say nothing – she had no intention whatsoever of objecting. She was also desperate to check up on Adam's welfare.

They glided out of the grounds of the station and onto the main road, turning right in the direction of the level crossing.

"He knows more about Donohue than any of us put together," Nick continued by way of an explanation. "His input will be invaluable to this investigation. Plus ...." His face instantly softened.

"Plus?" she urged gently.

The car came to a standstill at the crossing. Nick focused blankly on the flashing red lights. He barely blinked as the train thundered past.

"Plus, I really need to find out how he's doing," he replied sadly. "After all, despite what he's done, he is still my friend." Amanda nodded in understanding and reached across to squeeze his knee.

CHAPTER THIRTY ONE

A tenuous peace had settled over the Kent household, now that Sophie had finally run out of steam. After thundering up the stairs, she had slammed her bedroom door behind her with such force that the entire house had shaken. Thankfully, Luke and Paige were far too young to comprehend the reason for her fury or the seriousness behind her words, just that she was upset. A few cuddles and a couple of choccy biscuits had quickly restored their equilibrium, and they were now happily playing as if nothing had happened.

Much like people after their world had been convulsed by a terrifying earthquake, the adults cautiously set about trying to return to normality, unsure whether Sophie would reappear in her fury and rattle them with more aftershocks. They tiptoed around the children with pained smiles on their faces – anything to keep them safe and blissfully ignorant for a little while longer.

Carol went back to the kitchen to make yet more tea, and Rosemary was relieved that her parents had offered to stay the night. She was in no fit state to deal with anything, particularly Sophie's distress. Her father was sitting beside her, lost in his own morose thoughts as he stared blankly down at his grandchildren. She guessed by his face that he was trying to make sense out of this catastrophe without the benefit of all the facts – a futile exercise. Rosemary had only divulged the bare bones of what had occurred, and neither of her parents had pressed her for more. For that, she was grateful. She couldn't handle the shame. She hadn't told them about Guy Kane raping her and that Adam had probably confessed to killing Jason in a state of temporary madness because he believed she was having an affair. She cursed her stupidity. She should never have given in to Guy's threats. She knew that now.

The fact that their son-in-law had committed murder was plenty enough for Rosemary's parents to deal with. They knew what Jason Sadler had done to Sophie and that she had been seeing a counsellor, but they never would have believed Adam to be capable of seeking the ultimate revenge.

"Why don't you go upstairs and have a bath?" Patrick said gruffly. "You need to relax. Me and your mum can watch out for those two," he added, nodding towards the kids.

Rosemary sniffed and forced a smile. Yes, a bath would be great. She needed to escape for a bit, gather her thoughts and try to come to terms with what had happened. Right now, everything felt surreal – only pinpricks of adrenalin occasionally pierced the shroud of numbness that engulfed her.

"Do you mind?" she whispered. Her dad patted her knee, just as Carol emerged with a tray of drinks and set them down on the coffee table.

"Go on," he said.

* * *

Rosemary turned on the taps and poured in some lavender oil, before exiting the bathroom and crossing the landing towards her bedroom. On passing, she warily eyed Sophie's door, straining to hear if she was still crying. Despite everything the girl had said, and the hatred with which she had said it, Rosemary felt desperately sorry for her. She longed to offer comfort but knew she was the last person Sophie wanted to see. So she slipped into her own bedroom with a heavy heart and gently closed the door.

This room offered no sanctuary – its harmony sadistically crushed by Guy Kane's assault. Rosemary rested her back against the door and trembled. She squeezed her eyes shut, trying to stem a fresh deluge of tears. She hadn't slept here last night; she couldn't bear to and had chosen to sleep on the sofa downstairs. The bed was in exactly the same state as when Guy was here, although she had cleared away the debris, especially the vile condoms and their wrappers. Even so, the room was still tainted.

Rosemary inhaled a shaky breath and held it for a few seconds. The essence of the trauma she'd suffered was all around – the memory of Guy above her, behind her, touching her so intimately, taking her every way he could. All the time, he wore that same smug expression on his face. And then Adam standing on the threshold – his features contorted by heartbreak. The memory would be forever scored on her mind. Adam believed the worst, of course he did, and there hadn't been enough opportunity to explain. Would he ever forgive her? It had been rape, she kept telling herself; she hadn't wanted it. She would never want anyone but Adam. Surely her husband would eventually understand. But Rosemary had no proof now. Guy had discovered and destroyed the recording she had secretly made. The crushed remains of the little cassette still lingered in the pocket of her dressing gown.

Knowing that the bath would soon be ready, Rosemary tried to clear her mind of the day's wretched events. She had to look to the future, whatever that meant. She tore off her clothing, dropping it where she stood and reached for the same gown, wishing she had another so that she could burn this one. She wrapped it around her body plunging her hand into the pocket as she did so, her fingers seeking out the remnants of the tape. Really, it was useless, but she'd risked so much to record the rape, she wasn't ready to let it go. Carefully she took hold of the mangled evidence, the flimsy tape coiling around her fingers as she placed it in the drawer of her bedside table. One of the plastic spools slipped from her grasp and slid down the skirt of her gown before bouncing onto the carpet. Uttering a quiet curse, Rosemary fell to her knees to retrieve it. Her OCD insisted on keeping everything together, even if the rest of her life was falling apart. Just as she picked it up, she noticed something pink protruding from the hem of the valance sheet and recoiled in disgust. Another one of them! She thought she had destroyed every last one of Guy's used condoms but this had evidently escaped her sweep of the room. With the tip of her finger and thumb, she gingerly plucked the disgusting object from beneath the bed. She almost vomited at the sight of the semen trapped inside the rubber – Guy's semen.

She struggled to her feet and opened the bedroom door. She could hear Sophie talking softly on her mobile. Who would she be calling? Her boyfriend, Dale? Her other grandparents? Or Ruby? Ruby Taylor had been attacked and was in hospital, so she was probably the least likely candidate. Anyway, it was none of Rosemary's business and she was in no position to find out. She raced across the landing, holding the offensive item at arms-length.

Rosemary locked the bathroom door behind her, turned off the taps and lifted the toilet seat, staring down into the porcelain bowl. The warm fragrant scent of lavender rose from the bath and infused the air, but Rosemary needed to be rid of this thing before she could relax.

She dangled the condom over the toilet, preparing to drop it, but something made her hesitate. This was the only evidence that Guy had been here – it had both his and her DNA all over it. True, many people would conclude that the sex had been consensual. Rapists generally don't bother with the niceties of condoms. No, Guy was successful with women, and that's just what he was banking on. No one would believe anything else. If her own husband assumed the worst, what chance did she have to prove otherwise? But if she could make Adam believe that Guy Kane had blackmailed her into having sex against her will – that a crime had been committed – he might approve of her decision to keep hold of this wafer-thin piece of evidence. Rosemary decided to hang onto it, despite how much it disgusted her.

Slowly lowering the lid of the toilet, Rosemary placed the condom on the window sill before climbing into the bath. She rested back in the warm water and closed her eyes. No amount of scrubbing her skin would ever stop her feeling dirty. Only Adam's love and forgiveness could cleanse her. Thinking of him now, she wondered what was happening to him. Was he okay?

She seriously doubted it. How could he be? She desperately needed to see him and again try to explain. If she continued to put it off, nothing would ever get better. Tomorrow. She would go to the prison tomorrow and visit him.

Rosemary tried to block out the memory of his face in court that morning – the distant coldness in his eyes when he glanced in her direction. She knew he was trying to protect himself from the heartache she had inflicted, but it still hurt like hell. Indifference was so much worse than hatred, which at least was passionate. Witnessing the death of his love had the potential to send her over the edge. She had to get a grip, take the risk and visit Marden Prison.

But self-doubt threatened to thwart her plans. What if he refused to see her? Turned her away? What if he was deaf to her allegations of rape? What if her words bounced straight off his hardened heart? What if he didn't care anymore?

CHAPTER THIRTY TWO

Nothing could calm her racing heartbeat nor the sickening churn of her stomach. Her body trembled. It felt as if thousands of needles were stabbing her skin. Shock had deadened her senses and made everything seem hollow and dreamlike, but it had gradually worn off, giving way to this unpleasant prickly sensation. Sophie rubbed her arms vigorously and shivered. She was almost giddy with terror – terror for her father and for herself.

Trying to keep the panic at bay, she lay wide-eyed on her side, staring unblinking at the framed photograph beside her bed. It had been taken during dinner last Christmas, – a brief happy moment captured forever on film. Her father beamed out at her, posing with a spoonful of Christmas pud in his hand. He wore a chunky grey sweater and a silly green paper crown balanced precariously on top of his dark blond head. He seemed carefree – with his blue, hazel-flecked eyes twinkling mischievously and a lopsided grin on his face. Sophie had snapped him with the digital camera she had unwrapped that morning and was pleased with the result. Her dad had consumed a couple of glasses of red wine before the shot was captured and, for once, appeared relaxed. But, her mind screamed, it wasn't true was it? How could he have been? Three months before this photo was taken, he had killed Jason Sadler. His soul must have been in turmoil – his smile a thin disguise.

Downstairs, she could hear the muffled sound of voices – the kettle coming to boil for the umpteenth time. Rosemary's mum had taken refuge in the kitchen, trying to keep busy. Occasionally, Luke or Paige would squeal in delight, totally oblivious to the funereal atmosphere in the house and Sophie's attempt at fracturing their innocence long forgotten. She regretted her outburst. That had been cruel. And she envied them their peace, wishing that she too could share their blissful bubble of ignorance.

She heard the soft tread of footsteps ascending the stairs, the squeak of a door opening across the landing and the taps on the bath being turned on. Sophie blinked once but her eyes didn't stray from her dad's image. A solitary tear rolled slowly down her cheek, wetting the pillow beneath her head. Her mind refused to believe that her father was now out of her reach. She couldn't just call him whenever she wanted to. And there was no point in waiting up for him to come home from work. He wouldn't be coming home – not for the foreseeable future anyway. A desperate need to scream built up in her throat as her battle against the rising panic began to falter. Sophie buried her face in the pillow and silently expelled her misery. That was how it was at the moment – her urge to lash out at the injustice of life, swiftly followed by the blessed sense of numbness before the pressure welled up again.

Where was he now? Was he okay? Would they hurt him? A host of unanswered questions swirled around her brain. She heard the door next to hers open and close again. It must be Rosemary wandering around. At the thought of her stepmother, Sophie swallowed another surge of rage. She tasted bitter hatred on her tongue. None of this would have happened if it hadn't been for *her*. Her dad wouldn't have killed Jason, if *she* had kept her word. Adam may have fired the gun, but Rosemary had driven him to do it by leaking the secret. For Sophie, she might as well have loaded the weapon.

The drizzle that had cloaked the world in grey gradually began to gather momentum, echoing Sophie's sombre mood. Rain fell hard and persistent against her window. Would the sun ever shine again? Thinking how this moment could have been avoided continued to taunt her. If only she could just go back and change a few things, alter the course of history and steer them all down a different path, her dad would now be safe. If only time travel were possible.

But as she lay there a totally new and disturbing idea niggled its way to the forefront of her mind. It was so easy to lash out at others – to lay the blame elsewhere. But perhaps it was nobody's fault except hers.   Maybe she shouldn't have said anything about Jason in the first place and dealt with it by herself.   None of this would have happened if she'd handled it better.   There would have been no visits to the counsellor or the ups and downs between herself and Rosemary, which would have made Adam's life easier. Sophie's blood chilled when she contemplated this shocking revelation.   That was it!   Her dad was in prison, and it was all her fault!

She sat up in bed and pressed her hand to her mouth, stifling another cry of dismay.   Oh my God, oh my God, oh my God. Her eyes darted everywhere – the pink walls, the white furniture, the photos of her mother Jessica, her dad and her half siblings.   The room was compact but cosy – decorated with love.   Her dad had done this – made this her home – and what had she done to repay him?   She had ripped a ragged hole through his happiness with her revelation.   Everything she had done had a consequence.   Divulging the secret of her rape to her stepmother had given her a fleeting sense of solidarity – a problem shared and all that but, because of her childish need to be comforted, she was responsible for a catastrophe.

Sophie reached for her mobile.   She desperately needed to talk to someone – anyone.   She wanted to hear a kind voice and wished that she was still seeing her boyfriend, Dale.   But his behaviour the day before showed that he was no longer interested – that their short time together had ended as quickly as it had begun.   It was no good calling her father's parents either. They would be in no fit state to offer her sympathy when they themselves were trying to deal with the shock of their son's confessing to a murder and now being in jail.   Even though Carol and Patrick were downstairs, they had nothing to do with her.   Instead, Sophie decided she would phone her other grandparents – Jessica's mum and dad.   She didn't see them often because her resemblance to their deceased daughter caused them significant pain.   Still, they were her blood relatives.

She located their number on her contact list and dialled. Because everything had been such a whirlwind, they probably had no idea what had happened, but she was sure they would want to see her once she had enlightened them.

The ring tone buzzed continuously. Sophie held her breath, mentally reciting what she would say, but she never got the chance. Her heart sank when the answering machine kicked in and the gruff voice of Grandfather Bradley invaded her ear. Totally dejected, she left no message and hung up.

Of course, there was always Ruby. Even though she was in hospital there was a chance she'd have her phone with her. Sophie quickly located her number and pressed the green button. She hadn't spoken to her best friend since she was attacked, and consequently felt a stab of guilt. But in her defence, by the time she did find out, Ruby had already been transferred to London. And when Sophie could have made the call, her own world had imploded when Dale dumped her, swiftly followed by her father's arrest. She hoped Ruby wouldn't be too upset by her lack of communication. The last thing she needed was to lose her friendship.

It was a long shot. Maybe mobile phones weren't allowed in hospital. Sophie seemed to recall something about this in a TV soap. It rang for several seconds before the call was eventually answered. Yet the voice on the other end wasn't Ruby's. It was male and sounded drunk.

"Whadyuwant?" the man slurred.

Sophie cleared her throat.

"I need to speak to Ruby," she rasped, half wondering if she had hit the wrong contact.

The man expelled a bitter laugh – a sound so chilling it frightened her.

"My daughter is dead," he spat. "The real Ruby is gone."

CHAPTER THIRTY THREE

Vince Taylor stared down at the phone in disbelief. Where in hell had that come from, saying Ruby was dead? No wonder the caller had rung off. He was shocked himself by the vehemence in his voice. He'd been asleep when the phone rang – one of those deep alcohol-induced slumbers which managed to block out all reality. He was surprised he'd even heard the phone ringing at all! He needed to sober up. That girl asking for Ruby had brought all his demons to the surface, leaving him with a harsh choice – either carry on drinking in the vain hope of obliterating his misery or start dealing with his ever-increasing mountain of problems.

Vince groaned and rolled off the sofa with effort, hitting the floor with a thud. He swore loudly. Some fucker was playing the drums inside his head, and he winced in pain when he tried to open his eyes. Thankfully, the curtains were pulled across, had been for days, casting the room in a shroud of gloom. He could only just make out the shape of the furniture but refrained from turning on the light. He knew there would be empty bottles and cans all over the place and overflowing ashtrays. He'd been living like a tramp in his own home. Plus, everything had been made worse by the rain – he could hear it now, the endless tap, tap, tapping, like an evil witch drumming her gnarled fingernails against the glass.

Vince wanted to shut out the world and grieve over his shattered life. While he had been in France, his wife, Christine had disappeared and was feared to have died mysteriously in a house fire. His mistress, Anna had dumped him and Ruby had been brutally raped and nearly killed. And to add insult to injury, he had since been told that Ruby was not even his daughter! Vince Taylor was on overload, although he took some comfort that not even the strongest man would be able to cope in his shoes. So what if he needed a drink? Who could blame him?

He struggled to his feet and stumbled out of the room into the hallway, tripping on a pair of abandoned work boots as he went. The answering machine was flashing – six messages were pending. He chose to ignore them. No doubt, there would be more bad news, and he couldn't face it. Somehow he made his way to the kitchen, coughing like an old man who had smoked eighty fags a day for fifty years.

Vince's eyes widened when he saw the state of the place. Piles of dirty crockery were stacked high on the draining board, smothered in congealed leftovers. It would take a chisel to lever some of that off. Had he eaten? He couldn't honestly remember, but there again he wasn't alone in the house. Vince felt a pang of guilt when he considered Jamie – his son. He had another child! Where was he now? Upstairs? At school? Vince glanced at the clock on the microwave and, despite still being under the influence, managed to calculate the timings. Jamie should be home soon.

Shit, he thought, raking his fingers through his unruly mop of wavy black hair. At this rate Social Services would be on his back, threatening to take the kid away. He had to pull himself together. But where to start? Housework was always Christine's thing, and she wasn't here. He struggled to stave off the fear that she wasn't coming back. That police woman, DS Black, had mentioned finding a body – a body so burnt that identification would only be possible through dental records. In his heart of hearts, he knew it was Christine. The fact she hadn't taken her passport or anything else suggested she wasn't leaving him or the children for good. She had simply disappeared off the face of the earth. It was the waiting game that crucified him the most, although DS Black had promised they would have an answer to the deceased's identity very soon. How he'd deal with the reality of Chrissy being dead he had no idea. Was the answer contained in one of those messages? Would the police tell him over the phone or do it in person?

The house stank of stale food, body odour and cigarette smoke. Vince licked his lips as he eyed the half bottle of whisky sitting by the sink. "It would be so easy", the devil on his shoulder whispered. Ignoring the voice, he chose to drink a tall glass of water and left the kitchen before he could be tempted further. It was no good to anyone, much less his son, to hide from these problems. As he passed by, Vince pressed PLAY on the answering machine and moved into the lounge to fling open the curtains. Dust particles danced on the air but daylight barely touched the room, the weather was far too miserable.

Apart from a couple of well-wishers and a woman from the press who wanted to talk to him about his daughter's assault, the rest of the messages were from work. His boss was a nice guy and had bent over backwards to get him a flight home from France following the news of Ruby's attack. Vince had been forced to leave his lorry overseas, and it had taken major logistics to get it this side of the Channel. Now the goodwill was wearing a little thin – he could detect strands of frustration in the other man's voice. He said all the right things, of course, offering the company's support, but the crux of the matter was, Brendan Forrester wanted to know when his driver would be back to work. However, worrying about his boss was the least of Vince's problems. He had to get this place shipshape now and provide a decent home for Jamie, then hopefully tomorrow he'd have a better idea about Christine.

Vince spent the next half hour clearing up. The ashtrays were emptied, the beer cans and spirit bottles thrown away. He had even tipped the remains of the whisky down the plug hole. He ran up the stairs, stripped off his clothes and jumped into the shower. By the time Jamie slipped timidly in through the front door, his father was washing up.

Jamie had always been frightened of Vince because of his dad's notion of what a son should be – everything he wasn't. Being small and arty never measured up to his father's football-loving, rough and tumble ideal. Ruby was clearly the favourite. The boy widened his eyes in surprise to see Vince looking so active after days of being holed up in a drunken stupor.

"Hi Jamie, you hungry?"

Jamie nodded. He'd been feeding himself for days, anything he could lay his hands on that didn't require too much cooking. He'd half expected to be scolded for leaving so much washing up but now could see clean dinner plates glistening on the draining board, under a film of soapy water. In his dad's hand was a tea towel.

"What would you like?" Vince asked as he made an exaggerated effort of opening and closing the kitchen cupboards. He spun around and tugged at the freezer door. Jamie watched in awed silence as a fog of cold air escaped before the door was once again slammed shut.

"We have sausages and some oven chips. Would that do you?" Vince continued.

Jamie nodded, pleased that his dad had finally decided to be a parent. He had been so lost lately, having had no one to comfort him. His mother had left and his sister was in hospital. There were just so many questions he wanted to ask but words failed him. He was constantly frightened and unsure – sensed the very foundations of his world cracking beneath him. Hopefully, now that his father had cleaned himself up, he might be able to explain what was going on.

"Go to your room and get changed out of your uniform," Vince said, attempting a weak smile. As he watched the boy obediently turn on his heel towards the stairs, he had a fierce urge to wrap him in his arms and never let him go. But that would be totally alien to Jamie and probably scare the living daylights out of him. Vince had to be patient. If it transpired that Ruby was not his flesh and blood and Chrissy really was dead, he'd have the rest of his life to get to know his own child. He knew he mustn't let his obsession for the truth about Ruby push the boy out of the limelight and back into the shadows. Even so, if someone had cocked up when she was born, they deserved to pay the price.

A bubble of anger rose in his gut. Vince closed his eyes and took a deep breath as he fought to control it. It still didn't answer the question of his own daughter – the baby Chrissy had given birth to sixteen years before. What had happened to her? He had mentioned his suspicions to Amanda Black, but would the police do anything about it, especially when some billionaire was involved? The thought of never knowing rankled deep, and then something occurred to him.

Vince walked back over to the answering machine and pressed fast-forward until he found the message from the journalist. Perhaps this Alice Monk would appreciate having a go at investigating this meaty subject on his behalf. Journalists were great at uncovering the truth and, if there had been some kind of conspiracy, she'd find it. That way, Vince mused, he'd have all the answers regarding that fateful night with minimum effort.

CHAPTER THIRTY FOUR

They say that time drags in prison. They were right. It didn't seem possible that just this morning Adam had been in court – so much had happened since. He would never before have believed that he'd find solace being locked in a cell, but the events at lunch time had proven just how precarious his situation was. The men in here were dangerous and unpredictable. One slip of the tongue, one wrong move, and it was Goodnight Vienna.

According to Azz, Adam had passed his 'initiation' by not fighting back. He had been allowed a few minutes to clean himself up before returning to his cell. That evening, he had had to endure another ordeal with another trip to the canteen. This time there had been no attack, but he could sense them all watching him, trying to suss him out. He kept his eyes averted, had even managed to eat some of the less revolting food, and only spoke when he was spoken to. It was much easier that way. And he stuck close to Azz, despite being unsure if his cellmate trusted him.

Not for the first time since his arrest, Adam wished he hadn't been so spontaneous. Why the fuck had he confessed to Jason's murder? What Guy Kane thought he had on him was probably only circumstantial. It was just seeing Rosemary and Guy together that had made him lose all sense and reason. Adam winced at the memory of his wife and the look of shame on her face when he'd walked in on them. God! It still hurt like hell – much worse than the bruises he had received at lunchtime.

Logic told him he was on borrowed time. How long before Azz remembered him as one of the arresting officers of his youth? The bloke was strangely quiet, undoubtedly mulling things over. As unnerving as this was, Adam resisted the urge to punctuate the silence with inane conversation. It would be best to play it cool and go with the flow. He'd more than likely cock up anyway and rat on himself if he began gabbling nervously. It was a relief when he finally saw the lighting dim, signalling that blackout would shortly follow. It must have been all but nine o'clock but Adam didn't mind. At least the night would give him a chance to think. Azz was busy making another cup of tasteless tea. He turned towards Adam, waving the used teabag between his finger and thumb.

"Do you want one before I throw this away?"

Adam, who was already stretched out on the bottom bunk, nodded. The tea was pretty foul, but he had to be sociable. The fact Azz had offered this at all meant he was trying to meet him halfway. Adam watched as he squeezed out what flavour there was left in the bag into a cup of hot water and handed it over.

"Cheers mate," Adam murmured, taking the cup. Azz hoisted himself onto the upper bunk.

"So, how was your first day?" he asked from above.

"Long," Adam sighed, trying to establish a bit of camaraderie between them.

Azz laughed.

"You'll get used to it, that's if you're convicted. When's your court hearing? Any idea?"

Adam sipped the tea and grimaced before placing the cup carefully onto the cold, tiled floor. Suddenly, the lights went out and they were plunged into darkness. He blinked rapidly, trying to adjust his eyes and focused on the door. Through the gaps, he could make out a faint orange glow that lit up the walkway just beyond their cell. He would have thought the prisoners would have settled down, but the dark only seemed to excite them. They began making noises – some were shouting, some singing, others creating sounds that were quite inhuman. He shivered and pulled the blanket over his shoulders, closing his eyes, trying to block it out.

"I don't know," he replied to Azz's question. "I'm seeing my brief tomorrow morning, I think."

"You married?"

Adam's eyes snapped open and his heartbeat quickened. It was obvious his cellmate wanted to chat. He swallowed, wondering if he should keep all aspects of his private life under wraps. But the best way to lie was to stay as close to the truth as possible, so they said. Just be economical with the facts.

"Yes," he replied, hoping that Azz wouldn't continue to interrogate him about his personal situation.

"You did well today. I'm sorry I didn't warn you about the lunchtime thing, but that's not allowed," he said instead, switching subjects.

"I suppose it had to be done," Adam replied diplomatically.

Azz laughed.

"Reginald was pleased with you. Had you retaliated, things would have escalated and everyone would have suffered."

Adam paused for a moment before saying anything else. He couldn't afford to risk relaxing in this man's company for even a second, no matter how friendly he acted. He sensed Azz was still suspicious, and the last thing he wanted to do was to give him any rope to hang him with. This little tête-à-tête was perilous ground. Adam decided to steer the conversation to the other inmates, thinking that it was perfectly natural to get the gen on the people he'd already encountered. After all, it would probably be considered a bit strange if he didn't.

"So I take it this Reginald guy pretty much runs the show?" he asked.

"Pretty much," Azz replied, turning over and thumping some life into his pillow. Adam heard the thud of movement above him.

"So, who's the big bloke seated opposite us in the canteen?"

Azz broke wind but didn't excuse himself.

136

"That's Toy. He's like Reginald's pet."

"Really?"

"Yeah. He probably shouldn't be in regular prison, but I don't think anybody wanted him."

Adam was intrigued. Toy didn't look completely on this planet. On both occasions that Adam had sat at the same table, the man appeared totally zoned out. He hadn't spoken, and only concentrated on feeding his face.

"Do you know what he did, why they put him here?"

Azz said nothing. For a moment or two, Adam feared he had crossed the line by asking too many questions. Eventually, Azz replied.

"Toy killed someone, but he didn't mean to," he whispered. Adam had to strain his ears to listen, but appreciated Azz taking him into his confidence. "Basically he's a large child who don't know his own strength. He don't think like we do – he's not wired up the same way. For one thing, there's no malice in him. He just likes to play."

"Play?"

Azz laughed softly before explaining.

"Let's just say, it wouldn't be wise to be alone in the shower with him. In fact, he's banned from showering with anyone else. The thing is, if he sees something he likes, he wants to play with it."

Adam was intrigued but said no more. He suspected he knew what Azz was insinuating and found the whole concept rather disturbing. So he made a note to keep out of Toy's way. Azz then went on to tell him about the screws.

"They're okay, most of the time. Watch out for Callum though."

"Which one's he?"

"Skinny, pock-marked face, shifty eyes."

This description fit the officer who had been holding the dog when Adam arrived.

"What's up with him then?"

Azz fell silent for a few seconds.

"You'll be okay, because you're a bit older, but my advice is, don't trust him."

Although his voice was tight, he didn't elaborate further.

CHAPTER THIRTY FIVE

For what seemed like the first time ever, Guy Kane left work that day feeling at a complete loss. His relatively short spell in Chichester hadn't exactly earned him the title of 'Mr Popular' with his fellow policemen. Frankly, nobody liked him. But that didn't really bother Guy. He'd been too focused on nailing Jason Sadler's killer to play best buddies with his colleagues, and if they chose to ignore him outside of work or give him the cold shoulder whilst on duty, he really didn't give a shit. All that had mattered was achieving the objective he had set himself – to be the arresting officer in a high-profile case, which would not only gain him respect, but maybe the chance of recommendation for an eventual promotion. And for that, he had taken risks – *major* risks. He had done things he didn't think he was capable of and, looking back, some of them made him cringe. He had left the Met under a cloud, the reasons for which had hopefully been buried under heaps of paperwork and red tape, although what he had done at Chichester was much worse, on so many levels.

Guy was a great detective, he knew this about himself, and he was a firm believer that rules set in stone sometimes had to be adjusted slightly to achieve the greater good. So he had plotted and schemed, committed burglary and blackmail and even forced a woman to have sex with him. As he climbed into his Ford Capri, he winced at the memory. It was Adam Kent's fault anyway. If he hadn't been the one to murder Jason Sadler, Guy would never have touched Rosemary – well, at least not under the circumstances he had. Yes, he'd have had a go, much like he had with Nick Marshall's wife. He couldn't help himself; he had a weakness for beautiful women. But if his colleague hadn't been guilty, temptation wouldn't have been put in his path. Pure lust and his irrational hatred for Adam had removed all logic.

As Guy drove out of the station grounds on his way home, he prayed that he was in the clear, despite that little stunt Rosemary had pulled secretly recording the rape. Yes, he had destroyed the cassette but now kicked himself for not taking the debris with him. Things could be repaired. There were skilled people out there who might be able to salvage this tape, and Guy could only hope that Rosemary wouldn't realise this and would toss it in the rubbish. So far, nobody had approached him with any rape allegations, so he was pretty confident he was going to be fine. It was time to move on.

But the one thing that bugged him more than anything was that, after all the risks he had taken, he hadn't been the one to arrest Adam. Fucking George Robins had got there first. Fucking George Robins would be the one to go down in local history as the arresting officer and would no doubt receive all the glory and respect that went with it. That was why he had contacted the press about Adam – sour grapes, pure and simple.

Also, for the first time in a long while, Guy was without a woman. He hadn't heard from Philippa Marshall for a couple of days, after he had bluntly told her to go away. She had finally got the message. Rosemary Kent was a no go, and she didn't want him anyway. Of course, there was always Cheryl Durrant, the woman he had managed to manipulate into bed with the sole intention of getting his hands on a particular file. Cheryl was a counsellor, and Adam's daughter, Sophie, had been one of her patients.

Guy suspected that whatever had been recorded in those sessions was the key to Adam's motive for killing Jason. He'd tried to lift it whilst Cheryl was sleeping but she caught him poking about in her private study and threw him out. That was why he'd had to break into her home. But Cheryl was no fool, and he knew she was suspicious. She had even challenged him, but he had denied her allegations, turned it around and made her doubt herself. In the end, she'd ended up crying and saying she was sorry.

Guy knew she loved him, and that was her biggest weakness. She was unaware of what he did for a living – he had given some spiel about being an insurance salesman. Why a salesman would want to pinch one of her patient's files didn't compute and only added to his defence. He picked up the phone. Perhaps he'd forgive her for accusing him, even though he was as guilty as hell. Guy was at a loose end tonight, he was dead horny and he needed a shag. He had every confidence that, when he said the right things and pressed the right buttons, Cheryl would fold and gratefully welcome him back into her bed. With that thought in mind, he decided not to call. Instead he drove. Common sense told him that he'd have more luck weakening her defences face to face.

CHAPTER THIRTY SIX

The Governor of Marden Prison was a man named Edward Hulder.   On the wrong side of fifty, he was usually found stressed up to his eyeballs and cocooned in his office, slowly losing his grip on reality.   He had a penchant for his wife's excellent cooking and, judging by the ever-increasing tightness in his waistband, the figure to prove it.

Edward had held the job for more than three and a half years now and was constantly teetering on the edge of giving it all up. But he knew he never would, at least not voluntarily, what with the excellent salary and pension scheme.   Leaving Marden wasn't an option if he wanted to maintain his status in life, but this meant there were times when he often likened himself to the prisoners he watched over. Trapped. So every day Edward would swing from barely able to cope to not being able to cope at all. The word 'challenging' couldn't even begin to describe the stress he was under and, by the look of things, his job was about to get a whole lot worse.

Spread open on the desk before him was a newspaper with today's date. It was just one of many tabloids carrying the same story, except for the Daily Sport, which was more interested in comparing the breast sizes of various celebrities.

Without taking his eyes from the headline, Edward did what he did on most days when things became a little too much to deal with. He unlocked his desk drawer, withdrew a half bottle of Smirnoff Vodka and unscrewed the lid. After swallowing two or three mouthfuls, he felt much calmer. He returned the liquor to the secret space behind a stack of books and secured the drawer.

Edward sighed loudly, threading his fingers through his curly grey hair whilst he consulted yet another paper. It was no good. He'd have to leave the comforting safety of his office and deal with the situation – something he rarely did. With a groan, he rose slowly from his chair and randomly scooped up a couple of newspapers. Before he could chicken out, he made for the door. Today was not going to be a very good day!

Just as he exited the room, Edward gazed lovingly at the photo of his wife, as if seeking courage and inspiration. He and Norma had been married for thirty years, and he loved her desperately. They had two children, a boy and a girl – both grown up. Norma didn't know about his drinking habit – not that it was a habit, of course. Edward knew he was in total control of the booze, not the other way round. But every minute he was in this job, he needed something to take the edge off. Especially after what he'd just read.

It was bad enough that his prison was labelled the worst in the country and that the powers-that-be had suggested more than once that his leadership skills weren't up to scratch. Edward was on his final written warning, which didn't exactly make him proud. All he'd ever wanted was to be able to hold his head high and receive praise for doing a great job. And yet, they continued to test him. He couldn't see any other reason for them sending a serving police officer, charged with murder, to his prison! Why not another establishment? Was this just another ploy to get rid of him? Make him jump before being pushed? Send in some ambitious new breed to take over?

Edward had read the paperwork on Adam Kent. As far as he could tell, everything was in order, but he wanted to make sure Rule 43 had been put in place. A crime such as this, committed by a copper, was always going to be sensational. In today's society, it was impossible to hide the truth. And once someone was charged, it became a matter of public record. All they could do was minimise the backlash. That's why Rule 43 was so important – to segregate the most vulnerable offenders from the mainstream.

And Edward didn't need the extra hassle of trying to keep this new prisoner out of harm's way. It would be much easier to get Kent transferred to another prison. Inmates died in here – usually because they showed weakness or had been banged up for harming the wrong kind of victim, like a woman or a child. Edward had tried all kinds of measures to curb the violence, but in vain. Marden somehow received the dregs of offenders, if there were such a thing, which was why it was madness to have someone like Kent here. There was no way Edward could afford to have a police officer's blood on his hands. He'd have to come up with a temporary solution before he could get shot of him. He intended to inform Adam of his plan when he saw him later that morning.

"I just hope to God he's been segregated," he muttered to himself.

Armed with his newspapers, Edward headed straight down to the briefing room, which doubled as the officers' break room. He needed to alert the staff as to what they were up against. He moved quickly through the corridors, puffing and panting from the unusual exertion, his shoes tapping loudly on the grey tiled floor. With luck they'd all be congregating before they released the prisoners for breakfast. He could smell it now, wafting up from the kitchens, the cheap sausages drowning in fat.

* * *

Half a dozen heads turned in surprise when the Governor blustered into the room. The guards were busy making teas and coffees, chatting amicably amongst themselves before their duty commenced. Edward Hulder's sudden presence was almost as outlandish as the Sugar Plum Fairy paying a visit, which was probably one of the main reasons the establishment was falling apart. Briefings rarely happened, probably because the Governor was as scared of his staff as he was of the inmates. Usually, if there was something to say, guards were summoned individually to his office.

For a second, nobody spoke. Mugs froze mid-air as everyone waited for an explanation as to this unannounced intrusion. Edward cleared his throat and closed the door softly behind him. He unfolded the first newspaper, losing his grip on the other which fluttered to the floor.

144

"What do you know about this prisoner?" he began.

Officer Thomas Hennessy squinted and leaned forward.

"Ah yes. He came in yesterday, straight from Chichester Magistrates," he replied matter-of-factly.

"And where is he now?"

"I put him in with Azz Secrett."

"You what?!" This was not good.

Thomas shrugged as his eyes travelled around the room. Everyone else appeared relaxed about his decision. Only the Governor looked as if he were about to combust.

"He's – a – police – officer," Edward said slowly, enunciating every syllable whilst prodding the front of the paper with his finger. "Why has he not been segregated? He's at risk from the mainstream prisoners. You should know that."

"I thought different," Thomas argued. "I thought it would spark unhealthy attention if we tried to hide him. They'd all presume he's a nonce or something but …"

"Nonce, police officer. It doesn't matter. I want him out of harm's way and no papers – for anyone," he ordered, glaring around at the sea of hostile faces. "All the while this story's in the press, and I suspect it will be for a very long time, Adam Kent is a sitting duck. I'll be getting him transferred as soon as possible."

"Reginald Samuels is going to go ape shit," Lucas Callum complained, crossing his arms menacingly over his thin chest. His colleagues nodded in agreement. "He always has his morning paper; he'll know something's wrong."

"I don't care," Edward hissed, his blood pressure soaring. "He'll have to learn to live with disappointment. Lie to him. Say the papers haven't been delivered yet. Be creative."

"There'll be reprisals," muttered Colin Woodard, a large balding officer who rarely spoke. Everyone nodded and chuntered in agreement.

"Deal with it," Edward bellowed, experiencing a rare ounce of courage and losing his temper. "It's your fucking job!"

* * *

"Fuckwit," Colin said when he was certain the Governor was out of earshot. The stunned silence broke as the officers began to voice their objections.

"Doesn't he understand that it's us lot who runs the prison, not him?" Colin grumbled.

"Clearly not," said Lucas, bending down to retrieve the newspaper Edward Hulder had dropped. He patted the pages neatly into place, his eyes coldly scanning the headlines – POLICE OFFICER CHARGED WITH MURDER. He rose slowly, smiling maliciously. This particular one showed a rather outdated photo of their newest inmate. Adam Kent looked much younger and was dressed in uniform and helmet, but it was obviously him.

"I think Hulder's got a point though," said Thomas, rapidly back-tracking as he read the paper over Lucas' shoulder. "If Reginald or any of the others see that, Kent's life will be in jeopardy." Everyone bar Lucas reluctantly agreed.

Lucas stepped away from his colleagues, jealously guarding the newspaper before carefully rolling it in a tube.

"And if not, we'll be getting earache that he hasn't had his daily," he argued. "All in all, this might be our one chance to get rid of Hulder. Think about it. Another death or beating on his watch? They won't stand for it, especially if it involves a high-profile prisoner. It will be Hulder who takes the fall. We'll just deny he ever gave the order. Who are they going to believe? Him or us? With luck, they'll get someone in who actually knows how to run this place."

"What are you going to do?" Thomas asked nervously, not liking where this conversation was going. Lucas Callum was evil and corrupt – the things he did and got away with beggared belief and not even the toughest guard felt confident enough to stand up to him. It was easier to keep in his good books.

Lucas laughed, beating the rolled up newspaper against the flat of his palm like a baton.

"After breakfast, I'm going to deliver this to Reginald," he said, winking at his colleagues.

CHAPTER THIRTY SEVEN

"So much for sneaking in through the back door," Nick seethed after they'd passed by the Canal Basin on their way to work and found a crowd of people congregating at the police station. Amanda slid down in the passenger seat of his car.

"What the hell?" she groaned, flipping the visor as they turned right into the grounds and crawled along at 10 mph, carefully negotiating a path through a swarm of reporters and cameramen. Several heads turned at Nick and Amanda's arrival before focusing again on the senior officer giving the press conference. Nick could see Superintendent Tarring holding court in the warm morning sunshine. The weather had changed for the better and looked positive for much of the week. Tarring was dressed in full livery, sunlight glinting off the crowns on his shoulders. Even from a substantial distance he appeared pretty pissed off.

"What's happened now?" Amanda murmured, shielding her face with her hand in an attempt to look perfectly natural and failing miserably. She and Nick had spent the night together, and the last thing they wanted was to come under close scrutiny so early in their relationship.

"My guess is, this is all about Adam," Nick replied soberly, swinging the Mercedes into his reserved parking bay. "It was always going to cause a shit storm." He turned off the engine and unclipped his seatbelt.

Amanda closed her eyes and rubbed her forehead, trying to massage away a headache. She'd drunk too much wine last night, which was a mistake. But the company had made it worthwhile.

"This is going to be serious for Adam," she groaned.

"I know," he said quietly, pushing away disturbing images of his friend locked up with a crowd of violent inmates. The two sat for several seconds, mulling things over before Nick finally

148

sprang into action. "Come on," he said, reaching over to squeeze her knee. "We've got things to do." He opened the car door and climbed out. Amanda followed suit.

Just then, a group of uniformed police constables wandered past on their way back from the smoking area.

"Morning Guv," they chirped, cheeky smiles plastered on their baby faces. It seemed the recruits were getting younger and younger. Amanda blushed and pretended to search for something in her handbag. Nick responded, silently cursing the fact it was practically impossible to keep anything private in this place. He hadn't planned to stay with Amanda last night, instead having every intention of taking things slowly. But they had enjoyed each other's company so much, one thing led to another and, before either of them realised what was happening, they were in each other's arms. So it seemed perfectly natural for her to ask him to stay.

This was the first time in a long while Nick had slept with anyone other than his wife. If he'd stopped to think about it, he might have worried about his performance, but that wasn't to be an issue. Neither he nor Amanda had been pressured, so what happened between them had felt good. No, rephrase that, Nick thought, suppressing a huge grin. It felt bloody fantastic! Not that it was anybody's business, but two people who were mutually attracted and shared the highest degree of respect for one another had made love. It was as simple as that. Yes, he was still married to Philippa, but divorce proceedings were well underway. He and Amanda had done nothing wrong.

He glanced across at her now, ferreting around in her bag, surreptitiously waiting for the officers to disappear from sight. It was inevitable they would be hot gossip for a while. Nick was prepared for this. He was also prepared for what was left of his marriage to come under scrutiny. After all, it was no secret Philippa had done the dirty on him with Guy Kane. In his mind, it was best to brazen things out. And this would do for starters, Nick thought boldly as he captured Amanda's hand and slipped his fingers through hers. She looked up at him with troubled eyes. He gave her hand a comforting squeeze, pleased that she didn't try to pull away. Hand in hand, Amanda and Nick walked into the building.

* * *

Amanda couldn't stop her face from burning. It seemed the whole place was awash with bodies to-ing and fro-ing. They ran a gauntlet of grinning faces and raised eyebrows. She almost died with embarrassment, only guessing what people must be thinking. It took every inch of willpower not to withdraw her hand from Nick's. They made their way into the lobby, just as Superintendent Tarring came blustering in through the door. He closed it quickly behind him, cutting off the voices from the crowd begging for more information. He paused for breath and began to brush imaginary fluff from his tunic. Only then did he lock eyes with Nick.

"That sergeant of yours has caused me no end of grief," he snarled, lifting off his cap and dragging his fingers aggressively through his thick crop of black hair, as if it were Nick's fault Adam had been arrested. He dropped his gaze and narrowed his eyes at their clasped hands. Immediately, Amanda and Nick separated – Nick burying his hand inside his jacket pocket whilst Amanda clenched hers into a fist at her side.

"I had to give a press conference, but that won't be the end of it," Tarring predicted, fixing them with his cold stare. "Mark my words, it's going to get a whole lot worse."

CHAPTER THIRTY EIGHT

At the end of the corridor, Nick and Amanda parted ways – he to the left and she to the right. They were in professional mode now. Amanda barely had enough time to remove her jacket when DC Aaron Hawker came bounding across the crowded CID office like an excited puppy.

"Where were you? I've been trying to call you," he said, dazzling her with a wide smile, his pearly whites a sharp contrast to his ebony skin. Amanda had never seen this officer look quite so animated. She scanned her phone, noting several missed calls. Then she remembered, she'd put in on silent last night.

"Sorry," she murmured, flushing slightly at the memory of her and Nick in bed. God, he was so amazing – so tender, so giving.

"Sarge?" She shook the delicious images from her mind and forced herself to concentrate on what Aaron had to say. All around them phones were ringing. The atmosphere was prickling with enthusiasm. Everyone seemed focused.

"Carry on," she urged, clearing her throat.

"Major turn-up for the books," he began, bouncing eagerly from foot to foot. "We've had the results come through. In a nutshell, it was Christine Taylor who died in the fire, and Craig Donohue's DNA is connected to the assault on her daughter, Ruby."

"Wow." It was all Amanda could think of to say. Last night, just before she and Nick left work, she'd received a call from the hospital telling her that their suspect was awake. Whether he was fit enough to be formally interviewed was unclear, but she had every intention of spinning round there today to gauge the situation. Firstly she'd have to clear it with Nick. And Vince Taylor was going to have to be told about the demise of his wife. Not good. This was the one part of the job she hated –

151

breaking bad news about the death of a loved one. She always felt their pain, and the task never got any easier. But Nick would want her to do it. After all, she had built a rapport with Taylor.

* * *

Nick was busy scrolling through his emails when he heard the knock on the door. He was still thinking about Adam and what Superintendent Tarring had said. For so long, Adam had been his blue-eyed boy, with a promising career ahead of him, and now … It was like a fairytale gone disastrously wrong. Nick had no idea how everything was going to pan out. Like scavengers feeding on carrion, the press were putting his friend in extreme danger. But they couldn't care less, as long as they had a story. Nowadays, prisoners had access to everything – newspapers, television, internet. He hoped to God they'd had the good sense to segregate Adam.

"Come," he shouted, just as the door squeaked open. He first saw Amanda and then DC Hawker, who was peeping shyly in behind her. Amanda was still flushed. Aaron was grinning like a ninny.

"Guv," Amanda began, biting her lip. After what they had shared the night before, formalities seemed a little unnecessary, but maybe she was right to lay boundaries. Work was work; home was home. It wouldn't be professional to blur the lines, and Nick certainly wouldn't want anyone suggesting they were letting their relationship interfere with their jobs.

"What is it?" he asked softly, peering at her over his half-moon glasses. God I was inside that woman a few hours ago, he thought, hardly believing it himself.

"I've sent you an email with two attachments. It is Christine Taylor – unfortunately," she said resignedly, her cheeks flushing as if she had just read his amorous thoughts. "And the results are back from the lab regarding Donohue's DNA."

"And?"

"It's a complete match to Ruby's attacker."

Nick expelled a sigh and began to swing backwards and forwards in his chair, something he only did when he was deep in thought. This case was Adam's baby. *He* should be receiving all the glory

"Guv?"

"Right, first things first," he said, snapping himself out of his musings. "We'll have a briefing, and then I want you to put Vince Taylor out of his misery."

Nick noted the pained expression on Amanda's face but ignored it. She was the best person for the job and she knew it.

"Secondly, I want you and Aaron to go to the hospital. See what state Donohue is in and find out when the doctors think he'll be fit enough to be discharged. We've had him under police guard since he was admitted, and I want that to remain in place. The more his health improves, the greater chance he has of trying to escape."

"Of course."

"By the time you get back from the hospital, I'll be on my way to Marden. I need to see Adam and get a handle on everything he knows about Craig Donohue. As I understand it, there are potentially a lot more historic crimes our suspect has to answer for."

After Amanda and Aaron closed the door, Nick picked up the phone. He had a very important call to make, to a DI Miles Button of Hampshire Police. Donohue's crimes stretched over decades and bled over into the neighbouring county, and it would give this officer some peace of mind knowing that the monster who'd eluded them for so long had finally been apprehended.

CHAPTER THIRTY NINE

"Mummy! There's lots of people outside," squealed Paige as she pressed her little face against the window pane. Luke scrabbled from the floor to the settee to join his sister, his eyes widening with excitement to see such a hubbub of activity outside their house.

"Come look, mummy," he called, eager to be included in his sister's discovery.

Rosemary, who was dressed in her nightwear and hungover from lack of sleep, extracted herself from her parents' company in the kitchen and hastened into the lounge. The children were giggling and pointing at something out in the street. Intrigued, she swept her dishevelled, long blond hair behind her ears and bent forward, only to be met by the flash of a camera. She gasped and stumbled backwards, dragging Paige and Luke away by their arms. They both cried out in shock and surprise. This was certainly not the reaction they were anticipating.

"Get back, get back!" she ordered them, inching forward enough to draw the curtains closed. The room was immediately cast in shadow, shielding the family from the eyes of the cruel world beyond but not the sounds. Rosemary could hear voices calling out to her.

"Rosemary! Rosemary!"

"What's the matter?" Patrick asked as he joined her in the lounge. He frowned the moment he noticed the tension on his daughter's face. He and his wife had spent an uncomfortable night in this house – Carol in Paige's tiny bed and he suffering the settee. Both of them were ruffled, their hair sticking up in all directions, their faces grey and creased with worry and exhaustion.

"I think the press are here. Outside," Rosemary replied in a heated whisper, as if the vultures beyond the walls could hear her. Suddenly very weak, she sank down on the rumpled duvet spread across the sofa and lowered her head in her hands. God! Would this nightmare ever end?

"What?" Carol asked, appearing from nowhere at her husband's side. She pulled her dressing gown cord tighter and charged across the room towards the window, preparing to wage war. Arms at the ready, she reached for the curtains to see what all the fuss was when Patrick's voice rang out, halting her in her tracks. "Don't!" Feeling as if she were about to step on a land-mine, Carol froze mid-stride and very slowly lowered her arms to her side. She paused for a moment, staring in bewilderment at the covered window, debating whether to be annoyed at her husband's abruptness whilst also contemplating what her impetuous actions might have led to. Eventually, sensing all eyes upon her, Carol inhaled a deep breath and meekly retreated, back to her distraught daughter. Wanting to feel useful, she pulled Paige onto her lap and stroked Rosemary's tangled hair.

"I don't think I can take much more," her daughter sobbed, barely aware of her mother's caress.

"What are they doing here?" Carol breathed. She could now feel her granddaughter trembling. Paige pushed her thumb into her mouth and laid her head on her gran's bosom. Luke, not wishing to be left out, also began sucking his thumb.

"Isn't it obvious?" Patrick seethed in disgust. "It's about Adam. They've found out where he lives. They're looking for an angle and they don't care how they get it." He huffed loudly. "They're a resourceful lot, I'll give them that much."

"What am I going to do?" Rosemary wailed. "I'm supposed to go to Marden today to see him. How will I get past them?"

"What's going on?"

All heads turned to see Sophie standing in her pyjamas on the threshold to the lounge. This was the first time she had been downstairs since all the upset the previous afternoon. She hadn't eaten anything in hours, skipping dinner and rebuffing Carol's vain attempt to comfort her.

"Hi sweetie, do you want some breakfast," Patrick asked, slapping on a bright smile which didn't look at all reassuring. Naturally Sophie wasn't convinced. She narrowed her eyes and looked at the scene with suspicion.

"What's going on?" she repeated, refusing to be deflected.

"The press are outside," Rosemary said with as much calm as she could muster.

"Press?"

"Newspapermen, cameramen, reporters," she explained.

"I know who the press are," Sophie retorted irritably, rolling her eyes.

"I'm going to see your dad later. I – I mean – *we've* somehow got to get past them. I don't know how..."

"Can I come with you to see dad?" the girl interrupted, suddenly very animated.

Rosemary shook her head. That's the last thing she needed. She had to see Adam alone in order to gauge his true feelings towards her and try to make him understand what had happened with Guy Kane. This was something that had to be done face to face. It was her first opportunity and, right now, the most important thing in her life. She couldn't do any of this with his child sitting alongside her.

"No. You've got to go to school," she said firmly.

"What? With all this going on?" the teenager protested.

Rosemary clenched her jaw and rose from the settee. Feeling a modicum of inner strength, she pulled back her shoulders and despite the utter contempt and disbelief on Sophie's face, refrained from buckling under the pressure.

"We have to try and behave as normal as possible. I know it's going to be difficult, but they're looking for sensation. We don't say anything to them, do you understand? Not even 'no comment'. Just ignore them, okay?"

Sophie nodded mutely, bemused by her stepmother's sudden show of spirit. She turned back towards the stairs and began to ascend. Rosemary allowed herself to relax a little. She had won this particular fight.

"Can I come with you the next time you go?" Sophie asked, pausing halfway.

"I'll take you soon, I promise," Rosemary said softly.

"Well, I won't hold my breath. I know first-hand what your promises are like," the teenager said tartly, cruelly reminding her that she had a long way to go before she actually won the war.

CHAPTER FORTY

Cheryl Durrant could almost hear her mother's voice, berating her for being such a stupid trusting woman. Maybe there would be an element of truth to that. She wasn't entirely sure if she had done the right thing either. Now in the cold light of day, last night felt like a dream. She rolled over to the other side of the mattress and touched the patch of warmth on the bottom sheet – evidence that another person had recently lain beside her. Now Guy was gone.

Cheryl sat up and combed her messy bed hair with her fingers. Her body felt sated and heavy with pleasure. Perhaps, yet again, she had been a fool to fall so easily for his charms – maybe she was serving her heart up on a platter to be broken but she couldn't help it. She was in love with Guy Kane and there was nothing she could do.

When he'd turned up out of the blue, her first instinct was to slam the door in his face, but rationality took over. A few days before, she had accused him of breaking into her house and stealing a patient's file. It had been a knee-jerk reaction, and he had stormed out, leaving her feeling not only very unsure but a bit of an idiot. She had absolutely nothing to back up such a theory and now believed her suspicions were completely unfounded. Guy Kane sold life insurance for Christ's sake! No wonder he had taken such umbrage to being accused a thief. She had most likely mislaid the file, or even accidentally shredded it. And as far as the window in the kitchen was concerned, she'd closed it by mistake. That was the most logical explanation. The fact that there was a police report of burglary floating around meant absolutely nothing. Judging by the officer's sceptical attitude whilst taking her statement, Cheryl had imagined the whole thing. She hoped the report would be buried somewhere, never to see the light of day. The whole situation was extremely embarrassing.

Last night, Guy had given her a second chance and she'd grasped it with both hands. Neither of them had discussed the 'burglary', or the horrible things she had said to him. It was time to start afresh. She needed him and wanted him. Life was too short to waste, and that was why she had happily welcomed him into her bed. It was just a pity he had to leave so early.

"Back on the road again," he said regretfully as he kissed the tip of her nose.

He told her that he would call when he was next in the area. Cheryl refrained from asking when, not wanting to come across as too needy. She revelled in the fact that, although he would be gone for the time being, he was now back in her life. She thanked God for another chance at happiness.

CHAPTER FORTY ONE

"Adam, I've thought a few things through and when the time comes, I want you to plead not guilty," Terry Brown began. They were seated at opposite ends of a small, square, stainless steel table in one of the pokier interview rooms at HMP Marden. A folder containing bundles of paperwork relating to the Jason Sadler case was stacked up on one side and, directly in front of Terry, a notepad was open at the ready.

Adam raised his eyebrows in surprise at his solicitor's suggestion and stole a quick uneasy glance at the door. Through the glass panel, he could see the bald head of the guard who had escorted him here. Maybe it was because his situation was so critical that the atmosphere inside this small room felt airless and congested. He pulled the neck of his sweatshirt away from his throat in a bid to breathe more easily.

* * *

It seemed that today was to be a day of meetings. After breakfast, which was mercifully uneventful, Adam had been taken to see the Governor. Edward Hulder was friendly enough but made no secret that he wanted Adam somewhere else.

"You being a police officer makes things very awkward," he told him, trying to remain diplomatic. "I am therefore making an application to get you transferred to another, more fitting establishment. Marden definitely isn't the place for you."

It was clear what the problem was. Hulder didn't want to take on the responsibility for Adam's safety. If anything happened to him, it would look bad for the Governor and the prison. And let's face it, Adam thought, Marden's infamous reputation suggested it was in severe need of a serious shake up. He suspected Hulder's job was already on the line.

"But surely it will be the same situation wherever I go," he replied. "After all, I am what I am." He didn't want to go through it again – the first-time nerves. At least he had suffered the initiation here and passed. Since then, two meals had gone by without incident. A new lock-up would have its own problems, and there was always the chance that someone there might recognise him.

"I hear you," Hulder sighed regretfully, clasping his hands so tightly his knuckles turned white. A sheen of sweat formed on his brow, and he seemed to tremble ever so slightly. Adam narrowed his eyes. The man didn't look well. He watched as he stared for several seconds at a framed photograph on his desk, as if seeking approval before continuing. "My officers tell me you're sharing a cell with Azz Secrett?"

Adam nodded. He was depressed, even more so than yesterday, if that was at all possible.

"Well, in my opinion, they made the wrong decision. I'd be much happier if you were segregated straight away – for your own safety – until I can get you moved."

Adam disagreed. "But the reason has already been explained. It would create suspicion among the other prisoners if they thought I had something to hide. I don't like it either – living a lie, pretending I'm just your average con, hoping not to say the wrong thing. But at least I can try to blend in a bit."

"But for how much longer, I don't know," Hulder replied matter-of-factly. He opened his desk drawer and, with a long resigned sigh, withdrew a newspaper and slapped it down in front of this problematic inmate. It only took a second for Adam to realise the gravity of the situation when he saw his own face adorning the front page. He reached over and picked up the paper. The headline "SUSSEX COPPER CHARGED WITH MURDER" swam before his eyes. He was vaguely aware of Hulder watching his reaction. No doubt he would see the colour drain from his face and the subtle tremor of his hands. The Governor almost looked pleased that his shock tactic had succeeded.

"I don't know how long I can keep the other inmates from knowing about you," he said softly as Adam scanned the details with mounting horror. "But I've taken steps to delay newspapers. I'll even curtail the use of the internet, although I can't protect your identity forever. You will be found out. I'm just glad that the television in the common room is broken. At present, I won't be applying for a new one."

Adam looked up and met his eyes. Hulder gazed earnestly across at him and not without pity.

"You will be safer in segregation. Do you understand that now?"

Since Adam's arrival the day before, he always knew he was sitting on a time bomb, but this was disastrous. He had been naïve to think the story wouldn't make headlines. If there had been a plane crash or a bomb going off in some UK city, only then would his crime have been bumped to the second or third page. But that wasn't the case here – which was a good thing for the country, but it meant no end of grief for him and his family.

Adam carefully placed the paper back on the desk and stared up at the ceiling, focusing on a patch of damp. That's the trouble with old buildings, he thought randomly as waves of panic threatened to engulf him.

"Adam, you're seeing your brief shortly. Please take my advice and agree to move to segregation. They will find a way to hurt you if you don't," Edward Hulder said, driving the threat home.

* * *

Officer Thomas Hennessy collected Adam from the Governor's office and escorted him part way to the interview room. Maybe it was his imagination, but the guard appeared less chatty than yesterday, and less congenial. In fact, he seemed positively shifty, as if he were waiting for something to kick off.

Then another officer took over and Hennessy dropped away. This man was heavy-set and projected an air of intimidation – he had a balding head and wore a permanent scowl, like a rhinoceros in uniform. He also had very little to say, and Adam was starting to feel very isolated. The guard delivered him safely to the interview room and closed the door behind him. After the troubling meeting with the Governor, Adam was relieved to see the familiar, if not deeply concerned, face of Terry Brown.

"What's the point? I did it. I admitted it," he replied, in response to Terry's suggestion of going not guilty. He laid his palms upright on the table, symbolising that he had nothing left to offer.

"Do you trust me, Adam?" Terry asked, staring fiercely across at him, looking more impassioned than he'd ever seen him.

Adam shrugged.

"Of course, but you can't perform miracles. So why even try?"

"Our justice system is the best in the world," Terry reminded him. "You have your expertise, and I have mine. A few days from now, there'll be a preliminary hearing where we'll have the opportunity to enter a plea. That is when I want you to go not guilty. In the meantime, I will collate further evidence and witnesses. Expect a backlash. After all, they're expecting you to plead guilty."

Adam looked unsure. As much as he wanted to get out of here, the task his solicitor had set himself seemed virtually impossible.

"Come on, cheer up," said Terry, trying to lighten the mood. "I have my game plan. For now, all you have to do is plead not guilty. I can't be clearer than that, can I?"

Adam shuffled in his chair. It was hard and unforgiving, making the small of his back ache and his backside sore. He wondered if Terry felt the same way but, there again, he would have slept in his own bed last night and not on some sorry excuse for a mattress in a prison cell. He thought about what his solicitor had said, not just about the plea but the time it would take to even get to trial. How many weeks or months would pass before it began? Reality hit him hard. He could barely survive a day.

"Look," Terry said softly. "At least let me build a case, give it my best shot. You know as well as I do that a murder charge carries mandatory life imprisonment. Therefore, you've got nothing to lose if a jury hears you out. And that's what you'll get with a not guilty plea. There'll be twelve people, from all walks of life. Some may even be sympathetic towards you – that's what I'm banking on, although obviously, there will be some who won't. I know you're on self-destruct mode right now. That was evident at the Magistrates yesterday, but please trust me. Please let me try to lessen the chances of you throwing your entire life away."

"And if you can't win the case?"

Terry pursed his lips, his expression darkening with the gravity of the situation.

"Then here you will stay. Yes, you've been candid, even handed yourself in, but that won't help you, it won't lessen your sentence. For God's sake, you've admitted on tape to killing a man. I want to try and minimise the damage. As far as I can see this is the way forward. I know it goes against your deep-seated principles to enter a plea of not guilty when you're anything but. But Adam, this is last chance saloon. I can only advise. You tell me what you want to do."

Shit, Adam thought, staring down at his widespread fingers. He dragged his elbows from the table and dropped his hands into his lap. Yesterday he had accepted his fate, that life as he knew it was over. Terry Brown had made no promises but had still put him in a bit of a quandary. Adam needed time to digest.

"Do I have to answer now?" he asked meekly.

"Talk to your family and friends, but don't leave it too long. I need to carry out some research. I've got a lot of reading to do – people to see. I'll make an appointment to come back and give you some idea of where I'm going with this. Then, I'll need to know your decision."

* * *

Adam left the interview room in a bit of a daze. This time, the large officer who had guarded him was accompanied by Thomas Hennessy. Flanking him on either side, they proceeded to escort him back to the cell. They didn't speak and, once again, Adam got the distinct feeling they knew something he didn't. He was still reeling with shock about the story in the newspapers. What this meant for him and his family one could only imagine. The Governor had promised to keep the rest of the inmates in the dark regarding his identity, and Adam desperately wanted to believe him. Yes, they may kick off about the lack of newspapers and internet but hopefully wouldn't figure out that he was the one to blame.

A series of heavy doors were opened and then clunked closed as the trio passed through. Very soon they were in familiar territory. Echoes of shouts and banging noises became more pronounced as Adam was escorted into his wing. Everyone was on lock-down until lunchtime. In spite of the fact he hadn't been here long, he appeared to be losing weight. The food was terrible, and he couldn't stomach eating much, although Azz had promised that eventually something would click and he'd actually begin to look forward to meals. How long before I'm completely institutionalised, Adam wondered miserably and then realised with dismay that he was already halfway there. The first twenty-four hours he had spent here consisted of counting the minutes between breaks.

They continued to amble towards the cell he currently shared with Azz. It made him feel as if he were walking The Green Mile. Pockets of daylight streamed in through the slit windows thirty or so feet above them, casting a mottled effect on the floor. For a brief second, a rare beam of sunlight penetrated the mist and touched his face. Adam felt a heavy ache in his heart. He so desperately missed his freedom.

As they approached the wing, the noise from the other inmates began to peter out, which was unusual. Adam was too focused on his own problems to care. He was less intimidated than the day before and merely shrugged off the silent stares from the succession of caged faces. So far he had shared three meals with these people and was still in one piece, but this unexplained silence was becoming a little disconcerting. Hulder's warning about moving to segregation once again slid into his mind. It was another decision he'd have to make, but as long as Azz was being pleasant, it wasn't a worry.

He could now see his cell and wondered whether Azz would be making tea. He was getting used to that too. Then he noticed a couple of guards approaching and clocked their serious expressions. One of them was shaking his head as if trying to convey a silent message. In an instant, Adam was surrounded by uniforms. At first, he was bewildered by what was happening. What had he done? What were they going to do to him? But then a voice called out from behind – chilling him to the bone.

"Oi copper – you're in our world now."

CHAPTER FORTY TWO

Well, at least my wife's happy, Brian thought glumly as he wandered around the empty incident room for the last time. He stood for a moment with his eyes closed, conjuring up a host of memories, and imagined how everything had looked several days ago when the investigation was in full swing with everyone in place. Six months ago, he'd been seconded from Bognor Regis CID to head up this murder case and had been more than willing to come to Chichester to embrace what would be his grand finale.

In his mind's eye, Brian saw a room full of people, eager to come together and share information. Photos and charts were pinned to the walls, lists of various names and places scrawled in red and black ink across several whiteboards. Brian opened his eyes again and his heart felt leaden. It seemed like a dream – a colourful dream full of energy. He gazed around, wishing he could turn back the clock. The grim reality was a stark contrast to how he would like to remember things; the present atmosphere was washed-out and grey, almost ghostly. It certainly hadn't ended well.

He wondered if buildings or rooms ever retained feelings – positive or negative; whether somehow, the moods of their inhabitants soaked into the walls. Would anyone sense these vibes the next time this place was used as an incident room? Would the sadness seep out of the plasterwork, or would business just carry on unaware? Perhaps he was just feeling melancholy about the twilight of his career, not to mention horrified at what had happened to Adam Kent.

It was over. Within hours of Adam's court appearance, Brian's team had melted away – off to tackle matters far removed from Operation Crossword. The surfaces and walls were now bare and the boards wiped clean. All that remained of his final investigation were the computers on the desks, and even they were switched off. Brian should have been elated that the case was finally solved. Instead, he felt cheated. With a sad shake of his head, he closed the door and walked away from the past.

Yes, his wife Jane was ecstatic, although not without feeling. She knew how unhappy he was about how the investigation had turned out, but couldn't hide her excitement that she was finally getting her husband all to herself. All those years of marriage, waiting for him to come home, having to cancel on friends because of some last-minute disaster, not having a social life because he was too tired. He couldn't really blame her. Last night he'd found her perusing travel brochures. Her heart was set on a World Cruise, but that wouldn't be until the beginning of next year. It would take a big chunk out of his lump sum but, hey, she more than deserved it, and Adam Kent's fate would be decided well beforehand.

And Brian? What would Brian do now that he wasn't a copper? How would anything ever measure up? If Jane had her way, he'd be trekking over the Andes, mountain biking across the south of Spain or white-water rafting on the Zambezi. She was one adventurous woman, and he should probably go with the flow. What was the alternative? Shuffling around in his slippers, watching daytime TV and waiting to die?

Depressed as he was, there was one person he wanted to see before he headed back to Bognor Regis. Poor George Robins, he kept thinking. If there was anyone more disappointed about finding Jason Sadler's killer than me, it's poor George. Adam Kent's best friend and the man who'd arrested him. No wonder he was too stressed to work. His girlfriend, Natasha had phoned in to say he wasn't fit to come in. Brian decided he would swing by and see how he was. Maybe they could commiserate together.

* * *

George and Natasha didn't live too far from the station, just off of Kingsham Road. It was a small flint-faced terraced property set in Grove Road. Brian parked his car and wandered up the path. The front door was part-glazed timber and in desperate need of some TLC.   Some of the woodwork had bubbled and split, and the frame looked pretty wonky.   Brian cupped his hands and tried to peer through the bevelled glass before knocking.   The world beyond was distorted, and he couldn't see any signs of life. He gave the brass knocker a firm rap, which was answered by the low throaty bark of a dog. Brian stood back and waited.   He strained his ears over the noise, trying to imagine where George was.   Eventually he heard a man's voice cursing at the animal to be quiet. A few moments later, the door creaked open and a familiar bald head peeped shyly out.

Brian was taken aback by the sight of his officer.   George's eyes were heavy and swollen as he squinted in the sunlight, looking like the undead with an aversion to the daytime. His breath reeked of booze, and he had a full day's growth of pale beard.   Brian half expected to receive a mouthful of verbal abuse, but George looked somewhat sheepish seeing his boss standing on the doorstep.

"Sir?" he mumbled.

"Can I come in?" Brian asked.

George opened the door wider, bending to capture the collar of a red and white Basset Hound, which was growling and wagging its tail at the same time.

"Claymore, let my boss in," George said, pulling the dog away.   Brian stepped into the hallway, where the stench of alcohol was even more pungent.

"Come on through," he said, pointing out the way to the lounge. "Sorry the place is in a bit of a mess, Natasha's doing a double shift and I, well I can't face anything at the moment."

It wasn't too bad, considering. The TV was on in the corner – Jeremy Kyle Show. Come on George, snap out of it please, Brian thought. A few cushions lay scattered on the floor, and several dirty mugs and glasses littered a central table covered with sticky ring marks. There was half a bottle of whisky by the settee on the floor and an empty one in the waste bin. The curtains were drawn, blocking out the brilliant sunshine. This officer was in mourning – there was no doubt about it.

"Take a seat," George said, running his hand over his whiskers. He relinquished his hold on Claymore who made a beeline for Brian's crutch. "Want a coffee or something stronger," he asked, with a bitter laugh.

"Coffee's fine, George, thank you," he replied, patting the dog's pointed head. "Milk, no sugar, please."

George nodded and disappeared. Brian cast his eyes around the room. There were feminine touches everywhere and a lovely photograph of George and Natasha on a side table which looked to have been taken at a wedding. Brian really didn't know what he could achieve by coming here but felt it might help George if he talked to someone who understood his pain. George returned within minutes. He handed Brian a mug and sat down, reaching for the bottle of whisky and pouring himself a generous measure.

"Sure you won't join me?" he asked with a twisted smile on his face. Brian shook his head.

"Have you seen a doctor yet?" he began.

"Nope."

"Well, I think you should. This is bad George. You can't afford to lose control like this. Adam wouldn't want that."

"It's Adam's fault that I feel like this," George spat. "Why did he choose me? Why make me do it?"

"He obviously had his reasons."

George didn't reply. He took a mouthful of whisky and wiped his lips on the back of his hand before lowering his head.

Claymore scratched a flea on his ear, toppling over in the process.

"How's Natasha?" Brian asked, changing tack.

"Fed up with me," he murmured, glancing up. He breathed a sigh. "I can't help it. I can't stop the pain. She doesn't understand. She'll leave me, I know, but there's nothing I can do. We were going to file it weren't we?"

"File what?"

"The day it happened, we'd just arrived back from London. We'd hit another brick wall. I know it was going to be filed in unsolved cases. We didn't have the funds to keep the operation going. That's right isn't it?"

Brian shrugged.

"Perhaps."

"If only he'd held on. Said nothing. Why did he tell me? He'd kept his secret for months. What made him confess?"

"I don't know," Brian said honestly. "Maybe the sheer weight of guilt; he couldn't take it anymore."

"No, there's more to it. If only he'd waited. He thought Guy Kane knew something but even so …"

"Look George," Brian said, setting his mug on the table amongst the rest of the dirty crockery. He placed his hands squarely on his knees. "You can't feel guilty for making that arrest. Adam gave you no alternative. It's not your fault."

He noticed George's bottom lip tremble before the officer buried his head in his hands.

"I'm not ready to come back, sir," he sobbed. "I can't do this anymore."

"Please go and see a doctor," Brian begged him. He didn't want to leave him like this. "I'll call one for you."

"No, please."

"I don't care. I'm calling one out. You need help. I can see that, and I'm not leaving you alone until I know you're okay."

CHAPTER FORTY THREE

Lucas Callum possessed a sadistic streak, and no one around him would possibly disagree. He was cold and cunning, which he considered a blessing. It gave him an edge, gave him strength. The pleasure he took from another person's misery satisfied a craving – it was like feeding an addiction.

Nobody knew what had made him this way. Perhaps he'd had a rough upbringing and suffered at the hands of an abuser. Or maybe he was just born bad. It was a delicate balance. Lucas could have so easily turned to a life of crime but inexplicably ended up in a position of power. That was why he loved his job so much.

In short, everyone was a little afraid of Lucas Callum.

Working at HMP Marden provided the perfect environment in which to feed his twisted desires. He could sniff out weakness like a bloodhound, be it in the prisoners under his care or his fellow officers. Nobody was immune, especially the more vulnerable younger prisoners. If anyone suspected what he did during those quiet hours on a night shift, they just kept schtum and turned a blind eye. It was so much easier that way. There were rumours, but they never led to a full-scale investigation and ended up being passed off as nothing but urban myths.

Because of his reputation, Lucas was allowed to go on unchallenged, so he considered himself top dog amongst his peers. Never mind the Governor. Edward Hulder was weak, and whenever he did venture out of his office to brief the staff, his requests usually fell on deaf ears. Lucas was the man they listened to and, right now, he intended to make trouble. Going against orders and delivering the forbidden newspapers to one inmate in particular seemed the ideal way to cause copious amounts of grief for the Governor. There was no way the prisoners would accept a police officer into their fold and, once they found out who Adam Kent was, all hell would break loose.

But while Lucas may have been a conniver, he wasn't the brightest star in the firmament. Not that any of his colleagues were brave enough to point this out. If the end game was to get Edward Hulder dismissed, it wouldn't be Lucas who would take his place. He was a grunt – nothing more, nothing less – and what he thought he wanted by way of a new Governor might end up being a tougher nut to crack. Hulder could be easily manipulated with very few repercussions so was perfect for a man with Lucas Callum's needs.

Nobody told Lucas that his scheme might backfire on him, that it could be he who was left standing out in the cold. Instead, his colleagues went along with the plan, waiting for the inevitable explosion. They had no desire to see the police officer harmed and, if Lucas cocked up, so be it. Marden would be a much better place without him. Not that they told him that, of course.

CHAPTER FORTY FOUR

"He's a fucking copper," Reginald Samuels seethed as he scanned the story on the front page of the newspaper. Even though the photograph was in black and white and several years out of date, Reginald could clearly make out who it was. His arms trembled with indignation. That a copper had sat opposite him during meals and fooled them all! Shit! He almost liked the guy. Thank God for Callum putting them straight.

"The Governor wanted the papers confiscated," Lucas had said as he slid the prohibited article through the hatch in the cell door. "But I thought you had a right to know."

Reginald turned to his brother and flung the newspaper onto his bunk in disgust. He'd barely digested why Adam was on remand in the first place. All he was concerned about was that he represented the enemy, whether he was inside or out.

"What shall we do?" Albert muttered as he read the story. Adam Kent was on remand for murder, quite a weighty charge. He must have thought he was above the law, killing some poor bastard. Well, they'd teach him a lesson he'd never forget. Using his profession to snuff out someone's life. It wasn't right. He looked across at his brother, who was now standing with his face pressed hard against the opened hatch.

The two men were similar in looks, with balding heads set upon wide shoulders attached to squat bodies. Pit Bulls, that's what they likened themselves to. Reginald had his hands stuffed into his pockets and had adopted a defensive stance. Albert knew the signs. He wanted action now, and being cooped up in this cell wouldn't help his mood.

"Fucking copper," he mumbled, turning back to his brother. His eyes were bulging with repressed rage and his face was beet red. He'd been made to feel like a dick, and that didn't rest easy. The cell was compact, and there wasn't enough space for the amount of fury he needed to expel. He leaned back against the door and withdrew his hands from his pockets. Albert watched the fingers on his right curl into fist. Reginald began to softly punch his left palm. He wanted to do some serious damage. Once again, he twisted his head towards the cell door and angled his mouth to the opening.

"Aye, guess who I had breakfast with?" he bellowed down the corridor to no one in particular. The sound of Reginald Samuel's voice immediately stimulated interest.

"Who d'you have breakfast with?" someone replied, thinking he was about to hear a joke.

Reginald paused for effect before delivering the punch line.

"A copper! That Kent bloke is a copper."

"No fucking way," someone else screamed.

"Where the fuck is he? I'll rip his fucking head off."

"Yeah, set Toy on him Reggie," was another suggestion.

"He's gone to see his brief," came Azz Secrett's astonished voice. "It's a joke right? Don't say I've been sharing my cell with the Filth."

"Yeah, like I've been sharing my fucking meals with the bastard," Reginald spat.

And thus it went on. The news bled through the walls of Marden, making the prisoners restless, trapped as they were in their cells with their murderous thoughts. The air prickled with violence. Even the most placid of inmates was incensed at having been deceived. They were all bored and frustrated, and their aggressive feelings began to escalate – not against each other but at their restrictive surroundings. They wanted revenge for being tricked, as well as for the person who had died at Adam Kent's hand. And there was to be no swift remedy to quell this sense of outrage. So they pounded on the walls, kicked at the doors and stamped on the floor, each desperate to make his feelings known about HMP Marden's newest resident. Eventually, Reginald Samuels called for calm. As quickly as the corridors had been filled with the sounds of rage, they went silent, briefly confusing the approaching guards. The uproar seemed to have passed like a flash storm.

The guards carried on with their patrols, aware of the lingering hostility. No sound came from the cells, not even a stray cough or a whisper. One could easily be forgiven for thinking the building was deserted. That was what was so unsettling. Aggression clung to the silence. The guards could almost taste the bitterness in the air. They knew the reason, having been present when Callum announced his intention to disobey orders. Thank God, it was still lock down, and Adam Kent was away from his cell. But it wouldn't be long before he was back. Then what would happen?

The waiting game didn't last long. Doors opened and closed in the distance. There were footsteps – several pairs approaching, echoing across the tiled floors. The officers scurried to meet them, exchanging looks of concern with each other. This prisoner would certainly not be returning to his cell. The news was out, so they'd have to head him off before he came any closer. Just the mere sight of this policeman would cause further ructions.

The uneasy silence continued to bear down like an invisible force. Everyone, inmates and guards alike, held his breath. Adam Kent walked around the corner, under the protection of Thomas Hennessy and Colin Woodard. The officers flashed warning glances at the trio not to come any closer. Faces, tight with emotion, began appearing at the hatches, pressed against the unyielding metal to afford a better view. Adam seemed baffled when they suddenly ground to a halt. He gazed around, surprised by the unusual quiet. The guards began to whisper frantically amongst themselves. They could almost read the confusing questions spinning around his head. What was going on? And then someone spoke, and they saw him flinch. Adam Kent now knew that the game was up.

"Oi copper, you're in our world now."

Immediately the officers encircled him and ushered him away. Thanks to Lucas Callum, their work would be cut out keeping Kent safe.   Every one of them knew the prisoners would stop at nothing to get to him – that even being segregated from the mainstream was no guarantee of his safety.

CHAPTER FORTY FIVE

"Father, I rarely speak out of turn, but surely you have to see how impulsive you're being," Oliver Sinclair argued as he stood helplessly by, watching Sir Robert being wheeled towards the front door. Oliver never openly questioned his father's wishes, so this must prove just how important his need was to be heard now. In a last-ditch effort, he had been trying to put his point across and was becoming desperate. Despite his endeavours, the front door yawned open and sunlight streamed into the foyer.

As always, the handful of staff present kept their lips tightly closed, their eyes respectfully averted. They didn't make judgments about what went on around them. It was easier to see nothing and hear nothing within the gilded walls of this mansion. Today was the day the family were about to receive a new member – the long lost granddaughter of Sir Robert and Lucinda May Sinclair. A bedroom suite had been prepared in her honour, along with a healthy monthly allowance. Lucinda was looking forward to taking Ruby shopping. Having borne two sons, it would give her great pleasure to turn her granddaughter into a princess. Even the press had been alerted with the 'lite' version of events – how the hospital was responsible for the mix-up sixteen years ago but that the Sinclairs had chosen to be magnanimous and would not seek retribution.

Oliver danced behind the driver, Briers, trying to get in front of the wheelchair. They knew nothing about this girl, only that her upbringing had been common. She wouldn't fit into their world; she wouldn't know how to conduct herself in public. No doubt, she'd do something outrageous and let them all down. Oliver had done some research of his own. It didn't seem to matter that she was Lawrence's kid – Ruby Taylor was a slut. She didn't belong here. Not that he used those words in front of his father. Sir Robert Sinclair was stubborn and had to be handled with sensitivity. Right now, the old man gazed blankly ahead, purposefully blocking out his son's protestations. Suddenly it occurred to Oliver that, if he weren't careful, he could see his name being removed from the will and that teenage bitch inheriting the entire family fortune. He bit his tongue and took a step back, his narrow shoulders slumping in defeat. His mother was already settled in the car, glittering in unnecessary jewels. A smattering of press had gathered outside the house. Cameras flashed and reporters leaned in, desperate to get a hold on the story.

A breath of wind tugged at Sir Robert's snowy white hair as the rear door to the Mercedes Pullman was opened. Oliver watched as he engaged briefly with some woman thrusting a microphone in his face and then wave, all smiles, just before Briers assisted him into the plush interior of the family car.

Oliver kept to the shadows lest his true feelings be captured by some intrusive camera. It seemed it was only he who was being negative about his niece's arrival. But for public consumption, he had to pretend he was just as excited as everyone else. However, that didn't mean he had to be so accommodating in private. The old man was losing it big time, and this dogmatic attitude was testimony to that. In his prime, Sir Robert had been a force to be reckoned with – not even suffering a stroke could curtail his drive – and it was no accident that his company made millions. But, in Oliver's opinion, he had become soft and his judgment had deteriorated since Ruby had appeared on the scene. Somehow, he had to be stopped before he destroyed everything.

CHAPTER FORTY SIX

"What the hell are you doing here?" Ruby Taylor hissed the moment her father popped his head around the door. For some reason she had thought she could shed her former life – a life that had caused her nothing but misery – like an unwanted coat. Vince Taylor was a wife beater, Christine Taylor had abandoned her family and Ruby's perverted boyfriend had used her as a sex toy. There was absolutely nothing from her past that she wanted to keep hold of except, of course, her little brother Jamie. Maybe Vince suspected this when he journeyed to London to the exclusive private hospital in which she lay. Maybe that was why he pressed his finger to his lips and opened the door wider so that Jamie could barrel into the room.

* * *

It had been an emotional rollercoaster for Ruby. Not only had she suffered at the hands of those she trusted, she had been raped and left for dead. And now, she was recovering from aborting the child conceived from that rape, and this left an acrid taste in her mouth. Having a termination didn't rest well with Ruby but, the moment she'd discovered she was carrying, she'd panicked and wanted shot. It was as simple as that.

Before Vince had shown up, she was lying quietly in bed, a small pile of leaflets on the covers beside her, reflecting on what she had done. There were telephone numbers she could ring and websites she could visit, should she ever feel the need. Right now, it was all a blur. Ruby hadn't had a chance to think about the life growing inside her. It should never have been there in the first place, and she hoped that her rash decision wouldn't spoil her future – damage her insides in some way that would prevent her from bearing children. Would she always wonder what her son or daughter would have looked like, or could she push this unsettling thought back into some dark recess of her mind, along with the rest of her emotional baggage?

This was why she was so determined to grab hold of that new start in life that fate had offered her. She was leaving hospital today to live with her long-lost grandparents. She was rich and would be able to afford anything she desired. It was like a fairytale come true. Very soon, Sir Robert Sinclair would arrive and whisk her away to her new home. Home – a mansion of a townhouse in one of the most exclusive streets in London! He had shown her pictures and told her the press were lapping up what they were calling her 'Rags to Riches' story.

Ruby wondered what Simon would think if he were to see her in the newspaper or on television. Would he follow her to London and threaten her with that damned sex recording he'd made? Her mouth went dry when the gruesome memories flashed through her mind. It was far from consensual, but Simon had such a hold over her that she had felt she had no choice but to let him do what he did. In a moment of weakness, she had opened her heart to Sir Robert and told him about the power her boyfriend wielded over her. If the footage were ever uploaded onto the Internet, it would not only ruin her future but stain the reputation of her new family. Her grandfather told her not to worry.

Without her mobile phone, Ruby had no idea if Simon had even tried to make contact. What she was certain of was that any love she'd ever had for him had died. She crossed her fingers and prayed that she would never set eyes on Simon Richards or his revolting brother, Leo, ever again.

* * *

Now the man she had grown up believing to be her father hovered awkwardly before her – a dishevelled mess. Jamie, meanwhile, had propelled himself into her arms. He smelt of apple shampoo and bubble gum. Having gotten over the shock of their unscheduled visit, she could tell by their demeanour that something was seriously wrong. Jamie was sobbing quietly into the crook of her neck, wetting the cotton collar of her hospital gown. Vince just stood there, a broken man.

"I'm sorry to barge in like this," he said hoarsely, his troubled eyes cast downward. "But I felt you should know that the police have found your mum, I mean Christine."

Ruby stared at him, wincing at the way he referred to the woman who had brought her up. After the attack, she had angrily pushed her family away, and that was probably why Vince thought it advisable to call his wife by name rather than risk provoking another vitriolic outburst from the girl he once believed to be his daughter. But despite everything else, Ruby still considered Christine to be her mother.

"What's happened?" she gasped, hugging Jamie tighter. Vince opened his mouth to speak but then crumpled. Ruby waited, suddenly unable to breathe. She knew. She knew before any more was said.

"Mummy's dead," Jamie sobbed, filling the silence.

"What?"

"They found a body," Vince managed to say as he pressed his hands over his wretched face. "They've checked dental records." He swallowed. "It's her."

It didn't seem real. An icy calm washed over her, dulling her senses. Soon she'd wake up from this nightmare and go back to hating Vince for the way he'd been throughout her childhood. But right now, she felt only pity, not just for Christine and the son she'd left behind, but also for him. Not even Ruby, for all her tempestuous passion, could hate him right now.

She began to shake and hugged Jamie tighter.

"What happened?" she whispered, burying her lips in her brother's fair hair. Vince sank down on the foot of her bed, and she didn't stop him.

"There was a fire – that much I do know. What she was doing in that house, I have no idea. I don't think the police have told me everything yet." He raked his hair and shook his head,

183

staring at nothing. "When they release her, there'll be a funeral. You will come won't you?"

He sounded so pitiful. It was like a knife through her heart. Ruby's stomach performed a somersault as reality slapped her in the face. She pushed Jamie's heaving body away so that she could breathe. Oh my God, oh my God, she thought, leaning over the side of the bed. It isn't a dream. My mum is dead.

The word 'funeral' had stripped away the protective layer of shock, leaving Ruby exposed to the crushing pain. For several moments, she was unable to speak. The lump in her throat swelled to such a size that she thought she was going to choke. Then a short whimper and a strangled sob escaped her lips and she began to cry.

It was a scene Sir Robert and Lucinda May were not expecting when they entered the room, each carrying a festive armload of balloons and flowers. As they turned the corner they encountered a cluster of bodies embracing each other.

"What is going on here?" Sir Robert exclaimed. He recognised that brute of a man as Ruby's 'father', but he'd never seen the boy before. At first, he thought they were attacking his precious granddaughter but now saw they were trying to console one another.

On hearing the old man's voice, Vince broke away, all his fight deserting him. It was a battle he couldn't win with his fists. He intended to find out the truth about this multi-millionaire, after he had mourned his wife. He had already contacted Alice, the journalist, and made an appointment with her.

"I've just found out that my mum is dead," Ruby gasped over the top of Jamie's head.

"Oh dear God," said Sir Robert, as Briers pushed him forward to take her hand. Vince bristled but said nothing.

"You poor child," echoed Lucinda, staying put at the end of the room. She was disappointed that her carefully planned homecoming wouldn't be quite the fanfare she had hoped for.

"Please come back with us," Jamie wailed, pulling at Ruby's heart strings. She squeezed her eyes tightly shut as her past and future clashed inside her. She could feel her brother's hot frenzied breath against her neck – the desperate need for his sister's love now that his mum was gone. God! But how she craved this exciting new life, surrounded by wealth, as well as the need to discover the truth about her real father, Lawrence. Everything she'd ever known still resided with the name Taylor – with Vince and Jamie – but her blood was Sinclair. Surely she owed it to herself to take a step into this uncharted future?

Ruby stole a glance at the figure at the end of the bed. The woman was a stranger to her – petite with coiffed silver-blond hair and twinkly blue eyes. She looked expensive, with her fingers and ears glittering in precious jewels, but there was also a kindness radiating from her. Ruby could be just like her if she chose what was rightfully her destiny.

"I'm sorry," she whispered against the crown of her brother's pale-blond head. Jamie stiffened at her rejection and began to sob louder. "I'll come and see you and you can come and see me," she promised, seeking silent approval from her grandfather. Sir Robert gave a perfunctory nod but only Vince noticed the hardness in his eyes.

"There's something else," he said, ignoring the frosty vibes.

"What is it?" Sir Robert snapped, reaching out to possessively stroke Ruby's long, dark hair. "Can't you see how upset she is?"

Vince clenched his jaw, trying to keep his temper in check.

"They've got him, Ruby. They've got the man who did this to you."

At that point, Vince reached over and began to pry his distraught son from her arms. She relinquished her hold on her brother, her mind preoccupied by this last statement.

"Come on lad, let's get home," Vince said gruffly, keeping his eyes focused on his son. He couldn't bear to look at Ruby or the people who were stealing her from him. He pressed Jamie against his hip and held him tight whilst rummaging in his jacket pocket.

"I brought your phone," he mumbled, passing it over. "You might want to contact your friends."

Ruby robotically took hold of the mobile and sniffed, her fingers briefly brushing Vince's hand.

"I'll let you know about the arrangements," he added, steering his hysterical son towards the door. "And I'm sure the police will be in touch."

Ruby lifted her head and watched, through a veil of tears, as they left. Neither looked back, but she could hear Jamie's cries echoing down the corridor long after he'd gone.

CHAPTER FORTY SEVEN

When flies are found congregating en-masse, they're a complete giveaway that something is untoward. When a person dies, especially when the body lies undiscovered, the first to appear on the scene are the blowflies. With their extraordinary sense of smell, they can detect decay from a great distance, sometimes as much as ten miles, and arrive within minutes of death.

The flies set about laying eggs, hundreds of them, in any open wounds and orifices and on other exposed parts of the body. When the maggots hatch, they begin to burrow their way beneath the skin, feeding on flesh. If the temperature rises, the process accelerates, and the carrion insects rapidly multiply.

Such was the warm spell that provided the perfect breeding and feeding conditions for decomposition inside a vacant property in Bognor Regis. It was only when a sharp tap-tap-tapping sound could be heard at the downstairs window that Ali Mack, a local courier, was alerted to the problem. She'd heard the noise whilst delivering a parcel to the elderly neighbour next door. Ali knew the property in question had been unoccupied for several months – a local estate agents' 'To Let' board was erected just outside. It was like someone was throwing pellets at the glass from within. Ali, who was on her way back to her vehicle decided to change course, her curiosity getting the better of her. She walked the few steps down the short path towards the front window and peered into what she assumed must be the lounge.

The room was cast in shadow, so it was quite difficult to see. There was no furniture to speak of. She pressed her face to the pane of glass. Suddenly, an angry large fly launched itself at her head, smacking against the window. Ali freaked out and stepped backwards, almost twisting her ankle in the process. It was only then that she noticed a line of winged black insects converging on the sill, settling for a few seconds respite before returning to the focus of their obsession.

Ali, a no-nonsense lady in her mid-forties with short, spiky blond hair, was experienced enough to know what an infestation of blowflies meant. There was something dead in there. Shaking a bit, she extracted her phone from her pocket and dialled 999. Who or what it was, Ali had no idea. Perhaps a homeless person had found a weak entry point and since perished within. She calmly told the police call taker everything she knew, such as it was. It would only be a matter of time before Ali discovered she had inadvertently stumbled on the scene of a double murder.

CHAPTER FORTY EIGHT

Guy Kane was driving around aimlessly in one of the CID cars between Chichester and Bognor Regis when he heard the controller's voice crackle over the radio. The request was to attend a property in Longford Road, where a death was suspected to have occurred. Guy was bored. He was returning from taking a witness statement relating to a burglary and was at a loose end when the alert came through. He had been travelling back to base via the A27 and was about to enter the Hunston/Selsey roundabout when he quickly changed his mind. So, instead of turning off into Whyke Road, Guy travelled back on himself, making a hard right and heading in the direction of Bognor Regis town centre.

It wasn't really his patch, him working out of Chichester, but he figured he'd spin round and take a look to see if it was anything worth his while. If it weren't, he'd let the Bognor Boys clean it up.

The pleasure of his night with Cheryl had temporarily distracted Guy from being pissed off that his plan to arrest Jason Sadler's killer had monumentally backfired. Now he was left scratching around, following up leads in thoroughly unexciting cases, and he had nothing really meaty to get his teeth into. Guy needed something else if he were ever going to advance his career – something like the murder case that had slipped through his fingers. He was more than relieved that Brian Proctor was going to retire soon – it was evident the man had it in for him, and he'd make no progress all the time Proctor was in the force. Maybe he'd ask for a transfer to Bognor. He wasn't exactly in Nick Marshall's good books either, having screwed his wife. No. Guy needed a fresh start and this call on the radio could well be the chance he was looking for.

Thankfully, the traffic was fairly light – a short lull between the morning rush hour and the lunchtime mayhem. In less than fifteen minutes, he was indicating right over the 'square-about', a local colloquialism for the angled shape of the roundabout, before turning off past the railway station into Longford Road. This assortment of town houses stretched all the way down to the Victorian 'Picturedrome', which had been a cinema for nearly a century. A selection of modern residences nestled comfortably amongst their period neighbours, and Guy noticed that many of them were fronted by small courtyard gardens. As it transpired, it was at one of these more traditional properties where the action was.

The road was fairly wide, with plenty of street parking. Guy could see two marked police cars at the scene and one officer talking into his radio whilst setting up a cordon. As far as he could tell he was the first member of CID to attend, although he couldn't take it for granted. Any one of those plain cars parked close by could belong to the Bognor team. Guy crossed his fingers that this wasn't the case. He didn't want to be cast aside from something so potentially juicy. If he could at least have some involvement in an investigation this side of the Division, it would give him ample reason to seek a transfer. He seriously doubted that anyone would care if he left Chichester, which should be an extra incentive for them to make the transition as smooth as possible. It would be a win-win situation. Everyone would be happy.

Guy abandoned his car and hastened up to the uniforms. Despite the morbid circumstances, the town had a distinctive holiday feel about it. Butlins had built a major resort here, which contributed to this. Seagulls dominated the pale blue sky, screeching incessantly. Guy breathed in the salty air, suddenly feeling nostalgic. It reminded him of his childhood and the family trips to holiday camps in Blackpool and Devon.

As Guy approached the scene, an older officer, with a large gut spilling over his waistband, wobbled forward. He lifted his hand, deterring him from coming any closer. Wisps of grey hair peeked from under his cap and a pair of deep-set brown eyes that had no doubt seen it all, glinted suspiciously at the stranger.

"Sir, you can't come through," he said authoritatively, his fleshy jowls jiggling as he spoke. Guy removed his warrant card from his jacket and flashed it at the man.

"CID," he said. "I was in the area. What have we got?"

The officer immediately stepped aside and allowed Guy through.

"It looks to be two dead bodies – could be suspicious," he explained, huffing and puffing as he tried to keep up with this over-enthusiastic newcomer. "We're in the process of trying to gain entry."

"Have SOCO been informed and Force Medical Officer? Who's taking charge of this? Who called it in? Don't set foot in there without coveralls," Guy rattled off, instantly taking control and sounding as authoritative as he could.

The uniformed officer pursed his lips in annoyance. He was a career constable. He knew the score and had probably attended hundreds of crime scenes long before this jumped-up cockney was out of short trousers. Yet he played the game. He'd never seen this DC Kane character before but everything seemed aboveboard. They moved swiftly over to the house. Guy noticed a slender woman, dressed in a pale grey uniform with spiky blond hair, sitting on the bonnet of a marked car being interviewed by a female officer. She looked ashen and was shaking as she gave her account.

"That's the witness who called it in," PC Gregg explained to him.

"Great, I'll have a word with her after," Guy said.

The house in question was located towards the cinema end of Longford Road. A 'To Let' sign advertising 'Matharu Properties' had been erected within the small courtyard garden and was leaning over to one side. The tired cream-coloured paintwork of this Edwardian property was flaking in several places, and weeds had pushed through cracks in the path. The front door was partially glazed. There were no nets up at the windows.

As Guy walked closer, he could see something moving across the lower pane. He squinted. It looked to be flies. Two uniformed officers were in the process of gaining entry. It wouldn't take much to smash through that flimsy door, he mused.

"Because the double glazing is blown, the glass is cloudy. To begin with, it was difficult to see in but with the presence of insects, I am convinced there are at least two bodies inside the house," PC Gregg told him. Guy quivered with anticipation. He was the first member of CID on the scene and it was highly likely it was a double, if not multiple murder. Even when the boys from Bognor turned up, there was no way he was going to be ousted from this case. This is perfect.

Out of the corner of his eye, Guy could see the arrival of other units but he was clad in protective overalls long before they'd managed to slip through the cordon. He put his foot over the threshold, making sure he was the first man to enter the house.

The smell was sickening, but he was used to it. He'd attended many deaths before, all in different stages of decomposition. This wasn't the worst he'd seen, but it was pretty close. The recent warm spell had expedited the process. Flies swarmed around the room in an excited frenzy, buzzing back and forth towards the source. Guy heard the crunch of insect bodies beneath his covered shoes. He only took a few moments to assess the scene.

The front door led straight into the lounge. The room wasn't furnished, but he could tell it was the main living space. A flight of stairs, located directly opposite the entrance, ascended to the upper floor. There was a doorway leading off to another room, situated towards the rear – possibly the kitchen. Straight away, Guy could see two bodies, both male. One was lying on his back, in an almost perfect starfish position – the other had collapsed like a marionette at the base of the stairs. He noticed a dark spray of blood on the wall behind.

Guy stepped further inside. There were plants – hundreds of them in their infancy, swamping the entire floor space. They were also dead, their small, spiky leaves crispy from thirst. Straight away, he recognised their withered shape as cannabis.

"A drug hit, would you think?" said a gruff voice. Guy turned to see another officer clad in the same protective gear, wearing a mask over his face.

"It looks to be the case," he concurred.

"SOCO are here and the Force Medical Officer. We'd better give them room to work," the other man suggested.

Guy agreed. He had achieved his objective – he was now part of this investigation whether they liked it or not.

CHAPTER FORTY NINE

In the end, Sophie had gone to school. She didn't feel any better, but just had to get out of the house and its oppressive atmosphere. Rudely pushing a path through the scrum of excited reporters congregating outside, she had practically run all the way to the bus stop, hoping she wouldn't be pursued. Apparently, most of them were far too focused on trying to corner her stepmother to pay her much heed. Even so, a couple of voices half heartedly rang out, inviting her to make a comment.

Most likely they thought her leaving was a ruse to take their eye off the real target, who still wasn't thinking clearly or acting rationally. After first insisting that Sophie go to school, Rosemary quickly changed her mind. She said she didn't want Sophie even leaving the house until the reporters had left. Of course, she planned to visit Adam, but considered it better for the rest of the family to stay put. That was the last thing Sophie needed. Besides all the suppressed panic and the sombre mood, she thought she would drown in all the tea she had drunk. If Rosemary wouldn't let her go and see her dad, then she was going to fuck off out of the house – maybe hitch a ride and go and see him herself.

* * *

Any bravado Sophie might have brought with her disintegrated the moment she entered the school grounds. What if everyone already knew about her dad's imprisonment? Sophie faltered. After all that had transpired during the past forty-eight hours, everything else faded into insignificance. She'd barely even given her break-up with Dale Samuels any thought, not that they'd been seeing each other for long.

Sophie hovered for a moment, staring blankly at the red brick building, chewing her bottom lip and wondering what to do. Perhaps Rosemary was right and she should have stayed home – hidden away with the rest of them.

It was still relatively early, but the warm sun was already beating mercilessly on top of her head and she could feel beads of moisture trickling down her spine. It didn't help that she had her blazer on. Most of the kids weren't wearing theirs. Yet Sophie couldn't summon the energy to peel it from her shoulders. Instead, she stood in a daze as she began to wilt under the burning rays.

"Hi Sophie," somebody called, breaking her from her reverie. It was Sandra, one of the girls from her English Literature class. Sophie forced a smile, searching the girl's face for any hint that she might know something. But no, Sandra just flashed her usual pretty smile and walked past into the building.

Sophie sighed and turned back. A hoard of students were now advancing towards her. Because she was carrying such a monumental secret, she felt intimidated, as if they were enemy troops marching forward. Her heart hammered as she studied each of them for signs that somebody had found out about her father. It might be the odd whisper, or a furtive glance. Her mind was filled with images of being surrounded and taunted, and she decided that if she saw even the slightest indication that this might happen, she was going to bolt.

Some of students smiled and acknowledged her, others totally ignored her presence and some looked at her as if she had a problem. As they passed on by with no adverse comments, Sophie felt a little calmer and began to breathe normally again. Not one of them had turned and pointed their finger or made disparaging remarks about her dad. Even Dale, flashed a sheepish smile before disappearing from view. If he had known something, she was certain he would have approached her. After all, they were now in the same boat.

Dale came from a troubled family and it was common knowledge that his father and uncle were also in prison. But he didn't seem to have a problem at school. He was still Mr Popular. The difference was, Sophie's dad was a police officer and had murdered someone, so people were bound to be more critical. For now, it seemed as if she was safe. Everything was as normal as it had been yesterday. But for how much longer? Thanks to those pesky reporters, it wouldn't be long before everyone found out.

As Sophie stood on the threshold, debating whether or not to go in, she was reminded of her early days at this school. Her father and stepmother couldn't afford the expensive private school that Jason Sadler had paid for, and so she had been put here. Initially she had bridled at the change, and made herself a loner in the process. Over time, though, she'd come to terms with being here and had settled in, made a few friends and was doing well.

She entered the building, though it took every ounce of willpower she possessed before heading towards her first class.

* * *

The class had ended without anyone treating her differently. Sophie allowed herself to relax slightly. Somebody asked if she'd heard from Ruby. She shook her head, remembering the strange phone call the day before, when the drunken man had told her that her best friend was dead. Sophie didn't think so. She was sure he was lying, but she couldn't imagine why. As much as she missed Ruby, she had to concentrate on her own problems – first and foremost, finding a way to see her dad.

She entered the next class – English Literature. Once again, she acknowledged Sandra, who was busy removing her books from her bag and organising her homework on her desk. Homework! Shit! She was supposed to have written a 1,000-word essay on the character of Angel Clare in '*Tess of the D'Urbervilles*', which had completely slipped her mind. Filled with renewed panic, Sophie glanced around. Everyone had their papers in front of them – everyone except for her! She had never *never* forgotten to do her homework. And though she was one of Mr Barley's favourites, he always came across so wounded if a student failed to deliver. In her present state of mind, Sophie was convinced she'd die on the spot if she were

196

humiliated in front of the entire class. After all, what excuse could she possibly give?

Mr Barley entered the room, a short, balding man with a pot belly who reminded Sophie of a timid little mole. He bustled around, removing his creased fawn linen jacket before hanging it carefully on the back of the chair. As she squirmed in her seat, Sophie noticed sweat marks on his cotton shirt beneath his armpits. Mr Barley cycled to school every day and regularly got caught out by the weather. Hot, cold, wet or dry – it seemed he was always either squelching in his shoes or drenched in perspiration. One would think that by now he'd remember to keep a fresh change of clothes at school! Presently he was still wearing his bicycle clips! Yet he was a nice man, and Sophie wished that somehow she could magically conjure up the perfect essay for him.

As she watched Mr Barley prepare the lesson, she felt sick. Not for the first time today did she regret not taking Rosemary's advice. If she had, she could be at home with the duvet over her head, avoiding this catastrophe. After a few moments, her tutor nervously cleared his throat and turned his attention to the class, resting his buttocks on the desk. Sophie's stomach flip flopped.

"Before I start, I'll collect the homework. I take it you're all up to date?"

Sophie winced and raised a shaky hand.

"Miss Kent, is there a problem?" Barley asked, peering down at her in disbelief. She instantly felt the smug scrutiny of her classmates and her face became hot.

"I'm sorry, I-I forgot," she stammered.

Sophie braced herself, waiting for the inevitable fallout. She had seen this happen only a few times. It was very rare that anyone let Mr Barley down, probably because he was such a good teacher and they hated to upset him. Mr Barley shook his head, his mouth downturned as if he couldn't deal with her lack of commitment – as if it were a personal slight. Maybe this display of mortification was all an act, but it made Sophie feel even worse. Tears pooled in her eyes. She blinked them back and bit her lip. The knock on the door couldn't have been timed better. Without waiting for permission to enter, the head teacher, Ms Blanchett, flung the door wide open and strode in. Saved by the bell, Sophie thought as she released a deep breath and fought for composure. Instinctively, everyone sat up straight. Mr Barley turned from Sophie and hastened over to greet his boss.

Ms Blanchett made a formidable sight, the stereotypical head. It was difficult to judge her age. With her mousy hair dragged severely from her pale face into a tight bun and her heavy-boned frame, she could be anything from thirty to fifty-years-old. And she always wore navy blue, usually skirt suits that skimmed the mid-calf. Sophie imagined that Ms Blanchett's wardrobe consisted of all the same stuff. Sensible shoes and horned-rimmed glasses completed the puritanical image. In spite of her austere appearance, she was not as fierce as she looked. In fact, she was very kind and approachable, although she seemed rather agitated right now.

"If I may have a quick word," she said to Mr Barley, making no apology for this interruption. Her eyes rested for a second or two on Sophie, which immediately kick-started her racing heartbeat. Both adults left the room.

With no supervision, everyone relaxed and began to whisper amongst themselves. Somebody laughed and made a funny noise. Sophie stared fiercely at the door. She could see the outline of their bodies through the glass panel. They conversed for a couple of minutes before Mr Barley returned, slightly red in the face. He pressed down on the levered handle until the door clicked shut and walked very slowly and deliberately back to his desk, lost in an ocean of thought. Then he shook himself back to the present and cleared his throat.

"Where was I?" he said, almost to himself.

Nobody spoke.

"Ah yes – homework," he continued, rubbing his chin. He then asked for the homework to be passed forward and began to collect up the pages, taking time to shuffle them into one neat pile. Sophie said nothing. Had he forgotten about chastising her?

"Ah yes, Miss Kent," he said with a pained smile on his face. "Would you bring it in as soon as you feel able?"

Sophie nodded, totally dumbfounded. Sandra caught her eye and smiled as if to say, you got away with it, you lucky thing. Mr Barley began the lesson, asking everyone to turn to their copy of *Tess of the D'Urbervilles*. He began to read. Sophie tried to settle down and concentrate on the rise and fall of his voice as she followed the text. Although focusing on Thomas Hardy's masterpiece, she was certain she could feel the heat of her tutor's gaze upon her. At one point, she caught his eye and read something akin to pity on his face. She blushed and clenched her jaw, her wild heartbeat returning.

Feeling hot then cold, Sophie fidgeted in her seat. She rubbed the back of her neck, perspiration wetting her palm. It seemed as if the walls were suddenly closing in, stifling her. She tried to concentrate on breathing – Mr Barley's voice now sounded distant and tinny. A rush of noise filled her head until she could no longer hear him.

She began to panic. She had to get out of here. Something told her that he knew her secret, that Ms Blanchett had told him. If they had found out about her dad's arrest, then surely so had the rest of the staff. How long would it be before word spread throughout the whole school?

She managed to sit through the entire lesson but, the moment the bell sounded, she bolted from her seat. As she raced through the door, she heard Mr Barley calling out her name, asking her to stay back. But Sophie ignored him.

Ahead of the lunchtime crowd, she ran through the corridors, dodging other students emerging from their classrooms. Within seconds, she was outside, colliding with a wall of heat. She couldn't go back. There was no way she could go back until this nightmare was over. Sophie ran past the car park and the leisure centre, towards the roundabout, sweat pouring from every pore.

Only then did she hesitate, unsure of what to do next – turn left and go home or right and go into town? Her golden locks clung damply to her face. She stood for a second or two, trying to catch her breath. Glancing behind, there was no sign of the other students but she could hear their distant chatter.

The sky was cloudless. Several convertibles had their roofs down. People were out enjoying the sunshine. Sophie stood and waited, watching the world go by and then, decision made, she turned right. She needed to get away. She needed help.

CHAPTER FIFTY

Nick Marshall was still smiling as he put the phone down after speaking with DI Miles Button from Hampshire Constabulary. He could almost hear the relief in the other officer's voice when he informed him that they now had Craig Donohue under guard at St Richard's Hospital.

"There is no doubt – the DNA results match those taken from our latest victim. I have every reason to suspect that when comparing samples relating to the other women, we'll have hit after hit," he had told him confidently.

"When will you be able to question him?" Miles asked impatiently.

Nick took a sip of his coffee.

"Members of my team are at the hospital now trying to gauge a timeline for him to be brought into custody. Hopefully I should have an answer shortly. The problem we're facing right now is that the suspect is very sick. He suffered severe burns from a house fire and almost lost his life."

"My heart bleeds," came the sarcastic reply. "Keep me informed, and well done on catching this guy. He's managed to elude us for decades," Miles added good-naturedly.

It was true – many of Donohue's alleged victims had died in the early eighties. That was years before the miracle discovery of DNA testing had been introduced, although blood and tissue samples were held on file. After deliberating for several minutes, both officers were quietly confident that all related historic crimes would soon be put to bed.

As he hung up, Nick promised Miles that he would stay in touch. He was in a fairly good mood today, especially after last night. The dawn of a new relationship made him feel young again. Plus they were making substantial progress with this investigation – Ruby Taylor's attack and Eva Bennett's murder had technically been solved. Now they had to look forward to the complicated task of actually convicting the offender. They had to make sure that this case was watertight, with every 'i' dotted and every 't' crossed. It was imperative that Craig Donohue not slip through the net on a technicality. And, Nick thought smugly as he drained his coffee cup, while they weren't in competition with Hampshire, it was very satisfying to know that it was Sussex Police who had apprehended a serial killer. He couldn't wait to question this Donohue character and see what he had to say for himself. *But you wouldn't have anything if it weren't for Adam,* the voice in his head taunted.

Nick's smile instantly faded and he felt humbled. Yes, it was thanks to Adam Kent's tireless investigations that Donohue had been caught in the first place. If Nick had had his way, he would have let him go, simply because he was a doctor with an upper class accent! Adam had managed to see through this respectable façade and gone after him anyway, sometimes against orders. Mostly against orders, Nick thought as past conversations came to mind. He remembered the bollocking he'd given his sergeant after discovering Adam had deliberately relegated his duties to Amanda, just so he could follow up on a hunch. Nick cringed. He knew deep down that Adam Kent was a better detective than he would ever be. And where was he now? Rotting away in a prison cell when the department desperately needed talent like his.

Nick moved a stack of files over to one side and began hunting around the cluttered surface of his desk for Adam's notebook. Flinging drawers open, he rummaged frantically through them until he found it amongst some paperwork. Nick flicked it open and scanned the contents. The entries were neat and detailed, although sometimes impossible to decipher. Adam had abbreviated many words, and Nick knew that this little notebook carried all the evidence his colleague had on the suspect. Because Adam had researched the doctor so thoroughly, he would play a key role in nailing Donohue once and for all. So he's on remand, Nick thought matter-of-factly as if that was just a mild irritation. Doesn't mean he can't do some fucking work and translate his own bloody scrawl!

Suddenly filled with energy and a sense of purpose, he rose from his chair and snatched up his jacket, keys and mobile. It was the perfect excuse to visit Adam in Marden. There was no way the powers-that-be would refuse an audience with him. After all, it was official business. Though, just to be on the safe side, Nick decided to give them a call from his car and alert them that he was on his way.

As he exited his office, his personal phone warbled again. It had been ringing incessantly that morning. He knew who it was without even looking. *Philippa*. His mobile was choked with voicemails and texts, asking him where he'd been last night. Bloody cheek, Nick thought, after what she had put him through. He was half tempted to reply that he'd been in the arms of a beautiful woman but dismissed the idea. That would be immature and petty, and he considered himself a better person than that.

He gave his team the heads up, telling them that he'd be contactable via mobile, then stepped out into the warmth of the day and made his way to the car park. He breathed in the scent of freshly mown grass. Heaven! The weather was gorgeous – perfect for lazing about in the garden with a bottle of beer. Pity it was still the middle of the working week.

He unlocked the door to his Mercedes, just as the much anticipated call from Amanda came in.

"What's the news?" he asked climbing into the driver's seat.

"Donohue is awake but sleeping on and off quite a lot," she told him. He could hear the frustration in her voice.

"What did the doc say?"

"That he's on morphine for the pain and that, most of the time, he's away with the fairies. I'm worried that he'll slip from our clutches somehow."

"Have some faith, Mand," Nick said affectionately, smiling down the phone. "And tell me what the doc said."

She sighed.

"It's going to be a while before they feel he's fit enough to be questioned."

"Can he walk? Get out of bed?"

"He's badly burnt on the face and arm and, as I understand it, out of immediate danger. I'm no expert but I don't see why not."

"Shit," he cursed. "That means we'll still have to guard him. That's going to cost." He knew the moment he arrived back, he'd have to go upstairs, begging bowl in hand and put this case to the hierarchy.

Neither of them said anything for several seconds until Amanda broke the silence.

"I informed Vince Taylor about Christine." She sounded depressed.

"How did that go?" He turned the key in the ignition.

"It was awful, as these things always are. I'm having a horrible day, Nick," she said softly. Nick sighed.

"Do you want to go out tonight?" he asked, in an attempt to cheer her up.

"No."

Amanda's response was abrupt, and he panicked. Was she having second thoughts about the time they'd spent together? They had entered the critical stage in their relationship. Perhaps she was suffering from first-night regrets.

"What do you want?" he ventured to ask. It was a loaded question – Nick Marshall didn't play games. If Amanda had changed her mind about being with him, he'd rather know now before he fell deeper under her spell.

"I want to stay in, watch some television. Have a bath and an early night," she said decisively.

He nodded down the phone, feeling a bloom of disappointment. He then backed out of his parking space and spun the car, ready to commence the two-hour journey to HMP Marden. Two hours alone with his thoughts. Two hours to cogitate on what could have possibly gone wrong.

"Are you okay?" Amanda suddenly asked.

"I guess," Nick sighed, trying to disguise the despondency in his voice and project an air of nonchalance. He inhaled a deep breath, instantly putting protective barriers in place around his damaged heart.

"You are coming round tonight aren't you? I still want to see you."

"You do?"

"Of course, silly. When I said, I wanted a bath and an early night, I didn't mean alone."

CHAPTER FIFTY ONE

Adam's gloomy new accommodation was approximately seven feet by five feet. With almost no natural light, it was more like a dungeon than a cell. The narrow barred window looked directly out onto an exercise yard surrounded by high brick walls grimy with age. Once or twice, he peered outside at the square of concrete, infested with weeds and empty cigarette packets that had been collected by the wind and shoved into the far corners. Adam guessed that he'd never see the sun from this angle but, having felt the warm breath of air against his face, figured it was a beautiful day.

His mental torment was all encompassing. After the shock of being denied bail and being sent to one of the worst prisons in the United Kingdom, Adam had braced himself for a precarious life amongst hardened criminals. Until now, he'd been doing reasonably well. It had been a game of survival, but he'd managed to build a rapport with Azz, passed their initiation test and was preparing to tiptoe his way through some kind of existence until his trial. His solicitor had a plan which gave him a glimmer of hope but somehow, between leaving his cell that morning and returning less than two hours later, it seemed that his cover had been blown. So much for all those so-called safeguards!

Because of his profession, the threat to Adam's life was very real, so he had always assumed he'd be segregated. It was Officer Thomas Hennessy who'd dismissed his concerns, and he'd bowed to his greater experience when he was first booked in. The experiment had backfired monumentally. No matter how much Adam had wanted to believe in Hennessy's protestations that everything would be okay in the short term, there was no escaping the truth. He was a copper inside. Except for child molesters and such like, he was the lowest of the low and didn't deserve to live. And, having been deceived, the entire prison population was really riled up now that they knew the truth.

So, before he realised what was happening, Adam was ushered directly to segregation – precisely where he should have been in the first place.

"I'm sorry mate," one of the guards said as they encouraged him inside the narrow dark space. "It's for your own safety." Adam had barely had time to explore his new lodgings when the door to his cell was unlocked again by Officer Hennessy, who told him he had a visitor. The man looked a little sheepish but didn't apologise for his error in judgment.

Because of the danger, Adam was escorted to another part of the building, far from where the other prisoners received visitors. He was back in the interview room where he had met Terry. During the short excursion, neither he nor Hennessy spoke. Whether it was embarrassment on his part, Adam didn't know, although he didn't feel much like talking either. Thomas remained ever vigilant. Not all the inmates were locked up; some were out of their cells performing mundane tasks. Adam could feel a thick bank of animosity closing in from all sides. He kept his eyes cast downwards, trying to keep in step with his escort and not get left behind. Thankfully no one threatened or tried to attack him. Even so, throughout the five-minute journey, he could sense the underlying hostility. He knew and they knew that having a guard at his side didn't mean he was necessarily safe. They had just chosen to bide their time.

To Adam's horror, he found his parents waiting for him, and a lump formed in his throat. His mum and dad were doing their utmost to appear positive, but their masks were transparent, and Adam could see the true pain behind their eyes. They all took their seats – he on one side of the table, his parents on the other. He longed to hug them and kiss his mother but knew this was against the rules.

"Hello son, how are they treating you?" his dad rasped. Adam glanced up at Thomas, who flashed him a sympathetic smile and then looked away.

"I'm okay," he lied. "It's not too bad." His dad nodded and swallowed hard. Adam turned his attention to his mum who sat with a frozen, almost manic smile on her face. Her bottom lip quivered as she fought to control her emotions. They both seemed shell shocked and, much like him, wading through a nightmare they were sure would never end. He was their only son and they idolised him. He had always made them proud – from the day he had taken his first steps to the time he had risked his life to save someone from drowning in a tumultuous sea. It's what he did, and they were the type of people never to withhold their affection. Seeing their son like this must be killing them.

"Have you seen Rosemary?" his dad asked. His mum continued to sit in silence, not trusting herself to speak lest she break down in front of him. Adam struggled to keep his own emotions in check. There was no reason for them to know what had happened between him and his wife – he didn't want to shovel further misery onto their broken hearts. Looking at them now, he knew they couldn't take much more. Adam shook his head.

"Not yet," he managed to murmur.

"We've brought you some things," his mum suddenly announced with forced cheeriness. She turned in her seat to address Thomas. "It's only a couple of magazines and biscuits. That's allowed isn't it?"

Thomas smiled.

"We'll take a look and pass them on," he promised.

"Have you seen your solicitor yet?" his father pressed.

"Yes," Adam sighed.

"And you're pleading guilty?" It was clear how difficult it was for his dad to utter those words. The mischievous twinkle in his eyes once so familiar was gone, the vibrant blue replaced by a dull flat grey of hopelessness.

208

"Terry wants me to enter a plea of not guilty," Adam replied with a shrug.

"Oh?" said his mum. She looked across at her husband in confusion.

"I don't know what he's got up his sleeve," Adam confessed.

"So what will that mean? A proper trial?" his dad asked.

"I think that's what he wants. I'm seeing him in a couple of days. I'll know more then."

And so the stilted conversation went on, none of them able to relax under the pressure of such scrutiny. Those happy carefree days of family life, which they had all taken for granted, belonged to another time and place. This hour with his beloved parents was slipping by so fast, Adam could sense it. It wouldn't be long before Hennessy called a halt to this meeting, although he suspected in his case, he wouldn't be quite so stringent. But when Adam caught his eye and saw the subtle nod from the guard, he turned reluctantly back to his mum and dad.

"I'm afraid, times up," he said with as much enthusiasm as he could muster. He forced a smile.

"Gosh, that went so quick," said his mum. They all stood to leave, struggling to rise from the confines of the chairs that were, as usual, bolted to the floor. There was an awkward moment when nobody really knew what to do. Under normal circumstances his dad would have shaken his hand and his mum would have kissed his cheek. Instead they hovered for a couple of minutes as Adam fought for control. It was pointless to even wish for them to stay but he really didn't want his parents to leave him here. And then the unspeakable happened – something that he vowed he'd never do. As they all began to filter out of the room, his mum turned back, her eyes moist. That's when she told him she loved him. Something shifted inside and all the defences Adam had built up to protect himself suddenly crumbled, leaving him open and vulnerable. No longer was he their grown son, always so capable and strong. In his place stood a defenceless little boy. So much misfortune had befallen him, some of his own making, granted, but the life he'd loved so much was already a memory. The future looked hopeless. It wasn't what he wanted – he might as well be dead. Before he could regain his composure and rein in his anguish, Adam burst into tears.

CHAPTER FIFTY TWO

How do you win back your wife's heart when she hates you? That was the question dominating Gavin Peterson's mind as he tried to write a letter to Tracy. He'd been sat at his desk for what seemed like hours. His arm was aching, his shoulders had seized up and he was dying for a cup of tea, but he refused to move until he'd completed his task. It was far too important to push aside.

Evidence of his discarded attempts was scattered around him. The waste bin was overflowing with balls of screwed up paper that had tumbled out onto the carpet of Gavin's study, rolling under the desk as well as his chair. It had to be right – carry enough sincerity but, at the same time, not be too mushy. Yes, he could journey to London and try to beg for forgiveness face to face, but what was the point if she refused to see him? All that wasted effort and expense. Been there, done that, he thought miserably. How would he ever be able to express what he was feeling when Tracy continued to put up barriers? Guilt would almost certainly prevail the moment he saw those green eyes filled with so much hurt and accusation, undoubtedly preventing him from saying half the things he wanted to say. He'd probably end up babbling like an idiot and make her despise him even more.

Say what you want in a letter – that's what his mum always told him. Easier said than done, Gavin thought, grimacing at the state of his handwriting. But what else could he do? If he typed it on the computer, it would come across businesslike and impersonal. So, it looked a bit scruffy, but Tracy wasn't totally unreasonable. She'd understand. Besides she knew his right hand was out of action, and it might even soften her a little to know he had made the effort with his left. Um, he thought sardonically, even if I could write normally, I'd still probably choose not to. It was an excellent ploy to wheedle his way into her good books. He did wonder about buying a pretty card but then decided against it. The letter had to be humble and in no way embellished. Tracy was no fool.

Gavin glanced at his watch. Time was moving on and the boys would soon be home. He stared at the blank sheet of paper, seeking inspiration. The first challenge had been the salutation. He had begun with 'Dear Tracy', changing it to 'Dearest Tracy', then 'My Darling' and finally 'Sweetheart' before deciding to keep things simple.

Then there had been the question of how forthcoming should he be? Should he tell her about Jenny being dead and therefore permanently out of the picture? Or would that be construed as him conveniently trying to return with his tail between his legs simply because his mistress was no longer available? Only Gavin knew that wasn't the case. He had chosen Tracy over Jenny long before she'd topped herself. It wasn't his fault Jenny had lost the plot and set out to destroy him and to poison Tracy's mind. Maybe he shouldn't mention Jenny at all. God, love was full of pitfalls!

Gavin closed his eyes, trying to encapsulate everything he felt about his wife into some literary masterpiece – words she could devour and take to her heart, words she wouldn't be able to resist. He pictured snatches of their life together as man and wife, to a time long before he had strayed. Countless, happy times they'd enjoyed as a couple flowed freely into his mind – the day they'd got married, the joy of bringing their sons into this world, family picnics, days out, Christmases, birthdays, making love. But all these images were tinged with shadow, like photographs burnt around the edges. He could now see it as Tracy saw it. How his deceit had crept around the margins of her world, slowly infecting her precious memories.

Gavin felt humbled. He'd had it all and he'd thrown it away. He swallowed and once again confronted the page through a watery haze. Then he picked up his pen and began to write. Seeing things from Tracy's point of view, he now knew exactly what he wanted to tell her.

CHAPTER FIFTY THREE

Nothing and nobody was going to stand in her way, or at least that was what Ruby kept telling herself. Though putting this into practice wasn't easy, especially when every morsel of guilt and self-doubt conspired to prevent her from doing so. She was determined to ignore her heartache and leave behind her old life, so with a resolve she didn't know she possessed, Ruby forced herself to stop crying over her mother and the family she'd callously cast aside. It was regrettable, but what could she do? Her damaged past had no place in her glittering future. With that thought in mind, she washed the misery from her face in preparation to embrace the wealth and excitement that went hand in hand with the Sinclairs. There was the small matter of dealing with her attacker, but Ruby was confident that, because her grandfather was such a force to be reckoned with, she'd handle it fine when the time eventually came to face him.

"My name is Ruby Sinclair". Like a mantra, Ruby had been rolling this sentence around in her head for several days now, ever since she'd discovered her true identity. She liked it. It sounded so much better to her than Ruby Taylor – more sophisticated for one thing. Of course, as it had recently turned out, she was never Ruby Taylor in the first place!

Ruby was still in the dark as to how this mix-up at her birth had occurred. Her grandfather, Sir Robert, had promised that he would explain everything – warts and all, when she was ready. This would include some information about her real father, Lawrence. Ruby hoped so. She didn't like being lied to, even if it were done with the best intentions.

From the snippets she had gleaned so far, she had been switched with another baby. The question burning in the back of her mind was – had it been a terrible mistake or was the act intentional? Sir Robert had once confessed that he was ashamed about something he'd done in the past, which suggested the latter. Ruby already knew the police had a vestige of interest in what had happened the night she was born. He'd made no secret of this fact. Even so, deep inside, she really didn't want to believe her grandfather capable of deserting her.

Ruby was old enough to realise that no one was perfect, but the voice in her head continued to whisper controversial questions such as – who was the other baby and where is he or she now? There had been no mention of the infant since. It was almost as if it had disappeared. Thinking of the missing child made her uncomfortable, and it was proving to be a constant battle to shove aside her gnawing suspicions. These unsettling accusations had a habit of rearing up out of the blue, drip feeding doubt and dampening her spirit. Her future was bright – she was a wealthy young woman and her life was changing for the better, so why did these dark thoughts make her want to re-evaluate her choice? After all, whatever her grandfather had done back then, she was with him now, and Ruby was certain he'd make it up to her.

"My name is Ruby Sinclair. My name is Ruby Sinclair," her brain screamed defiantly.

She believed she had more or less conquered her reservations to let go of the past. Seeing Vince and Jamie so distraught today had been the ultimate test, especially when she was informed of Christine's death. This shocking revelation could have so easily weakened her resolve and sent her spiralling back to her former life. It was a natural reaction. They had played a major part in her everyday existence, and their devastation affected her deeply. Even though Ruby didn't belong with them anymore, it was still right and proper to weep for the woman she had once believed was her mother.

"Never feel guilt for mourning someone you love," Sir Robert had crooned gently as she buried her head in the pillow and sobbed, all the time whispering, "sorry sorry" for subjecting her new family to her anguish. She was embarrassed for crying over people who no longer mattered in her future. Hours later, Ruby could still hear the echoes of her brother's cries in her head, tugging at her heartstrings, making her question the decision to leave them at all. But he really wasn't her brother was he? Jamie, Vince and Christine had nothing to do with her. She should never have been with them.

Pushing aside the recent memory of their desolation and the strange emptiness inside her where her aborted baby had once nestled, Ruby was determined to be happy. Reaching across, she took hold of her grandfather's hand, wanting to feel some human contact. He raised his eyebrows in surprise and squeezed her fingers. She could sense a smile from Lucinda. Ruby sighed deeply, in a bid to quell another wave of rising doubt that told her she was making a giant mistake. It was imperative to focus on her newly found good fortune. Any girl in her shoes would grasp this with both hands, wouldn't she? Whatever the consequences. For the umpteenth time that day she glossed over the negativity and thanked her lucky stars she was being given another chance at happiness. She might as well have been flying over London on a magic carpet, the journey towards her dazzling future was that exciting.

Now swathed in luxury and cushioned by her grandparents, Ruby forced herself to relax as she pressed her head against the plush leather of the chauffeur driven car. It all felt like a dream, or a fairytale. As the car meandered its way through the streets of London, passing many great landmarks, Ruby had to pinch herself that this was to be her new life – her heritage. She was aware of everything – the vibrancy of the world beyond the tinted windows, the smell of the upholstery and of the expensive perfume inside the car. It was almost as if she had travelled the length of a rainbow and was now enjoying her pot of gold at the other end. And this way of thinking is the key to everything, she told herself. Just relax and enjoy it.

Already she felt safe and cosseted. Being the granddaughter of such a prestigious family meant that nothing bad would ever befall her again. She had conversed many times with Sir Robert, but her new relatives and the world they inhabited were still unfamiliar to her. For instance, she'd never lived with anyone else besides the Taylors. They knew the good Ruby and the bad Ruby and loved her regardless.

Before leaving the hospital, Ruby had also been warned about the press. Not only was she the rising new star in the Sinclair empire, she had also survived a vicious assault. Her life was newsworthy – the stuff that made headlines. Like broody females around a newborn, they wouldn't be able to resist.

"Just smile, my darling," Sir Robert had advised, long after Ruby's former family had departed and she'd wiped her eyes. "Naturally, they're curious about you, but I beg you to say nothing."

There had been a smattering of reporters gathered outside the Primrose Hospital when they left. Cameras flashed the moment she emerged into the sunshine. Carrying the festoon of balloons and flowers that her grandparents had bestowed on her, Ruby was escorted directly to the waiting car – a handsome stretch of sleek black and highly polished chrome. She felt like a celebrity. Before disappearing into it, she had smiled sweetly at the braying press, hoping they had managed to capture her beauty on film – that any evidence of her former grief was no longer visible to their inquisitive eyes.

"Ruby – how do you feel about being an heiress?"

"Ruby – is there anything you'd like to say to your attacker?"

Lucinda and Sir Robert had politely waved and smiled but neither issued a comment. The Mercedes pulled unhurriedly away from the kerbside to whisk their granddaughter off to her new home.

Ruby quickly realised that tomorrow morning she'd be in all the papers. What would her school friends think? Naturally, they'd be green with envy. And Simon? The sudden thought of her ex-boyfriend instantly sullied her fragile happiness, dissolving it with another wave of anxiety. Sir Robert must have sensed her change in mood for he asked her if she was all right. Ruby forced a smile and nodded, concentrating on the scenes playing outside the window. She focused her attention on the back of the chauffeur's head, remembering the mobile phone her dad had passed to her in the ward. No, correct that. He wasn't dad – he was Vince. She really must stop referring to him as her father. Would there be any messages waiting for her? Would Simon be annoyed that she hadn't been in touch and was now out of his reach?

Ruby decided that, as soon as she was awarded a little privacy, she would switch the device on. Something told her that her precious mobile would be one of the possessions Sir Robert would encourage her to surrender, simply because it held connections to her previous life. So far he hadn't mentioned anything about the phone, which was stowed safely in her pocket. She would relinquish it and anything else relating to her life with the Taylors, but only after she had checked it one final time.

CHAPTER FIFTY FOUR

Cancún, Mexico

Dying for a cool refreshing drink, the young man lifted his head from the sun lounger. He squinted as he craned his neck left, then right in search of a waiter. Through the haze of heat, he spotted a familiar rotund figure in a black and white uniform standing next to the Copacabana Bar on the opposite side of the pool. His name was Antonio, and he was one of the jollier waiters at the resort. Antonio was busy loading his tray with an array of exotic colourful cocktails and was too far away to notice any signal. The man propped himself up on his elbows and scanned the immediate vicinity, his eyes briefly washing over the glistening bare bodies around him paying homage to the sun. What he didn't see was another member of staff.

He licked his lips and tried to swallow. It was no good, he couldn't wait a moment longer. He needed a sparkling water, with plenty of ice and a slice of lime. He glanced at the woman stretched out beside him – her firm young flesh pink from a morning's sunbathing. She was lying on her back, eyes closed, brow furrowed slightly against the rays. Her long blond hair was pulled tightly from her naked face and secured into a knot on top of her head. On the deck between them sat two redundant hi-ball glasses, melted ice and a bit of lemon rind at the bottom.

"Do you want anything to drink?" the man asked.

"Nuh-uh," she replied.

"I'm just going to get an iced water from the bar. Are you sure?"

She didn't reply, so the man pulled himself from the bed before stuffing his feet into a pair of flip flops. He stood and gazed lovingly down at the female, making a note to slather more sun cream all over her gorgeous body before she burnt.

Abandoning his crumpled towel on the sunbed, he took slow lazy steps towards the bar. The sounds of a steel band floated on the air, adding to the holiday vibe, along with the mouth-watering smell of barbecued meats. He circumnavigated the majestic, kidney-shaped pool with its tropical garden and waterfall, smiling dreamily at the dragonflies skimming its glittering surface. There were dozens of butterflies with brilliantly coloured wings – some as large as a man's hand – fluttering effortlessly from one exotic flower to the next. *Paradise.*

He'd only been here just over a week and already it felt like a way of life. Hot cloudless days melted deliciously into warm fragrant nights in a relaxed self-indulgent routine. It's funny how easily people can adapt to new surroundings, he mused as he appraised the beauty of the hotel grounds; how a mere room suddenly feels like home. The resort was full but never seemed crowded. It had been worth the money to come here and pay extra to be all-inclusive. Furthermore, no children under the age of twelve were allowed, and the man considered that a bonus.

Each day, after he and his wife eventually tumbled from their bed and emerged from their suite, they would enjoy a leisurely breakfast of fruit and pastries before making a beeline for the pool. They had no interest in taking excursions to smelly noisy cities or joining the throng of tourists clambering to see ancient temples. They'd come here mainly for the sun and food, and to dip their toe in the local culture without actually immersing themselves in it. Crime beyond the walls of this hotel was prolific, and the man needed a break from all that.

The bar had been designed like a simple grass hut with highly polished wooden stools abutting the counter. As he approached, the music became louder – strains of melodic steel emitted from the speakers. Adjacent to the bar sat two Macaws on a perch. One was scarlet red, the other cobalt blue. Each parrot was busy preening his long, glistening feathers with a beak so massive they could crush Brazil nuts.

On seeing the man approach, Antonio beamed a brilliant smile, his pearly whites a contrast to his bushy black moustache.

"Ah, Señor Talman. You want me to bring you something?" he asked, his dark face coated in a fine sheen of sweat.

"It's okay," said Matt to the waiter. "I just wanted a glass of iced sparkling water," he added to the lady behind the counter. She smiled politely and set about preparing the drink.

"Go and sit. I will bring it to you," Antonio insisted as he began to depart with his tray.

"All right then," Matt said turning to the bar lady. "On second thoughts, can we make that two?" He knew without a doubt Tina would change her mind the minute she saw his drink.

"No problem, Señor Talman," called Antonio, now several feet away. "I shall deliver these and be right back."

Matt gave a small shrug and stood watching him for a moment. Despite his bulky frame, the waiter glided smoothly among the sun loungers with the agility of a dancer, stopping only to distribute the orders amongst the guests. Matt turned and smiled at the bar lady before ambling back to his wife. But since he was up, he decided to pay a quick visit to the gents before he settled down on his sun lounger again.

He changed course, wandering past the parrots toward the hotel foyer where he knew the nearest toilets were located. The foyer had a roof but no walls to speak of and, as Matt entered, he noticed a people carrier parked out front with a new batch of tourists spilling from its side door. He smugly noticed how tired and creased they all looked, remembering the long arduous flight to get here. That seemed like a lifetime ago – the journey, the wedding and all, but it had only been a matter of days. And only a matter of days before the honeymoon was over and it was back to the real world. Matt shook his head to dislodge this disturbing thought. He didn't want to even contemplate it.

Right now, he was in paradise and he never wanted to leave. He and Tina were together twenty-four-seven, with no distractions – no work, no Tony Junior, no nothing – just the two of them and a hotel that catered to their every whim.

He entered the gents, took a leak and wandered back out. The newcomers were now sprawled over the chairs at reception, sipping complimentary cocktails whilst the staff booked them in. Matt veered off to the right towards the gift shop. They had been so consumed by each other, they hadn't even considered buying any gifts, but Tina would undoubtedly want to buy her little boy something. There was a variety of plush teddies wearing sombreros which would probably suffice. He picked up a brightly painted vase, said to have been made locally, thinking that might do for his parents. The shop was more than adequately stocked with souvenirs and of course there was always the airport. Shame to be thinking of home, Matt thought, but eventually they'd have to face it. He scanned the array of goods on offer and saw a stack of British newspapers. He'd made a point of not even looking at one since he'd been here, so intent was he to distance himself from the rest of the world's misery, but something had caught his eye.

Matt bent down and picked up a Daily Mail. He frowned. The photo on the front page showed a man he recognised and the headline beneath made him gasp in shock.

"You want to buy?" asked the assistant.

"What?" Matt asked as he scanned the story beneath the picture.

"The paper? You want to sign it to your room?"

"Yes. Room 420," he said, his mind absorbed.

He left the shop, his vision clouded by the horror of what he had just read. Clutching the rolled-up paper in his fist, Matt walked back to his sunbed in a trance, his disturbed thoughts at odds with the lush surroundings. How? When? Why? All at once, he didn't know which way was up or down. The real world had managed to find its way to paradise, no matter how hard he'd tried to keep it at bay and, worse still, it was personal. There was only one thing Detective Sergeant Matt Talman was certain about – the honeymoon was over.

CHAPTER FIFTY FIVE

"Hey, listen up. The copper is crying. Do you hear me? The copper is crying." It sounded as if some warped town crier was bellowing down the corridor.

Horrified at being caught out, Adam instantly glared up at the spotty youth peeping with unadulterated delight through the sliding hatch in the door.

"Fuck you," he seethed from the vicinity of his bed, wiping the tears aggressively from his face. Gone was all the pretence. They all knew who and what he was, and there was no point even trying to win their trust. On the contrary, *he* had to change. He had to become just as tough as anyone else, or at least give the appearance that he was. Enough to make them think twice before trying anything.

Since his parents had left, Adam had let his emotions go. He'd been alone in his cell, and there had been no one else to witness his breakdown. Yes, he felt sorry for himself and sorry he'd failed to shield his misery from his mum and dad. That had been a mistake of gargantuan proportions. They had so much wanted to comfort him, and all he'd done was pile pain on pain.

Suicidal thoughts had already begun to creep into his mind. Seductive and beguiling, they beckoned him to take the easy way out. His life was over. It was as simple as that. Even on the rash assumption that his solicitor could get him off, his job and marriage were lost. If it weren't for the fact that he would devastate his parents, he could so easily succumb to temptation. Perhaps that was why the prison officers had chosen this particular cell, situated conveniently close to the hospital wing. Adam suspected that they were keeping their eye on him. For the sake of HMP Marden's reputation, him topping himself was probably the last thing they needed. As he gazed around the soulless interior, with only a single bed, and a metal sink and loo, there was nothing to stimulate his mind. He really didn't know how much longer he could survive this. Whilst Adam accepted that he must pay the price for Jason's demise, being segregated from the rest of the prison only gave his inner demons room to play.

After seeing his parents, he had scanned the area, hunting feverishly for a way to end it all, his eyes finally coming to rest on the metal bars set firmly into the concrete frame of the window. Compared to other British prisons, Marden wasn't quite as stringent when it came to health and safety. This gave Adam strange comfort because what was there to live for? He'd rather do it to himself than to give some other prisoner the pleasure. And who could blame him? Despite her far-fetched explanation, his wife had cheated on him. Those images of Rosemary and Guy Kane would be forever seared into his brain, flashing up when he least expected it, especially as he had no other form of distraction. And he'd lost the career he loved, his liberty and, on top of everything else, now carried the guilt of seeing his parents in pain.

Adam had yet to spend a night in segregation and, whilst he knew there was little danger of him being attacked, he wasn't sure if he'd be able to sleep anyway. This section of the prison was extremely noisy. Prisoners, who he suspected were quite vulnerable, would often cry out for no reason. One man had started shouting "Help – don't hurt me." Adam doubted anything was happening to him, but it was still unsettling to listen to. Could the wrong person ever get inside one of these cells? Then, for a brief while, the deranged man would settle down before starting all over again.

The face now leering through the hatch offered no mercy. Adam could smell food and guessed it must be lunch time. He had barely eaten anything since he'd arrived the day before, but he wasn't hungry. He still couldn't believe he'd only been here twenty-four hours. Already it felt like a lifetime. Once again, thoughts of topping himself began to tempt him.

"I've bought your lunch, copper," said the voice. Adam rose reluctantly from his bed and moved cautiously towards the door. He was surprised that they'd allowed another prisoner to serve him. Whatever was on that plate, he'd already decided to leave it there. God only knows what they had done to it.

The other man was a gaunt fellow in his early twenties with a feral look about him. He licked his thin lips almost lasciviously, pinning Adam with his intense stare.

"It's corned beef, mash and beans," he explained conversationally. It had been served on a plastic plate, along with a plastic knife and fork. Something red and jellified wobbled in a pudding bowl beside the main course.

"And trifle," added the prisoner. He gave a crooked smile before hawking back a mouthful of phlegm and spitting it into the mashed potato.

"A bit of extra flavour for you, Pig," he snarled.

Filled with an intense surge of loathing and disgust, Adam launched himself at the door, shocking the other man enough to stumble backward.

"Get out of my fucking sight," he growled, his lip curled, fists clenched. He gave the contaminated food a shove and heard the plastic tray and crockery topple to the tiled floor.

"Shit," said the man as Adam retreated to his bed.

"Clean that mess up, Parsons," shouted a voice which sounded very much like Officer Hennessy.

"It wasn't me," the other prisoner complained. "It was him."

"Didn't you hear what I said? Clean that mess up."

An assortment of curses followed, along with the sound of plastic crockery being retrieved from the floor.

"Fucking starve Pig for all I care," he was heard to mumble. Trying to calm down and regulate his breathing, Adam rested his back against the rutted wall of his cell. Darts of adrenalin coursed through his veins, spiking his fingertips. He knew that if he chose to continue this existence, this was probably the first of many altercations he'd have to endure.

Eventually, the spotty face re-appeared in the hatch. This time, the man wasn't smiling.

"Fuck you copper! You're dead," he warned coldly, dragging his finger malevolently across his throat before disappearing from view.

Adam released a deep breath as the aftershocks reverberating inside him gradually petered out and his equilibrium was restored. He sat waiting for any repercussions for the part he'd played in creating the mess, but nothing happened. It would appear that he had won the first round.

Once again, as if on cue, the prisoner next door began to shout, "Don't hurt me. Please don't hurt me." Adam closed his eyes, trying to zone him out.

"Shut up, Finch," yelled another voice. Mercifully, the cries for help stopped. Just then, Adam heard heavy footsteps beyond his door. Seconds later, the clunking sound of metal on metal followed and he stiffened as the door to his cell was flung wide open. The large bald officer who had escorted him to see his solicitor clutched what looked to be a rolled up magazine in his fist. Adam sighed, guessing that perhaps after all, he'd have to endure some form of punishment for throwing his lunch over the floor, but what else could they do to him? He'd already been segregated.

The guard glowered down at him for effect and relaxed his facial muscles as he slowly shook his head. Then he tossed the magazines Adam's parents had brought him onto the bed. Where the biscuits had vanished to, he didn't ask.

"Don't be expecting all this fancy treatment every day," he warned.

Having no idea what he was talking about, Adam didn't move.

"Well, come on then," said the guard, rolling his eyes. "You've got another visitor."

"Who?" he asked, scrabbling eagerly to his feet. Perhaps his dad had returned and he'd get a chance to put his mind at rest.

"Your wife," was the reply.

CHAPTER FIFTY SIX

The moment Ruby set eyes on her new home, it felt as if she had just walked onto the pages of *Hello Magazine*. And as if the house weren't gorgeous enough, her bedroom really was something to die for. Her jaw dropped the instant she saw it.

"This is for me?" she murmured, turning to Sir Robert for confirmation. He smiled fondly up at her from his wheelchair.

"Do you like it?" he chuckled.

"Like it?"

It wasn't just a room – it was a huge suite, complete with a four-poster bed, wall-to-wall mirrored wardrobes and even a squashy sofa. A massive flat screen TV completed the scene. Ruby could see a door to the right which led off to the bathroom.

"Really? Is it really mine?" she breathed.

"Yes, my dear," Lucinda squealed in delight, her girly voice strangely at odds with her age. "Where did you think we were going to put you? In the servant's quarters?" She laughed at her own joke and clapped her hands.

Ruby stood swaying on the threshold, hesitating before entering. The carpets were snow white, and she was wearing shoes. She shook her head in amazement and glanced nervously at Lucinda before slipping them off. She was having difficulty thinking of this woman as her grandmother. For one thing, she was exceptionally glamorous – petite, with a head slightly too large for her nimble frame. A lollipop head, Ruby mused, common amongst female celebrities who failed to consume enough calories. In her opinion, grandmothers should be plump and bake cookies, much like Christine and Vince's mums. She doubted Lucinda Sinclair had ever cooked anything, let alone ventured into the kitchen.

Towering above this birdlike woman, Ruby felt buxom and awkward. She hoped she had done the right thing by removing her shoes and that her grandmother would be pleased. First impressions count. That's what Christine had always instilled in her. It showed a mark of respect whenever visiting someone else's home.

Lucinda didn't alter her expression and, now that Ruby was standing closer, she could see why. There was no way this lady could have retained the complexion of a twenty-year-old without undergoing surgery. Like a mannequin in a clothes store, her skin was unnaturally taut, as if the lines and crow's feet had been ironed out. Unfortunately, whenever she did try to smile, only the corners of her mouth twitched slightly whilst the delicate skin around her eyes remained frozen. From a distance, it was barely noticeable but up close and personal, the result was very false. At the hospital, Ruby had wanted to be like Lucinda. Now she had changed her mind. Christine was beginning to get lines around her eyes, fanning out whenever she laughed, but that wasn't a bad thing. In fact it only served to make her more beautiful – more real.

Thinking about the woman she'd always considered her mother and the cold realisation that she was dead, Ruby felt another wave of misery which threatened to overshadow her excitement. She closed her eyes for a moment and then blinked several times, swallowing hard to dispel the swell of grief clogging her throat. Soon she'd be alone and would have the freedom to cry. It might have to wait until bedtime, but she had promised herself that, sometime today, she would award herself the luxury of just letting go. She didn't really know either of her grandparents well enough to unleash her emotions in front of them. Whilst they were both very kind, they didn't seem to be the type of people to pull her up onto their knee and give her a cuddle. In fact, Ruby feared that if she tried to hug Lucinda, her bones might break. For the briefest of moments, she felt another overwhelming surge of homesickness as memories of Vince comforting her when she was a small child flashed through her mind.

"Please, go in and make yourself at home," Lucinda urged finally, snapping her back to the real world. "It is your room."

Sir Robert cleared his throat before he spoke.

"Please, take your time Ruby and, when you're ready, come back downstairs. You've met the majority of the staff but you have yet to make acquaintance with your uncle. I'm disappointed that he wasn't here to greet you when you arrived."

Ruby detected a distinctly disapproving edge to her grandfather's tone.

"Yes, my dear," Lucinda added. "Take this day to relax. You and I will be going shopping first thing tomorrow morning and then, in the afternoon, I've made an appointment to have your hair cut and styled."

"Oh," Ruby gasped, reaching up to possessively finger a long black strand. How much would they want to cut off?

"Come on Lucinda, I know you're excited but let's not try to overburden the child too soon," laughed Sir Robert as Briers, who had been present all along, wheeled him away. Lucinda pressed her hand to her mouth and giggled again. Then she gave a little wave and followed her husband down the hallway, leaving Ruby standing alone.

* * *

Ruby watched them go before turning back to her bedroom. Like a fantasy world, it seemed to twinkle enticingly, waiting to be explored. Really, she should be excited – it was a dream come true. Any girl would want this – surely? Ruby inhaled a deep breath, desperate to re-capture the earlier feelings of eagerness and anticipation she'd enjoyed each time she contemplated her new life. She needed to be strong and move on. For the sake of her future, it was imperative to dispel the doubt and uncertainty in her heart. Yes, it was devastating to learn about Christine and to let go of Jamie, and even Vince but, if she didn't get a grip, this negativity could ruin everything. It would only continue to make her feel as if she didn't belong.

And Ruby *did* belong here. She was a Sinclair. This wealth was her birthright. It didn't matter that she looked different to them. So what if she was tall with a generous bust, that her olive skin tone and exotic beauty was at odds with the typical English Rose. Evidently her looks didn't come from this side of the family. From what she had seen, they all had pale complexions, blue eyes and fair hair. Ruby guessed that she must therefore, take after her natural mother – whoever she might be.

Come on Ruby, she thought as she picked up her shoes and stepped into the room. You've won the lottery. Be happy. Her toes sank into the deep pile and she stood for a moment, curling and uncurling them, enjoying the sensation. I'm rich, she told herself over and over. This is my new life. I'm going to be beautiful and envied. I'll have the world at my feet.

She moved dreamily towards the bed, reaching out to lightly touch the drapes and quilt – all made of the softest, most luxurious fabrics she had ever seen. Ivory and golds, russets and bronze. Everything smelt brand new. Her fingers brushed a variety of velvets and satins – no expense had been spared. Like something from The Princess and the Pea, the mattress itself was so high up off the floor that, when the time came, she would literally have to clamber on top to go to sleep.

Still clutching her shoes, Ruby ventured towards the bathroom, which was twice the size of her bedroom back home. A claw foot tub took centre stage. There was a vanity sink, separate shower cubicle, a toilet and even a bidet. Again, everything looked to be newly installed and untouched. The pearly-white floor and wall tiles glittered under the halogen spotlights. Completely overwhelmed and not wishing to spoil the effect by even using the pristine toilet, she stepped backwards into the bedroom and lingered in front of the wardrobe.

The sliding door glided open, as if moving on air. It was empty, cavernous, waiting to be filled with pretty things. Ruby bent to neatly place her shoes in one of the storage holes, smiling at how forlorn they looked as she closed the door on them.

Suddenly remembering the mobile phone that Vince had passed to her, she hastened to pluck it out of her pocket and switched it on. Ruby didn't know how much longer it would be in her possession. Her new family were gradually taking control, and she welcomed that. Didn't she? Hoping that there was still enough charge, she shuffled over to the window to catch a signal.

Her bedroom overlooked the garden which was part courtyard and part lawn. At the far end, she spied what looked to be an impressive ornamental pond. The borders were full to bursting with a variety of vibrant blooms. A couple of stone benches had been strategically placed to enjoy the most attractive aspects of the garden. It was impossible to imagine that this oasis of calm was in the centre of a bustling city. Filled with a renewed sense of enthusiasm, Ruby couldn't wait to go outside and explore.

Her mobile phone buzzed several times, alerting her that she had some messages pending – a number of texts and one on the answerphone. She swallowed nervously, feeling the usual coil of fear as she wondered what Simon would have to say. Even though he was technically out of her life, he still wielded a certain power over her.

Her throat dry, Ruby scrolled through, noting that one or two of the texts were from Sophie Kent, enquiring how she was and that she was missing her. The remainder were from other school friends wishing her well. With a queasy churn in her stomach, Ruby bravely lifted the phone to her ear and proceeded to listen to the message on her answerphone. It had to be Simon, and if it wasn't, his not making contact would further unnerve her. She'd suffered his silent treatment many times and it could only mean one thing – something bad was about to happen. The sex recording, she thought with a fresh wave of terror. She squeezed her eyes shut in silent prayer but, as suspected, Simon's voice filled her ears.

"Ruby baby, it's only me. Honey, I heard what happened, but I don't know where you are. When you get this, call me back. I love you, baby, and I'm sorry I hurt you."

The endearments were hollow; she had fallen for them countless times before. Ruby released the breath she had been holding and stared wide-eyed down at her phone. Okay, she was confused. It wasn't that Simon was being nice. His primary objective would always be to entice her with his sweet talk but, if that didn't make her succumb to his charms, he would then become sulky and childish. Failing that, Ruby would have to endure Simon's nasty side and be punished. It was always the same, and she'd had the misfortune of experiencing every single one of Simon Richards' personalities. He had more facets than a diamond.

What was strange though was that the answerphone message was several days old. She would have expected him to have rung again, even if just to keep up the pretence that he cared. But there was nothing, and that wasn't like him. She feared that perhaps he had just decided to fast forward his usual routine to collect on his threat and had already uploaded the recording onto *YouTube*. If that were the case, everybody in the whole wide world would soon be watching her performing sexual acts with two men. It didn't matter that she had been coerced to do something she was unhappy with. It wouldn't be portrayed as such. She'd be labelled a slut by the public and, even though her grandfather had promised her otherwise, Ruby was terrified that she would be famous for a different reason.

CHAPTER FIFTY SEVEN

"Can somebody please tell me who the fuck that is parading about as if he's the one running the show here?" Detective Chief Inspector Trent Abbot asked of nobody in particular. He had only just arrived on the scene and, naturally having assumed that nothing would happen until he had assessed the situation, was thoroughly pissed off to find a stranger strutting around barking out orders. And on top of everything else, Trent wasn't even late. How dare this person have the gall to start proceedings without him! The cordoned-off area in front of the property in Longford Road was already buzzing with activity.

Hearing the caustic tone in Trent's voice, PC Gregg was more than happy to enlighten him. After all, he'd been the one to challenge Guy as he had tried to muscle in on the scene. Perhaps it was because of his vast experience from years pounding the beat that Gregg had a handle on this. He had dealt with all kinds of people, from all walks of life, and had taken an instant dislike to this detective. There was something slimy about Kane, and Gregg's instincts were rarely wrong. So he decided to be the one to answer the DCI's throwaway question.

"His name is Guy Kane, sir, and he's from Chichester CID," he explained conspiratorially, narrowing his eyes as he too homed in on the newcomer. "He happened to be the first on the scene and just took over."

The object of their discussion was currently standing on the pavement outside the house, waving his arms in the air, whilst conversing with a member of the SOCO team.

"Is that so," muttered the DCI through clenched teeth as he finished pulling on his protective overalls. Without further comment, he moved away from the cordon, striding purposefully towards the property. So far, the discovery of two dead bodies had not only attracted ghoulish spectators but also members of the local press. A couple of TV cameramen were jostling with the crowd to obtain a better angle, whilst a line of uniformed officers endeavoured to keep everyone at bay.

It was perfectly natural for Trent to bristle with annoyance at the intrusion, although he had to hand it to this detective – he did appear to know what he was doing. Without further ado, he approached Guy directly.

"Hello," he said, projecting his authority as he proffered his hand. "I don't believe we've been introduced."

Guy raised his eyebrows in surprise at this sudden interruption and turned away from the officer he'd been conversing with. Unexpectedly confronted by a domineering figure with dark wavy hair, he was then subjected to his firm handshake.

"Sorry, I'm DC Guy Kane," he said as his arm was pumped mercilessly up and down. He finally managed to prise himself free of the other man's iron grip, flexing his fingers to get the blood circulating again. "I work out of Chichester CID. I was in the area when I heard the call on the radio. Naturally, I couldn't ignore it," he said pleasantly with a modest shrug. "And you are?"

"DCI Trent Abbot – the man in charge," Trent replied dryly.

Slightly rattled, Guy took a moment to compose himself. The last thing he needed was to make a bad impression, especially as he had plans to transfer to Bognor Regis. He had no doubt that Nick would happily agree to this request just to get rid of him. But if he pissed off the wrong crowd here, he wouldn't be going anywhere.

Despite the seniority of his rank, Trent Abbot was so much younger and better looking than him, with a square jaw and an alluring dimple in his chin. Not only that, he was broad and muscular and stood a full head over Guy, who was still weakened from trying to compete with his crippling handshake. The fact Trent Abbot had achieved his commanding status at such a young age was mind blowingly frustrating. It proved that he must be able to impress the right kind of people in order to so effortlessly scale the ranks, forcing Guy to admit that he could learn a lot from him. After all, in his humble experience, it was a slippery pole to the top of the food chain. So he decided that it would be in his best interests to make DCI Abbot his new buddy.

"I'm sorry if I've stepped on your toes," he said apologetically, trying to appear suitably humbled. "Crime scenes are ingrained in me. I just leapt into action. No excuse, sorry." Better not over-do it with the arse licking, he thought.

Trent nodded and relaxed his facial muscles.

"So, what have we got?" he asked, gazing at the property in question.

Guy smiled and licked his lips as he too turned towards the house. Officers were everywhere, clad in protective white overalls, to-ing and fro-ing, carrying in various pieces of equipment.

"It's a double murder basically. Two males, each with a single gunshot to the head. In my opinion, it looks to be a professional hit."

"I see," said Trent as he peered up the street towards the crowd of onlookers. There was always a chance the killer could be in amongst them, revelling in his glory.

"Any idea who they are?" he asked, referring back to the victims.

"Leo and Simon Richards," Guy replied. "We carried out an initial search of their clothing, and both were carrying identification. The evidence inside suggests they were drug dealers. There are hundreds of pots of cannabis plants downstairs, which are also dead."

"Are the deceased known to us?"

Guy nodded. "Yes, especially Leo, but they've kept below the radar for several years."

"Let's go inside," suggested Trent.

Guy beamed, suddenly feeling matey. This was just what he wanted – a sense of being included. Brothers in arms, he mused striding side by side with his potential new boss, trying not to appear too smug. It was now more important than ever to remain professional. If Guy played his cards right, there'd be plenty enough time to ingratiate himself with the DCI who had the capacity to become a key player in any future promotion. As long as he kept away from this man's wife, he shouldn't have a problem. And just so long as he's not mates with Nick Marshall, whispered his subconscious, curtailing his excitement.

As they entered through the door, Trent recoiled at the stench and quickly cupped his hand over his nose and mouth.

"Sorry about that," muttered Guy as they were bombarded with bluebottles. "I should have warned you."

"It doesn't get any better does it," laughed Trent as he shuffled deeper into the room. He waved his hands in the air, batting away the frenzied insects.

Guy stood back, respectfully refraining from saying anything further and allowing the DCI ample opportunity to gauge the murder scene for himself. The Force Medical Officer, who was crouched over Leo Richard's body, rose shakily to his feet to greet Trent as he approached.

"Hi Trevor, when's retirement?" Trent asked, slapping the doctor on the back. Cameras flashed constantly, taking in every gruesome inch of the kill site.

"Can't come soon enough," the old man muttered. He gave a stiff smile and turned back to the job in hand. "Judging by the physical state, and given the recent rise in temperatures, I am guessing that death occurred approximately a week ago."

Trent nodded and urged the doctor to continue.

"Both men died from a single shot. See here?" Wakefield pointed to a small entry wound slightly off centre, just above Leo Richard's left eyebrow. "He wouldn't have known what had hit him," he added dryly as he and Trent moved over to assess the other body. "Rigor mortis has passed in both victims. Obviously, I'll know more when I get them on the slab."

"We have yet to establish the calibre of the weapon until the post mortem. There's no sign of the bullet casings," another officer who was working close by informed them. "Could be that the perpetrator took them with him."

Trent nodded. Everything pointed to a professional hit. His inquisitive eyes swept the room, taking in every minuscule detail. It was empty, apart from a host of withered plants and a soiled mattress, complete with rumpled quilt shoved up in the far corner. He was guessing, from the evidence, that these men were here on a temporary basis but the question was – had they broken in? Standing directly over the body of Leo Richards, trying to ignore the sickening stench, Trent gazed dispassionately down at the decomposing remains before focusing on the other victim who lay crumpled on the stairs.

"It looks as if they were in the process of leaving," Guy said, sidling up beside him. Trent nodded.

"This property – who owns it? What do we know about it?"

"There's a To Let board outside," Guy interrupted.

"I saw that," Trent replied sharply. "We need to contact the estate agent. Judging by the lack of furniture and the illegal paraphernalia, it appears that these men may have been squatting."

"I'm on it," someone else said.

"Have we found anything else on the bodies? Mobile phones, for instance, that could give us a list of their contacts?"

"We've bagged one mobile that was plugged into the wall," said another officer.

"Great," said Trent. "We need to go through the address book and get in touch with every person on that list. Carry on with the good work. I'm off to speak to the press."

Guy watched the DCI leave the property. He hesitated briefly before deciding that he too needed some fresh air. After several seconds, he followed in his wake. Somehow, he had to put across his ambition to transfer to Bognor before the moment passed and Abbot forgot who he was. Hopefully he had seen his potential and would want him on his team.

As Guy emerged from the house, he could see his future mentor talking to a couple of reporters. He pulled the hood away from his head and stood in the small courtyard garden, soaking up the afternoon sun as he watched the man converse easily with the press. Rank aside, Abbot seemed like a good bloke, solid, down to earth – someone who would appreciate his sense of humour. He envisioned them standing at a bar, swigging pints of lager, Trent doubled up with laughter at something Guy had said.

He reached inside his protective overalls to fish a packet of cigarettes from his jacket pocket. Guy knew that it was purely down to the old adage – it's not what you know but who you know. Still watching Trent, he nudged a fag from the stack. He hadn't had a smoke since arriving on the scene and now felt the urge to satisfy his craving. Moving away, so as not to contaminate any evidence, Guy ducked his head beneath a stretch of police tape and immersed himself in the crowd. He stuck the cigarette between his lips and lit it, dragging hard. He was standing a few feet from the reporters, enjoying his fag when the DCI caught his eye. Within seconds, Trent was beside him.

"Got a spare?" he asked.

Guy instantly fumbled within the layers of his clothing and produced the cigarette packet. He offered it to Trent who glanced covertly over his shoulder, scanning the crowd before taking one.

"Shouldn't really. My wife will kill me," he laughed. "Just checking that the cameras are facing the opposite direction."

Pushing the cigarette between his lips, he borrowed Guy's lighter to ignite it. Guy grinned. This was going to be easy.

"So, how long have you been at Chichester?" Trent asked conversationally, raising his face to blow smoke away from the heads of the crowd.

"About nine months or so," he replied, hoping this informal little chat would naturally lead on to his desire to transfer.

"Terrible news about Adam Kent," Trent said, swiftly changing course. "I've met him on several occasions. Really nice bloke, or so I thought."

"Yes. It was a shock," nodded Guy, trying to look suitably morose as he pondered how to steer the conversation back to him and what *he* wanted. "Just goes to show, you never know who you can trust."

"Well, I hope that was a one off," Trent snapped, frowning as he stubbed out his half-smoked fag. What a bloody waste, Guy thought as he watched the DCI pick up the crushed cigarette from the pavement and place it in his pocket. Trent then smiled pleasantly and extended his hand. Once again, Guy suppressed the urge to wince as the bones in his fingers were squeezed to within an inch of their life.

"Anyway, I'd like to thank you for your input today," Trent said, breaking away from Guy and moving back towards the cordon. "Naturally, I'll be in touch regarding the case." Shit, I'm being dismissed, Guy thought, suddenly panicking. There was nothing else for it but to just blurt it out.

"How easy would it be for me to transfer to Bognor?" he asked.

Trent halted in his tracks, his brow furrowed.

"Why do you want to move?

"I need a change basically."

"Why?" he asked, his eyes narrowing suspiciously. "You've only been there for a few months. Where was your last posting?"

Trying to ignore the intensity of Trent's gaze, Guy sucked the final remnants of his fag and discarded it on the floor, buying himself a little more time whilst he considered the best way to reply. It was now or never. Don't lie but be economical with the truth.

"Originally, I'm from the Met," he explained. "Came down here with a bucket full of ambition. I trod on a few toes – my fault entirely. I've learnt a lot but also made a few enemies in the process. I want to progress but, where I am, my superiors won't support me."

"Wow," said Trent. "I appreciate your candor. Give me a call over the next few days and we'll have a chat."

He then wandered away, ducking his head under the cordon. Guy watched him go, replaying in his mind what he had said. Everything he'd told Abbot had been the truth. There hadn't been time to lay all his cards on the table, but there hopefully wouldn't be any need to. If Nick Marshall was happy to get shot of him, it made perfect sense not to warn Abbot about his reputation. Guy smiled and waited a few moments before heading back in the same direction.

CHAPTER FIFTY EIGHT

Ruby could hear raised voices the moment she got downstairs. It had taken a while to find her way in such a labyrinthine house. Long hallways led off in all directions, with closed doors concealing heaven knows what. Her adventurous side wanted to explore, to push open the doors and unveil their secrets, but she didn't. That would have been the old Ruby – the fearless rebellious teenager. But with all the bad luck that had befallen her, she had lost her nerve. She might be related by blood, but this whole environment and the people who inhabited it still felt a world away. It would almost certainly be frowned upon if she were discovered poking around in things that didn't concern her.

Ruby's suite was situated on the second floor. There was a lift, but she had opted to use the stairs. Finally, her bare feet touched the cool white marble of the entrance foyer. During her descent she hadn't seen a soul and was wondering where everyone had disappeared to.

Standing at the foot of the stairs, Ruby tucked her hair behind her ears and gazed in awe around her opulent surroundings. She could smell fresh flowers, although she couldn't see any. Most likely, they were some of the bouquets given to her at the hospital, most of which were in her bedroom. Not an object was out of place and, despite the sunlight streaming in through the windows, not a speck of dust could be seen floating in the air. Everything reeked of money, from the gilt-framed oil paintings adorning the walls to the Ming vases balancing on plinths. Ruby was afraid to touch anything.

Her heart hammered violently as her emotions continued battling inside her. Heart ruling head – head ruling heart. She desperately wanted this life, to live in this luxury. But it was so different from her old house, where she used to slip off her shoes at the base of the stairs and sling her handbag or jacket over the bannister. If this new environment lacked anything, it was a sense of homeliness. Ruby knew that if she committed to these people and their way of life, her days of relaxing and slobbing around were over. No longer could she see herself kicking back and watching *Eastenders* or *Holby City* on the telly. That would no doubt be deemed as 'vulgar'. Ruby wrinkled her nose and shook her head in bewilderment. She just wished she could stop fretting about the little things and embrace the change.

Once again a wave of homesickness washed over her, and she stared down at the mobile phone. Still teetering on the brink of a life-changing decision, she half wondered if she should call Vince to come and get her. He could be here within two hours and take her back to normality. But what's normal? the other half of her brain cried. Your mother is dead. Nothing will ever be normal again.

The raised voices broke through her maudlin thoughts, piquing her curiosity. Ruby recognised one of them to be her grandfather's. She followed the sound, tiptoeing through an elaborately moulded archway which led on to further hallways and doors. This place was like a giant maze. The deeper into the house she ventured, the voices became louder until she eventually reached the threshold of what looked to be a study. The door was partially opened so Ruby was able to see through the gap. She raised her hand to knock but then hesitated. Never before had she heard her grandfather so angry. It sounded as if he was tearing a hole through someone. An unfortunate member of his staff perhaps?

Still clutching her mobile to her chest, Ruby was uncertain as to what to do. She desperately wanted to speak to Sir Robert about her fears regarding Simon. She didn't want to bring shame upon herself or her new family and needed some kind of reassurance that the recording would never be made public. He had given his word that nothing and nobody would ever hurt her again, and she wanted to believe him. But how would he ever stop Simon from doing what he had threatened? Money, I suppose. He could have offered him money.

"How must this look to her, after everything I promised? Your mother and I bring her home. The staff are welcoming, the press are excited, but where were you? Sulking somewhere, no doubt. You've ruined your mother's plans, and that's unacceptable. You have to meet her sometime. She is your niece, after all!"

"You know my feelings on the matter," another voice responded. "I actually have far more pressing information about Lawrence that you may find interesting."

Hearing mention of her real father's name, Ruby held her breath. Naturally, she was eager to find out more about him, and any morsel of information would be most welcome. Despite feeling guilty about hovering outside and eavesdropping, she couldn't bring herself to announce her presence until the argument had died down.

"Don't try to change the subject," growled Sir Robert. It seemed as if he were talking to a child, but the other voice was clearly an adult male. "I am disappointed in you, Oliver. You will make amends. Tonight at dinner, I want you to be charming."

"Fine," Oliver spat. "I will do as you ask but, please, take a look at this morning's paper. It shows a picture of the killer."

There followed a brief silence, after which the squeak of the wheelchair and the rustle of paper.

"Good Lord," breathed Sir Robert. "No wonder Proctor wasn't jumping for joy about the arrest."

It seemed that the worst of the altercation had passed. Ruby took a deep breath and once again raised her hand and gently rapped her knuckles on the door.

"Come in," barked her grandfather.

She slowly stepped forward, her wide inquisitive grey eyes hungrily darting around as the mystery of yet another room was slowly revealed. Wall-to-wall shelves were crammed with books. Ruby could smell the leather, the dust, the hint of a cigar. Sir Robert sat behind an expanse of mahogany. There was a window, dressed in rich burgundy drapes, directly behind him, which overlooked the street. His desk was clear, apart from an ornate gold lamp and an old-fashioned ink well. He was holding a newspaper in his good hand and was very preoccupied. Despite the bright sunshine, the room seemed gloomy, stuffy and disappointingly small.

As she entered, another man turned to face her. He was tall and thin, with slightly rounded shoulders. He coolly assessed her through pale blue eyes. Ruby tried to act natural and friendly, but he put her on edge. So, this must be my Uncle Oliver, she thought sadly – the only fly in the ointment, so to speak. Even though his features creased in a semblance of a smile, she could clearly tell it was forced.

"Hello Ruby," he said, reaching out. "Welcome to our humble family home. I'm Oliver and I hope you'll be happy here." The bitterness and ill feeling that exuded from him was almost tangible. Even so, Ruby gingerly took hold of his limp hand and they briefly shook. Oliver turned back to her grandfather, staring down at the old man with a look she couldn't quite decipher.

"So, I'll see you both at dinner," he said, making a hasty retreat before his father could detain him further. It might have been her imagination but, as soon as Oliver had left, Ruby noticed the room temperature rise – such was his frosty insincere welcome.

"I'm sorry about that my dear," said Sir Robert, placing the newspaper down on the desk. "It's a bit of an adjustment for him, finding out he has a new niece. In time, though, I'm sure he'll come around. He has his own place anyway, so you won't come into contact with him too often. Now tell me, are you settling in okay? Is there anything you need?"

Her grandfather still appeared a little distracted, and Ruby suspected it had something to do with the headlines in the paper. She held up her mobile phone and waved it in front of him. He must have forgotten she still had it in her possession, and now she had his attention.

"Ah, is that the device your – your adopted father passed to you in the hospital?" he asked.

She nodded.

"I'm worried grandfather, about Simon, about the recording. He hasn't been in touch to threaten me, and that's not his style. I'm scared he's already uploaded it onto *YouTube*. What if the press find out? It will cause such problems for you as well."

In spite of her best efforts, the tears came. She hadn't planned on crying in front of him – in front of anyone! She was reserving that little luxury for bedtime, when no one would be any the wiser. But now she had started, she was unable to stop. Great hulking sobs escaped as her heart broke in two. It wasn't just the fear of Simon's disclosure, it was all the grief of the past few days – from being raped and left for dead, discovering Christine's fate, losing her family and original identity, even aborting her baby. Everything had culminated in one emotional time bomb and the distinguished Sir Robert Sinclair was in the unfortunate position to witness the detonation.

He sat speechless for a moment, unsure of how to handle the distressed girl. A gentle pat on the hand would not suffice. Ruby needed to be held and, unbeknownst to her grandfather, it wasn't the first time today she longed for Vince. She didn't notice the way Sir Robert's right hand fluttered towards the top drawer of his desk. Nor how his gnarled fingers protectively stroked the protruding key.

"Dear girl, come now. It will be fine. I promised you, and you have to trust me," he eventually crooned, trying not to be too repulsed by the ribbons of snot escaping her nostrils.

"But how – how can you be so sure?" she sobbed, wiping the mucus on her sleeve. "You d-don't know what Simon's like. The things he-he made me do."

"I said, *trust* me Ruby. You're in my world now. No one will ever hurt you. You're safe with me. Just believe in yourself. This is your destiny."

Somehow his words managed to penetrate her misery, soothing away her fears and gradually diminishing her desire to return to her old life. It was true. She could be everything she'd ever dreamed of being. She just needed to get a grip. It was only the first day for heaven's sake. What did she expect? Tomorrow she would go shopping with Lucinda, to all the best stores where money was no object. That alone was a fantasy.

"W-where's Luc – I-I mean grandmother?" she sniffed, hiccupping her way through the question.

Sir Robert smiled gently, relieved that Ruby had finally calmed. He could never get used to all these female hysterics, and his wife was bad enough.

"She's gone to lie down with one of her migraines. All the excitement of meeting you has taken its toll. She should be fine by dinner."

Ruby nodded, her eyes falling on the newspaper on the desk. Sir Robert was watching her carefully.

"I overheard mention of my father," she murmured. "Is there something in the paper? I'm sorry if you think I was listening in. I didn't mean to." She dropped her gaze, embarrassed, her cheeks flaring red. She sniffed and wiped her face with her hand. She heard her grandfather sigh.

"There's no easy way to say this but you'll find out soon enough," he said, spinning the newspaper around. "Your father was murdered six months ago, and here is a picture of the man who killed him."

CHAPTER FIFTY NINE

"Why did you come here?"

This simple question, bluntly delivered, completely threw her off balance. It wasn't what he said, it was the way he said it. His tone was rude and unwelcoming, each syllable like a splinter of ice in her heart. She'd been nervous enough about coming here in the first place, and this was definitely not a good start.

Rosemary had expected Adam to be aloof towards her, but his hostility was bordering on ridiculous. After all, she wasn't the enemy. Surely he could see that. Whatever he thought he knew was clearly all messed up. As far as he was concerned, she had fallen for Guy Kane's charms like so many other women when, in fact, she was a victim of blackmail. If she achieved nothing else today, she had to somehow get through to her husband that she had only succumbed to Guy because she'd been trying to protect him. How could he possibly think otherwise?

After battling her way through the mob of reporters, photographers and cameramen camped outside her door, she had got in her car and driven off. On her way to Marden, Rosemary had rehearsed what she wanted to say to Adam. She practiced her opening line over and over, hoping that he would thaw enough for everything that followed to come naturally. She had been so preoccupied that she barely remembered the journey. The sat nav had guided her to a monstrous facility, fringed with barbed wire. It was impossible to imagine her lovely husband being held prisoner here. Rosemary had been directed to the visitor's parking area and then went through a security check before she was allowed inside.

There was so much she wanted to say, to explain what had really happened. Up until this moment there'd been no opportunity. But now sitting opposite Adam in this stark, utilitarian room, overshadowed by the presence of a prison guard, Rosemary's resolve began to weaken. It was clear by the emptiness in her husband's eyes and the way he clenched his jaw that he believed the worst of her. He couldn't even look at her properly. It was almost as if she repulsed him. Her actions had hurt him and evidently cost her his trust. If only she could have that time again, she would gladly re-write history and stand up to Guy Kane, instead of folding under the weight of his accusations. But what was done was done. She couldn't change the past.

Rosemary had never seen Adam like this before and it took her breath away. How could someone so warm and loving metamorphose into a cold distant stranger? I'd walk on fire for you, she thought sadly, struggling to hold back her tears. Please love me again.

Even if she wanted to she couldn't hold him, but it was probably just as well as he would more than likely recoil from her touch. Time was of the essence. He wasn't talking, so it was up to her to take the initiative. She chose to ignore his opening question. It was ludicrous anyway. She was his wife – for better or for worse. That was why she had come.

"How are you?" she whispered.

He sneered and folded his arms across his chest, like pulling up an emotional drawbridge to protect his heart.

"I'm having a ball actually," he said cuttingly.

Rosemary winced and closed her eyes. Sarcasm didn't suit him. This was going to be so much harder than she'd imagined. She inhaled a deep breath and tried again, clenching her fists and digging her nails into the soft palms of her hands.

"It wasn't what you thought, you know."

A smirk was his only response.

"The day before you – you know – found out, Guy visited the house. He told me he was looking for you and I believed him. I thought that his reason for being there was genuine so I made him a coffee. He was your colleague after all and I wanted to be hospitable."

Rosemary hesitated and studied Adam's impassive face. Was he even listening?

She bit her lip and continued.

"We talked about things in general. Then he started talking about Jason Sadler and that he knew who killed him. Adam, he tricked me. I wasn't prepared to be confronted like that, and he could see in my face that I knew what you'd done."

She swallowed hard, wringing her hands, trying to keep her emotions at bay.

"He told me he had evidence about Sophie being raped and that that was your motive for killing Jason. I don't know how he knew this and I didn't ask. Now I wonder. I mean, her sessions were meant to be confidential. Nobody outside of our family had any idea about what had happened to her, so how could Guy have found this out?"

She noticed Adam frown and something flicker in his eyes. She licked her lips and pressed on.

"He then suggested he could bury the evidence, and I grasped this possibility with both hands. That was my downfall. I was cornered. Guy said he would only do that on one condition," she paused and bit her bottom lip. "The condition was that I sleep with him. To be honest, I thought I'd have some time to warn you, but he forced me to do it straight away. Then he told me he was coming back the following morning and to call in sick from work."

A sob escaped her lips and she broke down. For a several moments, Rosemary couldn't speak but she felt the weight of Adam's gaze upon her. She kept her head hung low.

"I had a plan – to trap him," she murmured. "I used your recording machine to tape what he was doing but I had to go through with everything in order to make it work. And it would have worked but you came home and found us."

Rosemary paused and wiped her eyes. Slowly she raised her head and looked Adam directly in the eye. His expression had softened. She saw compassion.

"What happened to the tape?" he asked, his voice hoarse.

She shook her head and shrugged despondently.

"He found it and destroyed it."

"How?"

"He stamped on it."

"Do you still have it?" Once again, Rosemary saw the clench of his jaw and the hardness return to his eyes but this time, she knew it wasn't directed at her.

"Yes."

"Good girl," Adam said, leaning forward. "Now, listen carefully to what I have to say."

CHAPTER SIXTY

"I'm so sorry, Tina," Matt said again as he shuffled in beside her. He'd lost count of how many times he'd apologised during the past few hours yet her mood remained icy. She sat staring miserably out of the aircraft window, absentmindedly watching the hive of activity playing out across the apron of Cancun International airport.

Matt settled down and clipped on his seat belt. They'd been lucky to get on board at such short notice, and the plane was full to bursting. Though they were still on the ground, everything around them already felt cramped and congested – people squeezing past each other in the central aisle, kids squabbling, luggage that was much too large being forced into the overhead lockers. It was going to be one hell of a flight. A baby screamed directly behind him, setting his teeth on edge and making his eardrums buzz. Matt didn't like flying at the best of times and hoped the mother had some miracle remedy to ease the child's suffering, which would help to ease his.

He stole a glance at his wife. She looked uncomfortable, her upper body twisted away from him in such an awkward position – anything to avoid having to look at or talk to him. I suppose I'm lucky she agreed to come home with me, he thought sadly. She could have threatened to stay.

A large man, wearing a gaudy patterned shirt and stained beige shorts suddenly plonked himself down next to Matt, stealing what precious space there was left. He was sweating profusely and had a stale wet-dog odour about him. Tina's head snapped round and she wrinkled her nose in disgust, brazenly expressing her displeasure. Matt smiled at her and gave a small helpless shrug, hoping that the arrival of their unwelcome neighbour would at least go some way in uniting them. Unfortunately, it seemed to have the opposite effect. Tina just scowled at her husband and continued her scrutiny of the workers below.

Matt stared miserably at the back of the seat in front, listening to his fellow passenger grunting and straining as he fumbled with his belt. Gradually the hubbub around them settled down as the luggage was finally stowed away and people took to their seats. Members of the cabin crew drifted up and down the aisle, preparing for the safety demonstration. Matt closed his eyes – he didn't need to listen to it again. He kept thinking of the horror on Tina's face when he'd told her he needed to leave. Of course she was pissed off, having their honeymoon cut short, but what else could he do? Something terrible had happened to one of his mates – the best man at their wedding, no less! How could he relax and enjoy the delicacies Mexico had to offer, knowing full well someone he cared about was going through hell – and so publicly as well?

"I'm sorry Tina," he murmured, opening his eyes and turning his head towards her. "I will make it up to you, I promise. I just have to find out why this has happened. I can't be as carefree as you want me to be now that I know about Adam."

God, it was so frustrating, talking to the back of her head. In his defence, he had tried calling several people to get an update on what the score was but was unable to connect with either George or Nick Marshall. He had then phoned Adam's house, hoping to speak to Rosemary but ended up talking to an older woman who sounded nearly hysterical. It wasn't as if he hadn't made the effort to remain in Mexico, although the next call Matt did make was to the airline.

The safety demo began. Matt kept one eye on the pretty stewardess who was dangling a mock oxygen mask above his neighbour's head. He leaned across, putting his lips close to Tina's ear. Her hair tickled his cheek.

"If it was someone you cared about, I would have left gladly," he whispered before sitting back.

There was nothing like a bit of emotional blackmail to drive home his point but it seemed to do the trick. He heard Tina sniff as his words eventually sank in, knowing that if it had been her

253

young son in trouble, or even her parents, she would naturally expect her husband's support. Although still facing the window, Tina slowly relaxed her muscles and tentatively uncoiled her fingers, before groping around in search of his hand.

CHAPTER SIXTY ONE

Sophie had run out of options. After her dramatic exit from the classroom, she had been practically everywhere, hoping to find sanctuary from the cruel remarks about her dad she would inevitably have to face. With the press glued to the front of her home, along with the suspicious way the head teacher and Mr Barley had behaved, it wouldn't be long before everyone knew what had happened. Sophie loved her father but, just now, she couldn't handle the shame his arrest would create. It would be on the news, in all the papers. She knew she wouldn't be able to hide forever but desperately needed to find a haven from the maelstrom that had torn through her world.

She'd become quite proficient at reading bus timetables, and the most logical destination was to visit Grandfather and Grandmother Bradley's house on the outskirts of Chichester. Because their daughter Jessica was dead, Sophie thought they would be emotionally removed from the debacle surrounding their ex-son-in-law. They had kept their distance from her for quite some time, and Sophie suspected it was because of her startling resemblance to her deceased daughter. But it was high time they moved on, she thought. After all, she was their only grandchild. She chose not to call first so as not to give them the opportunity to fob her off.

But when she got there, no one seemed to be home. She'd rapped the large brass lion's head knocker several times to no avail. And she'd peered in through the lounge window, but saw no signs of life. They couldn't have been out shopping because Grandfather Bradley's Jaguar was still parked on the drive.

She sat down on the doorstep to think. They wouldn't be avoiding me would they? she wondered sadly. The sun was even hotter than when she'd left school and she was getting thirsty. A tall slender woman dressed in a floral blouse and tight jeans emerged from the house next door and enquired if she needed help.

Feeling extremely conspicuous in her school uniform in the middle of the day and so far from class, Sophie mumbled a brief explanation. Up close, the woman was much older than she first thought – maybe even older than Grandmother Bradley – and she was plainly but unsuccessfully trying to disguise it. Her skin was caked in face powder, the residue of which had settled in her wrinkles. She'd also doused herself with some kind of cloying scent, and Sophie tried not to breathe in too deeply for fear of breaking out in a coughing fit.

"Oh Sophie, it is you isn't it? Gosh haven't you grown up," the lady exclaimed, peering intently at her through vibrant purple-framed spectacles. "I haven't seen you in months. Or is it years?" She shook her head as her memory failed her. Her heavily made-up face creased into a smile, accentuating her advancing years. Sophie shrugged. She had no recollection of this lady, who evidently remembered her.

"Didn't you know? Your grandparents have taken to the high seas?" the woman continued, emitting a high-pitched laugh. "I expect you'll soon be receiving a postcard from them."

"When w-will they be back?" Sophie stammered, disappointment flaring inside her.

The lady sighed and pursed her lips. Bright pink lipstick had seeped like tributaries into the lines around her mouth.

"Well, not until the end of next week," the woman sighed. "Do you want me to call your parents?"

Sophie shook her head.

"Or come in for a glass of orange juice?"

Sophie contemplated the invitation for a few seconds whilst focusing on the neighbouring property. She licked her lips and tried to swallow. She was thirsty, but now that she knew her grandparents were away, she just wanted to get out of here. She politely declined the offer and walked back to the bus stop, deaf to the well-meaning protestations behind her.

Tangmere was her next port of call. Sophie made her way directly to St Andrew's churchyard, where her mother was buried. At least here she would find a little peace. Nobody would think to bother her in this place. She sank down beside the grave, pulling her knees up to her chest and reached over to pluck dead flowers from a small floral arrangement set at the base of the headstone. She had placed them there only a few days before.

Whenever possible, her dad always brought her to visit every Friday. He would respectfully stand off to one side and allow Sophie time to talk to Jessica. It had become their little ritual. She now closed her eyes, trying to imagine Adam standing quietly behind her. As always, she traced with her finger the inscription carved into the headstone. It was bad enough knowing that her mother was in the ground, but lacking her father's comforting presence was like a double-edged sword. Her natural instinct was to cry, but it seemed Sophie had cried so much over these past few months that there was nothing left. So she rested her head gently against the smooth marble and listened to the birdsong. Jessica's plot was set in the shade and, with the warmth of the afternoon, it wasn't long before Sophie drifted off to sleep.

* * *

She awoke with a start – disoriented and thirsty. Glancing at her watch, Sophie saw she had been asleep for nearly an hour. She gazed around, relieved the churchyard was still empty. It wouldn't be long until the end of school. There was nowhere else left to go. She had to go home.

She rose gingerly from the ground, her legs wobbling like a newborn foal, her skin crisscrossed from sitting too long on the grass.

"I'll see you soon, mummy," she whispered as she heaved her pink school bag onto her shoulder. It was like a miracle.

Sophie suddenly felt better – much stronger, ready to deal with her disjointed home life, school and the press. She didn't know how long this fortitude would last, but she had at least found somewhere to run to. The churchyard would become her sanctuary – her secret place, especially now that she had proven she could get here without her father. Rosemary and the others would be none the wiser about her little excursions, as long as she didn't make a habit of them.

Sophie hurried towards the bus stop, having no idea how long she would have to wait. But it didn't matter, a few minutes here or there. Her stepmother was too wrapped up in her own misery to pay her any attention anyway. Today, St Andrews churchyard, tomorrow a visit to her father. Sophie felt invincible, she could go anywhere, and when her mobile rang displaying Ruby's name, she almost laughed with delight. At last her friend had contacted her. Sophie had been so worried for her, and was terrified that she'd never see or hear from her again. Obviously, Ruby had recovered enough from her ordeal to read her texts.

"Hi. How are you?" she gushed.

There was silence. Sophie was afraid the caller would turn out to be that same drunk who had answered her friend's mobile before, but it was Ruby who spoke.

"Sophie?"

"Yes. Hi."

She had reached the bus stop and was gazing off into the distance, hoping to see the familiar hulk of a double decker lumbering towards her. The A27 was busy now. Sophie could feel the air move as vehicles thundered past.

She brushed a stray lock of hair from her eyes, smiling inanely now that she could finally talk to her friend. But what Ruby said tore that smile from her face.

"I don't want to see you ever again," she hissed. "Your dad murdered my dad. Goodbye."

CHAPTER SIXTY TWO

Ruby's eyes remained locked on Sir Robert's as she ended the call. The revelation that her natural father had been murdered, appallingly by her friend's dad, had shocked her to the core. She was so confused, nothing made sense anymore. After all, Adam Kent was no ordinary dad – not only was he a policeman, Ruby had once thought she was in love with him.

She had believed Adam to be the paragon of good – a man who battled against the evil deeds of others. So now what? What did it mean to her when the heroes became the villains? When black merges with white and darkness merges with light. What was right and what was wrong?

"Ruby darling, I'm so sorry you had to find out this way," Sir Robert murmured, peering intently across at his granddaughter. He cursed his thoughtlessness for exposing her so crassly to the truth and was surprised that she hadn't experienced a moment of weakness. After all, she'd just ended a relationship with a close friend. But despite worrying about her fragility, Ruby stood, her face completely devoid of emotion. If anything, there was a hardness in her eyes, turning the soft grey to flint. It was quite chilling to witness how a young woman, so outwardly passionate, could suddenly retreat inside herself.

Ruby wavered slightly and blinked, placing her hand lightly on the back of a tarnished, green leather chair to steady herself. Sir Robert continued to watch her, mindful that, if she fainted, he'd be in no position to break her fall. He hoped he hadn't pushed her too far, although he was also trying to come to terms with the fact that a police officer was responsible for murdering his son. There was a great deal of information for them both to digest. On the plus side, however, this might help to further distance Ruby from the people who inhabited her old life and more enthusiastically embrace her new one.

Sir Robert decided to allow his granddaughter a little time and space to get to grips with things. But not a lot. He couldn't handle her wallowing in self-pity when Lucinda was so looking forward to their shopping expedition. There was no way he could contend with two overwrought females.

Ruby's shoulders slumped slightly as her eyes wandered back to the newspaper.

"Can I read this in my room, please?" she asked, her voice no louder than a whisper.

His first instinct was to say no – this would undoubtedly lead to questions, uncomfortable questions such as an explanation as to why Lawrence had chosen to call himself Jason Sadler. Then again, the poor girl had a right to know part of her heritage. Of course, Sir Robert had every intention of telling her the truth. But only the censored version.

"That's okay, my dear. You go upstairs and rest. Take your time and I'll see you at dinner," he said, trying to raise a flicker of a smile on the teenager's face.

Ruby nodded and snatched up the newspaper. Then, just short of the doorway, she stopped and stared thoughtfully down at her phone. Sir Robert watched, barely breathing as she turned back and placed her precious mobile on the desk in front of him.

"I'm ready to let go," she said, jutting her chin out defiantly.

It was music to his ears. He refrained from speaking or even smiling. It was a delicate balance – too much too soon would prove detrimental. Only Ruby could relinquish her past and it had to be of her own free will. If he pressured her, it might not only backfire, but the future of his empire would ultimately fall to Oliver – not his ideal candidate as his son chose to dally with those of the same sex. Sir Robert didn't move until he was sure his granddaughter had left the room. Then he released a lungful of air.

The device was a Nokia and Ruby, like most teenagers, loved her phone. Her actions meant one thing – a declaration of acceptance. Ruby had chosen to become a Sinclair because it wasn't just a mobile she'd surrendered, it was all the contacts stored inside. Sir Robert rested back in his chair, elated. He would buy her another – an updated model, with all the functions. He turned the key in his desk drawer with his good hand and secreted his granddaughter's phone alongside another – that of Simon Richards, her recently deceased ex-boyfriend.

CHAPTER SIXTY THREE

"Hello Adam," said Nick as his former sergeant was led into the interview room, flanked on either side by a guard. Did they think he was dangerous or was this for his own protection? Nick shook his head in dismay as he regarded the man he thought he knew so well looking every inch a prisoner on remand. He was accustomed to seeing Adam dressed in a suit or, at the very least, smart casual clothing. This sloppy attire of tracky bottoms and sweatshirt, commonly favoured by inmates all over the country, was totally out of place on someone usually so immaculate.

Nick had had the misfortune of visiting Marden a number of times during his career to interview various belligerent oafs, and to be here for a man such as Adam – well, he had to pinch himself that this wasn't just part of some warped joke.

Adam smiled in surprise, but it did nothing to disguise the fact he was suffering. And he hasn't been here that long, Nick mused as he watched him settle down on the chair opposite.

"How are they treating you?" he asked, trying to project a nonchalant air to mask his own concern.

Adam shrugged as his haunted blue-flecked eyes rested for a moment on the guard standing by the door. Only one of them remained now – the tall skinny one with the permanent sneer. *Callum.* He hesitated before answering and turned his attention to Nick.

"Well, it's not great, to be fair, especially since the others know who I am."

"Shit," groaned Nick. "I'm so sorry mate. We did everything in our power to keep this quiet but you know how it is. I have to say, it's like a bloody circus at the station."

"I should imagine it is," Adam sighed, stroking his chin and feeling the first prickle of stubble. "So is this a social call or an official one?"

"A bit of both. I'd just like to say that despite you sitting on the other side of the table, I still consider you a mate and, between you and me, I sort of understand why you did what you did. I mean, if it were my daughter ..." Nick shivered as he tailed off.

Once again, Adam's eyes flickered nervously over to the guard. He shuffled in his seat.

"Because I'm here largely in an official capacity, I've been allocated extra time with you," Nick continued.

"Is that so?" Adam was still focusing on the man standing behind Nick. What was it with that guy? Nick thought, turning round in his seat just in time to see the prison officer smirking at them.

"What's going on?" he demanded, in his best authoritarian tone. "I'm here on official business and I require some help with an ongoing case. I don't know what you think you're doing with this intimidation crap but I ask you to desist or I'll make a complaint."

Lucas Callum narrowed his eyes, sizing up this new opponent for a few seconds before thinking better of it. He clamped his mouth shut and gave a small indifferent shrug before focusing blankly on the wall behind them. Nick turned back to Adam and smiled, no doubt glad he'd won that particular battle. What he didn't know was that his tough attitude had just sealed his friend's fate as far as Callum was concerned.

"So, I bought this." Nick removed a small notebook from his jacket and once again, turned to Callum. "It's just a book," he said bluntly, making matters worse by theatrically fanning the pages for effect. "Nothing concealed. You can read it if you like, but good luck with that because it's basically indecipherable." Callum gave a curt nod. Only Adam noticed the clenched jaw and the pulsating tick in the guard's left temple.

Nick rested the book on the table in front.

"It's my notebook," Adam said simply.

"Yes it is. And it won't be long before Craig Donohue is fit enough to be interviewed. You solved the case but you often write in this weird abbreviation that I can't understand. If we're going to lay this investigation to rest and obtain the result we need, I have to know everything about him and the women he allegedly killed. You mentioned his wife's mother for example. Take your time and walk me through it so that when I finally face him, I can hit him hard and fast with substantiated facts."

CHAPTER SIXTY FOUR

So it's come to this, thought George wearily as he fingered the packet of medication prescribed by the visiting GP. Fluoxetine, it said on the box. He pulled out the folded leaflet to scan for side effects. Feeling sick, blurry vision, constipation – great! Problems sleeping – wonderful! Sexual dysfunction – terrific! It also confirmed what the doctor had told him. This wasn't to be an overnight cure. It would take two to four weeks before he felt any differently. He'd also been signed off from work.

Detective Inspector Brian Proctor had been a rock, staying with him the entire afternoon. He had been the one to call the doctor, had waited whilst George was being examined and had even gone to the pharmacy to collect the pills. It really was going beyond the call of duty, and George was sorry Brian would soon be retiring. He had gained a great deal of respect for the man. Another good officer lost, he thought sadly.

He was alone now, except for Claymore. Brian had left fifteen minutes or so earlier. George checked the time. Natasha would soon be home – that's if she still wanted to be with him and hadn't high-tailed it back to Romania on the first flight out. He focused on the bottle of whisky sitting on the table alongside the empty glass. He could see a half inch of golden liquid at the bottom. The doc had advised him not to drink alcohol but he really *really* wanted to. It was going to take sheer willpower to tip it down the plughole, because that's what he knew he should do. He wasn't so far gone as not to know that was the sensible course of action, along with getting rid of the stash hidden in various kitchen cupboards and under the stairs. His accumulated Christmas presents had the potential for accelerating his journey to hell, if he weren't careful. But he had the taste for it now. George licked his lips, eyeing the bottle. Maybe just one more – just one wouldn't hurt. Claymore yawned and watched him accusingly from across the room. George unscrewed the cap, picking up the bottle with one hand and holding the glass in the other.

"Hey, I won't tell if you won't," he said to the basset as he began to pour. Just then, the doorbell rang.

"Saved by the bell," he said to Claymore as he placed the bottle and glass back on the table and rose from his seat. He shuffled out into the hall, wondering who on earth it could be. He was surprised to find Rosemary, Adam's wife, standing gazing up at him.

He groaned out loud. Christ what's she here for? To berate me for being the one to arrest her husband? He couldn't handle this – not stone cold sober. He held up his hands in surrender.

"Look. I had no choice. He gave me no choice," he began.

"George, I need your help," she said, interrupting him. "Adam told me to come here because he trusts you."

"Hang on a minute." He scratched his bald head, trying to play catch up. She looked desperate. This was not how he expected her to be. A slap around the face was more or less what he'd imagined.

"Can I come in?" she asked. "I don't want to have this conversation on the doorstep."

"Of course, of course," he said, standing aside and peering covertly down the street. Several school children ambled by on their way home.

Rosemary slipped past him and walked directly into the lounge, bending slightly to caress Claymore's head. She sat without being asked and began to ferret around in her handbag. George closed the front door and followed in behind her. He pulled back the curtains, sending motes of dust flying into the air.

"What's going on Rosemary? Why has Adam sent you?"

She removed a rather battered mini audio cassette, the tape spilling out like entrails and, to his horror, a used condom tied in a knot at the end.

"What the hell?"

"I'll be frank. Adam sent me because this is a very delicate situation." The words tumbled forth and Rosemary had to pause for a second to catch her breath. When she spoke again, her pace was more deliberate and controlled.

"We don't want to make a formal complaint until we have irrefutable evidence. As you can see, the tape is damaged and I need you to work under the radar to somehow get it restored." She then held the condom up between the very tips of her thumb and finger, her face contorted in disgust. "This condom contains vital DNA, both inside and out. This also needs to be done confidentially. It's a hush-hush investigation."

"Investigating what exactly?"

Rosemary bit her lip but held his gaze.

"Not what, but who. Guy Kane. In a nutshell, he blackmailed me with claims he knew what Adam had done, forcing me to have sex with him in exchange for his keeping his mouth shut."

George's mouth fell open as he flopped down on the sofa opposite. She gazed earnestly across at him, beseeching him to help her. In his befuddled state of mind, he was having trouble keeping up. He could now see insurmountable pain in her big brown eyes. Guy Kane capable of blackmail? Of rape? He hated the man, yes, but even so.

"George please! This is what happened. Somehow he found out about what Jason Sadler had done to Sophie. The only people who knew this were her family and her counsellor in Felpham. Guy said he had proof. He must have got it from her, but those sessions were confidential. I can't believe it was pillow talk. The woman would be struck off for one thing. Her reputation is second to none. Something doesn't add up."

"Okay okay," he interrupted, shuffling forward and resting his elbows on his knees. "Why don't you report it officially?"

"Because of the way Guy is with women. Everyone would believe I fell for his charms. Up until now, even Adam believed the worst about me," she explained sadly. "Guy stamped on this tape but Adam says it could possibly be fixed, at least enough to transcribe what happened."

"And what exactly is on that tape?"

Rosemary sighed and closed her eyes. When she opened them again, George could see tears. She blinked and they burst their dam, streaming down her cheeks. Rosemary aggressively brushed them aside.

"I taped his threats. I taped the rape. It's all here, and this condom contains his semen." She wrinkled her nose as she stared down at the revolting sheath of pink rubber now resting on the edge of her knee. "On its own, it proves nothing, but with the tape …" She pinned him with an intense stare. "I can't risk Guy finding out about this George, knowing that somehow he'll conjure up a way to destroy vital evidence. He's already tried it. He's sneaky, and he won't sit idly by waiting for someone to reveal his crimes. That's why we're turning to you – seeking your help. Please George, this won't make any difference to Adam's situation, but it may award us some justice for what Guy's put us through."

George stared thoughtfully at the bottle of whisky before focusing on his newly prescribed medication. He'd be no good to anyone either inebriated or off his head on pills.

"Thank you, Rosemary," he muttered out of the blue.

"For what?" she asked, clearly puzzled.

George held her gaze and offered a sheepish smile.

"For saving me from myself."

CHAPTER SIXTY FIVE

It was with a delicious sense of complacency that Cheryl Durrant awarded herself a generous glass of crisp white wine that evening. Since her recent reconciliation with Guy Kane, which had then led to a spectacular night of exquisite lovemaking, it had proven a highly successful day. She also wanted to give herself a huge pat on the back for all her hard work – five clients in all, including two new ones. Business was good and her love life was amazing. What more could she wish for?

During her counselling sessions, memories of herself and Guy would occasionally swim into her mind. More than once, she had to pull herself back from the daydream or, even worse, suppress a smile. That would never do whilst listening to someone else's emotional pain. After having been exposed all day to the misery and anxiety of her patients, Cheryl was tired but happy. She was content, and that was a positive thing. She decided to relax and eat her meal in front of the television.

She wandered through to the lounge, balancing a bowl of pasta and her glass of wine on a tray. It was a bit of a rebellion – Cheryl had been brought up to eat at the table. Her mother had ingrained this formality into her since childhood, saying it would be better for her digestion and also likely to keep her from becoming a slob. It felt almost decadent to break the habit of a lifetime. She knew Guy preferred to eat his meals on his lap and in the bedroom! She giggled. Her mother would have a fit if she could see her feeding him spicy noodles in bed.

Cheryl sat down and picked up the remote control. Once or twice, her eyes strayed to the phone, willing it to ring. Guy had told her he would call very soon. But when? It was virtually impossible to concentrate on anything when she yearned for him so much. She flicked through a few channels, trying to retain her upbeat mood but sensed a cloud of despondency hovering on the horizon. Then she asked herself, what advice would she give her clients if they were in her situation. Find something else with which to occupy your mind, carry on with your life and become your own person – that sort of thing. Well, it was time to practice what she preached. Otherwise she'd be reduced to becoming a middle-aged version of a lovesick schoolgirl, and that wouldn't be very attractive at all. She had to remember that Guy was often on the road and extremely busy. He said he would call her, and she had to believe him. End of.

Twirling a string of spaghetti around her fork, Cheryl switched on the local news – the lead story being a double murder in Bognor Regis.

"Good God," she mumbled, as she pushed a wad of pasta and tomato sauce into her mouth. She chewed robotically whilst watching an attractive officer in his early thirties with dark wavy hair explain how two men had been discovered shot dead in an unfurnished terraced property close to the town centre. What is the world coming to? she mused. Bognor Regis of all places! Cheryl shivered. It was all a bit too close for comfort. With her eyes still glued to the screen, she felt for her wine glass and swallowed a couple of large mouthfuls. The road looked familiar – was it Longford? She placed the glass carefully back down on the small table beside her chair and resumed eating.

The television cameras scanned the street, taking in the movements of the police in their white forensic suits, entering and leaving the house. Cheryl was busy trying to pinpoint exactly which house it was when the camera briefly focused on a man who was emerging from the doorway. The way the sun glinted off his red hair when he removed his hood snagged her attention. She leaned forward and squinted, then gasped in shock, dropping her pasta-laden fork onto her white rug and staining it with Bolognese sauce. In a flash, he was gone and the news reader moved onto the next story.

Cheryl stared blankly at the screen for a long while, her dinner cooling on her lap. That man had looked so much like Guy, it was uncanny. But it couldn't be him. She put her tray to one side and picked up her glass, holding it against her lips for a moment before tipping her head back and draining it in one gulp. She wandered into the kitchen to pour herself another measure. Her eyes must have been deceiving her. Perhaps he had a double, or maybe she was missing him so much, her mind was playing tricks.

She opened the fridge door and grabbed the bottle. Instead of just replenishing her glass, she took the bottle back into the lounge. There was nothing else for it but to wait until the next news update. Hopefully, they would show the same story. In the meantime, she didn't know what to do. She picked up her phone and called Guy, knowing he'd just laugh it off, saying that there must be someone else out there, equally as good looking. Unfortunately it went straight through to voicemail. Cheryl didn't leave a message.

She could almost hear her mother whispering in her ear. *How well do you really know this man?* Niggles of doubt began to rise up and infect her happiness. It didn't make any sense. Guy told her he sold insurance. Why would he lie? What was wrong with saying he's a copper or one of those forensic bods? Neither of those was what you'd call a hush-hush profession. Her mind must have been playing tricks on her, she concluded. After all, she had been thinking about Guy at the time.

There was nothing else for it but to go online. All the recent headlines would be available at the touch of a button. She hadn't seen the news for a couple of days now, so World War III could have started without her realising it. With a barrage of unsolved mysteries filling her brain, she hurried up the stairs to her computer to search for answers.

Cheryl logged on, tapping her fingers impatiently on her desk. The BBC news homepage eventually sprung up and she was faced with another headline – Chichester Police Officer Charged with Murder. Because that story was also close to home, Cheryl briefly put aside her quest to read this story. The world is definitely going mad, she thought. If you can't trust a copper.

"Branded a hero for saving a witness from drowning last month, Detective Sergeant Adam Kent of Chichester Police Station showed his true colours when he confessed to killing local businessman, Jason Sadler. Sadler was found buried in woodland at Whiteways, near Arundel last September. He had been shot. Kent has recently been charged and has since appeared at Chichester Magistrates where he was remanded in custody until the trial ….. "

Cheryl blinked several times before continuing to read but found it almost impossible – the words swam in front of her eyes as her brain struggled to absorb these facts. *Adam Kent*. She knew him. He was the father of Sophie, a former client. Cheryl remembered how messed up the girl had been about her stepfather raping her. She thought back to their sessions, and what she had seen and read in the past. She remembered the case now – how Sadler's remains had been found last autumn. There had been a massive police hunt for his killer but the media frenzy had quickly died a death as other stories took over. Maybe it was because Sophie had stopped coming to see her that Cheryl had completely forgotten about Sadler and the mystery surrounding his death. That is, until Sophie's file went missing.

Suddenly she felt very cold. What if the file was taken and she hadn't inadvertently destroyed it? What if a burglary had been committed after all? But who would benefit from obtaining all that sensitive information? She swallowed another mouthful of wine. Some of it trickled down the side of her chin, but she was far too preoccupied to wipe it away. Someone on the case? Someone looking for a motive for murder? Or someone trying to protect himself? Did Adam Kent break into her house? If he was capable of murder, then surely burglary would be a walk in the park. But before Cheryl drove herself mad considering this option, she needed to see if there was any information about the double murder in Bognor. With luck, there'd be a picture of the officer standing outside the house and she could zoom in and lay her suspicions to rest.

She quickly found the story but there was no picture of the man. Of course there was an easy way to rectify this – just call the police station and ask. If she didn't find out soon, she wouldn't be able to sleep.

So she dialled the number for the Sussex Police switchboard and asked to be put through to Bognor Regis police station. A woman answered. For a brief moment, Cheryl was in two minds about whether to share her suspicion regarding Sophie's dad being a burglar, but then decided against it. She didn't want to complicate matters further and perhaps would deal with that theory later. She rubbed her right temple, feeling the first indication of a headache.

"Hello, um, I just wanted to know if you could put me through to Constable Guy Kane please?" She felt stupid saying it and even more so when she was told that there was no one of that name at the station. Cheryl experienced a frisson of relief. He hadn't been lying to her after all. It really was high time she trusted him. She was just about to hang up when the woman spoke again.

"But there is a Detective Constable Guy Kane based at Chichester," she said.

PART TWO – (PERCEPTION)
SAMPLE CHAPTER
CHAPTER ONE

St Richard's Hospital

There was no question that Craig Donohue was guilty. That wasn't the issue here – all the DNA evidence pointed to the fact. And neither did Donohue's appointment have anything to do with the trauma of nearly dying after being badly burnt and partially disfigured in a fire. No, thought Dr Warren Phelps as he leafed through the contents of the man's case file. What needed to be established right now was the current state of the patient's psychological well-being and whether or not he remembered any aspect of his crimes. If Phelps could categorically state that Donohue was in full control of his faculties, then it would give the prosecution an overall advantage.

Naturally, the police were sceptical about his mental health, suggesting that he was deliberately acting vague and unresponsive, although this suspicion, combined with his fragile physical condition, was enough of an encumbrance to keep them at arms-length. Because they didn't want any unnecessary complications preventing them from achieving a successful conviction, they needed for him to be professionally assessed. Then, as soon as he was deemed mentally and physically fit, they would pounce on him, drag him in for questioning and build a watertight case.

Dr Phelps was pleased that he had been assigned this task and had every confidence that the truth about Donohue's mental state would soon be known. A psychiatrist at the top of his field, as well as a warm and personable man, he was highly regarded by his peers and patients alike. In short, nobody could help but like him. Maybe it was because his portly figure and massive white beard reminded everyone of Santa Claus, without the red suit, of course, that he was able to gain the trust of the most withdrawn and uncooperative subjects.

Phelps had seen it all – thirty plus years in the world of psychiatry, originally training in the U.S., as well as practicing in the UK, had made him an expert in evaluating disorders of the mind. Each subject posed a challenge and, from the very moment he encountered Craig Donohue, he sensed it would be no different. When the patient was wheeled into his office, Phelps had already read the case file on the man provided by the police.

Once inside, he closed the door softly behind them, shutting out the eyes and ears of the world, then turned to adjust the blinds at the window – anything he could do to make Donohue comfortable. He expected the session to be fairly routine, using his trusty formula for determining the truth. Even his office had been designed in such a way as to deflect any attempt at trickery. There were no dark corners or overbearing bookcases where lies could hide. Deceit would not be tolerated in its open airy environment whose walls were adorned with the colourful artwork of his five-year-old granddaughter. Cheerful stickmen with crooked faces peered out from behind the framed glass, creating a calm, reassuring ambience no more intimidating than a baby's nursery. Phelps was quietly confident that he would have Donohue's assessment pretty well sewn up before lunchtime.

* * *

But Craig was immediately on the defensive. He knew instinctively that this genial gentleman was trying to lull him into a false sense of security with the comfortable environment and the childish artwork. It was the certificates on the wall behind the desk that told him everything he needed to know – that unlike himself, Warren Phelps was no ordinary doctor – he was a psychiatrist.

Why they felt he needed to see one was totally beyond him. He wasn't in any way mad. God, until the fire, he'd been working quite happily and successfully in the Accident and Emergency department, with all the responsibility that went with the job. They wouldn't have employed him as a doctor in the first place if he weren't of sound mind. So he'd had a few issues, but who hadn't? Albeit none of these were of his own making. His friend Alex should really be the one sitting here.

Craig shuffled in his wheelchair, hating the contraption. He was actually able to walk but, because 'health and safety' deemed it necessary for him to be seated whilst away from his ward, he was made to feel like a complete invalid. He was aware that he had experienced some sort of trauma, though he couldn't remember what. There were things he knew but many that he didn't. He'd suffered terrible burns and almost lost his life. That much had been thoroughly explained. These injuries had not only robbed him of his sight in one eye but had also destroyed his right hand. There had been some talk of amputating it, which would be unavoidable if gangrene were to set in. The hand now lay uselessly on his lap, swaddled in dressings that had to be changed twice a day. Once Craig had risked a peek and immediately wished he hadn't. His fingers were soldered together, black and weeping, into a deformed clump. They might as well amputate it for all the good it was.

His days of practicing medicine were sadly now at an end and, if that wasn't bad enough, he couldn't bear to look at his own reflection. He had once been blessed with good looks. Now he had to face a monster in the mirror. So, yes, Craig Donohue was bitter and aggrieved by the cards life had dealt him, although he would defy anyone not to feel the same way under these circumstances. But that was certainly no reason to think him insane.

"Hello Craig. I can call you Craig, can't I?" Dr Phelps peered expectantly at him through a pair of half-moon spectacles. What if I were to say 'no', Craig thought sulkily as he shuffled his bottom in his wheelchair. That would really scupper the shrink's opening line. He stared resentfully back with his one good eye. Phelps smiled, taking his silence as a cue to continue.

"I'm so sorry about your accident," he said with conviction. "What, if anything, do you remember about it?"

In spite of himself, Craig couldn't help but try to envisage the circumstances leading up to the fire. His mind was full of holes – like a chunk of Swiss cheese. He knew he'd been with someone besides Alex – a woman. What was her name? His recollection of the event was disjointed to say the least, like an abstract painting that made no sense. However, trying to kick start that part of the brain where his memory was stored was too much like hard work. It wasn't that he was being awkward on purpose – his mind was severely fractured, and many of the key pieces were missing. The question was very straightforward – what did he remember of the accident? Unable to answer, Craig Donohue simply shook his head.

* * *

Dr Phelps sighed and rested his elbows on his knees before steepling his fingers. Pressing his lips tightly together, he observed the patient for a few moments, trying to gauge whether he was being deliberately obtuse. At such an early stage in the game it was hard to tell, but then it wouldn't be any fun if it were that easy. Donohue was a mess, and his memory loss was no doubt genuine. It could be that his mind was blocked due to shock – a common reaction amongst many trauma victims. The police had him in their sights for a host of violent offences, and Phelps suspected they would consider this little episode of amnesia somewhat too convenient. It was therefore imperative to shed light on the truth.

"Okay Craig. Let's try it another way. What can you remember?"

Craig shrugged and cleared his throat.

"The house – my home," he replied gruffly.

"Which house are we talking about? You have an address in Emsworth. Is that the one?" Phelps pressed, consulting his notes.

"No. My parent's house."

* * *

Those questions had unexpectedly unleashed a memory, and just for an instant, a true vision of Rosalind Hall flashed unbidden in Craig's mind. He saw it now for what it was – a faded beauty in need of complete restoration, not the rose-tinted ideal he'd always envisaged. He frowned, suddenly confused. Dr Phelps continued speaking quietly.

"Okay Craig," he said encouragingly, as if he'd been party to this major breakthrough and witnessed the light bulb flickering in Craig's head. "What do you remember about your parent's house?"

"I go there sometimes. The last thing I recall is that house," the man mumbled dreamily, lost in the past.

"And were you alone on that occasion?"

Craig shook his head, still bewildered by the harshness of his vision. Why take a woman to a house that was tumbling down? It didn't make any sense. What had I been hoping to achieve? Perhaps I'm insane after all!

"I don't know. I don't think so," he murmured distractedly.

"Okay," Phelps sighed, changing tack.

"The fire – what do you remember of the fire?"

Craig looked up.

"Nothing. I don't even know how it started," he replied candidly. "The house – has it gone?

He felt the first sting of tears. Rosalind Hall was the last link to his parents. What had he been planning to do with it? Just leave it there to rot?

* * *

Dr Phelps face creased in genuine sympathy. He wasn't obliged to answer the patient's question but suspected that Donohue already knew. Whether it was because of a recent memory flashback, or maybe a sixth sense, had yet to be determined. It was obvious that this property held great sentimental value.

He stroked his beard thoughtfully, allowing Donohue time to compose himself, whilst he bent his head to consult his case file. As he did so, his right ear suddenly buzzed from the stuttered squawk of the magpie that lived in the tree just beyond his office window. In fact, there was now a family of the noisy creatures out there!

Phelps stared at his notes, flicking through the pages. Donohue continued to sniff in the background. For a while, neither man spoke. Having now witnessed a hint of fragility in his patient, Phelps was convinced that this emotional display wasn't fabricated. He had seen his share of play-acting over the years, but Craig Donohue was unquestionably grieving over the loss of his childhood home. Right now he was debating the best way to clarify how much the patient remembered about the events leading up to the fire, without adding any undue distress. It did cross his mind that Donohue might benefit from a course of hypnotherapy, an avenue many of his peers were a little sceptical of. Phelps, on the other hand, liked to keep his options open. He decided to wait and see how this session panned out. Let's keep things simple for now.

Amongst the paperwork on his desk were a couple of photographs. One showed an attractive blond lady in her mid-thirties. The other was of a young girl with long black hair. These females were said to be Donohue's latest victims and, from what Dr Phelps had been told, the forensic evidence pointed overwhelmingly to his patient's guilt. They were obviously hoping to gauge some reaction during his therapy.

The man in the wheelchair continued to sniff loudly and wipe his face on his sleeve. He looked broken and pathetic and, despite what he was purported to have done, Phelps couldn't help but feel sorry for him. Whatever Donohue had or had not been, he was clearly no longer a threat.

Gingerly he plucked the photograph of Christine Taylor from his desk and expelled a long sigh. According to the brief, she had been present with Donohue at Rosalind Hall and had perished in the fire. He stared thoughtfully down at the image. Perhaps it would stimulate the patient's memory further if he showed him the photo. As a psychiatrist, he was trained to detect the subtlest of reactions and, if he noticed any defensive body language, he could steer the conversation accordingly. One way or another, he'd have a clearer idea on the patient's mental wellbeing.

"Craig, I'm going to show you a photograph and I want you to tell me the first thing that comes to mind."

Craig looked up and regarded him soberly through his one good eye.

"Okay," he whispered, suddenly sounding very childlike.

Phelps frowned for a second. Strange that he's speaking in this fashion but it could be an act. He presented the patient with the photo, all the time scrutinising Craig's reaction. He saw the colour drain from his face and heard the sharp intake of breath.

"Who is the woman in the picture, Craig?" he asked softly.

Craig swallowed, gazing pathetically across at Phelps before focusing again on Christine's image.

"Who is she Craig? Do you remember?"

"Yes," Craig squeaked.

"Tell me," he urged.

Craig closed his eye, squeezing out more tears before doubling over in his wheelchair and pressing his left hand to his ruined face.

"It's my mother," he cried.

Printed in Great Britain
by Amazon

81456412R00163